Derangements

Rajorshi Chakraborti was born in Calcutta, and grew up there and in Bombay. His first novel, *Or the Day Seizes You*, was short-listed for the Hutch Crossword Book Award, 2006. At present, he teaches Literature and Creative Writing at the University of Edinburgh.

Praise for *Or the Day Seizes You*

'A compelling debut novel... strongly rooted in the surrealist tradition. Running through *Or the Day Seizes You* are a continuous sense of dislocation, of time being stretched out to the point where it doesn't mean anything, and a paranoia based on uncertainty about where dream-life ends and waking-life begins.... This is a story about missed connections, about the vast spaces that can exist between people in close relationships, about being repeatedly distracted from important tasks.' *Indian Express*

'Rajorshi Chakraborti's debut spans two continents and many lives. It brings forth a colourful saga of love, sex, betrayal and dreams – both fulfilled and unfulfilled.... A refreshing novel, written with a fine balance between heart and mind, which dwells deeply into the true Indian psyche with great panache.' *Sunday Tribune*

'A dreamlike debut novel.... The narrative structure is fascinating. It's much more subtle than, say, magic realism, which often lends itself to excess. In contrast, (this) requires a careful reading to realise that it isn't a strictly logical narrative.' *Business Standard*

‘The narrative is fluid.... The characters are anything but flat or one-dimensional, which makes them that much more intriguing.... Not very often does one get to flip through a story in which the enigma of relationships is unraveled through men and women that don't live in a fool's paradise.’ *Dawn*

‘Journeys are... a recurrent theme running through Rajorshi Chakraborti's ambitious debut novel, taking us back and forth across time and time zones and bridging the divide between the realms of the physical, metaphysical and psychological relentlessly. Entertaining, absorbing and haunting.... A writer so promising and committed that one suspects he cannot help doing too many things too well.’

The Statesman

‘What's notable is the ease with which (Chakraborti) has created the sense of a life that's perpetually adrift in his compelling debut *Or the Day Seizes You.*’ *India Today*

‘His style owes something to surrealism, his content to Kafka.... It is a novel of ideas that, once lodged in a reader's mind, will firmly stay there. (He) seems to suggest that it is only through the prism of an absent identity that the world can accurately be described. This might not make easy reading, but for originality it's hard to beat.’

Edinburgh Review

‘One of the sleeper hits of Indian publishing in 2006, a low-profile title that became popular through word-of-mouth, acquired a cult following, and eventually made it to the Hutch Crossword Award short-list for best fiction title.’ *Life First*

Derangements

Rajorshi Chakraborti

HarperCollins *Publishers* India

First published in India by
HarperCollins *Publishers* in 2008
A-75, Sector 57, Noida, Uttar Pradesh 201301, India
www.harpercollins.co.in

2 4 6 8 10 9 7 5 3

ISBN: 978-81-7223-765-3

This novel is entirely a work of fiction. The names, characters and incidents portrayed in it are the work of the author's imagination. Any resemblance to actual persons, living on dead, events or localities, is entirely coincidental.

Typeset in 11/14.5 ElegantGaramond
Mindway Design Pvt. Ltd.

Printed and bound at
Saurabh Printers Pvt.Ltd.

For Didi and Kishoreda

Contents

Editor's Note

I have been associated with Raj's work for twenty-six years, from one brown paper envelope to another. The first one arrived without a return address on my desk in July 1980. I was an assistant at a small publisher's, and we had a hell of a time tracking down this crazy talent, which made it not entirely unlike the events of the last few months. This lad had troubled himself to inform us, in a long list at the bottom of his letter, of all the other houses to which he was sending his work, but omitted to mention where he was doing this fierce dispatching from. The ambitious and wide-ranging list seemed the outcome of dubious research – he'd included a pair of Californian soft-porn purveyors, and another mid-Western publisher of motivational fiction best known for fables illustrating the hard-won joys of premarital abstention, or the long way back to Jesus from hookers, wife-beating and drink – as well as motive: perhaps he meant to rush us all into signing him up pronto, terrified by the competition. The story goes that I actually had to take someone from a rival house out to dinner under false pretexts and later spend the night with her before I was passed on his whereabouts.

On rereading that I notice how I might be misunderstood. It sounds as though I'm grumbling. Therefore I should clarify:

sleeping with her was in no way a necessary or unpleasant part of the task. At my age I would hate to anger the gods of getting lucky. So if you're listening, no ingratitude is intended towards any favours shown me, past or forthcoming.

Perhaps this isn't the occasion to be silly, no matter how excited in anticipation I feel. Not knowing what I do now, I had to drive straight to the police, in order for the unopened envelope and its contents to be pored over, fingerprinted, analysed CSI fashion. After all, though no charges (against Raj, or anyone else) have been filed, a murder inquiry remains very much open. I experienced no sense of disloyalty: Raj would have been aware I had no other option. The resealed package was returned after a fortnight, and I was permitted finally to read, edit and publish as I thought fit. I have no idea about their findings, whether they kept any of the pages for themselves, or what it means, months later, that Raj remains without a return address.

There hasn't really been much editing for me to do here, not of the usual sort. Raj enclosed a handwritten note with firm instructions. Pay attention now: this might be useful. You'll find that the chapters alternate between two distinct books, the second of which is clearly fiction. Book One however is a memoir, and the idea of alternating chapters rather than publishing them as separate volumes was Raj's. In his letter he insisted on this particular sequence. Why Book One isn't chronological he justifies in his preface, and I've respected his demand to re-arrange nothing.

I guess all of this means he intended a confusion of categories: he wanted Books One and Two to meet, merge somewhere near the horizon. What he'll hopefully divulge when he is here again and taking questions is why – what began resonating so powerfully between his own plight and that of his character? Was it literary and thematic compulsion, or an urgency of a different order?

But none of those itches need scratching just yet. For now you can tell I'm pleased to an unseemly degree that he is safe, he is in the clear, and well enough to be writing. Beyond that, for those of us who've found it difficult getting on without him, this volume, whatever its status as fact or story, will be a welcome re-encounter.

At this point, before you begin, there are a few rumours I should lay to rest. Some of the stuff that's been coming up on search-engines to do with this matter has been preposterous (especially in the last couple of months, ever since news of this manuscript broke). To be specific, first, it was *not* found by a tramp inside a bin in Manhattan, who recalled another deadbeat scribbling away for the better part of three months in a doorway, before he jumped off Brooklyn Bridge to his death. Nor was it, as has been hotly speculated on at least a few blogs, delivered to me by agents of any corporation or government, friendly or hostile, complete with specific sequencing instructions, which might contain codes to various concealed parties. As I said before, it arrived through the post in a brown envelope, and you can be sure I'm on the job myself, nosing around for further information, hoping even to come across the right person to sleep with once more.

Ellery King
London, 2006

BOOK ONE

The Writer of Rare Fictions

(The Uncollected Memories of Raj Chakraborti)

He owns the world who knows its law,
He who feels its truth loves it.

– Rabindranath Tagore

One way or another the no doubt mad idea entered my mind that my own actions had historic importance, and this (fantasy?) made it appear that people who harmed me were interfering with an important experiment.
God has gilded me all over. I like that, God has gilded me all over.

– Moses Elkanah Herzog in Saul Bellow's Herzog

When such as I cast out remorse,
So great a sweetness flows into the breast.
We must laugh and we must sing,
We are blest by everything.
And everything we look upon is blest.

– 'A Dialogue of Self and Soul', *W. B. Yeats*

Preface

(August 2006)

Reaching out to people, reaching right inside of them – that's my thing, it's what I do, it's what I've been world-famous for. That's the legend about me, and there's no point in lying, God knows I loved that legend. For over twenty years, I nourished and watered it with more care than I ever invested in my own son. Yet I'm about to take an axe to it in public, to record my own fall and understand my numerous failings. Under such circumstances, you'll have to forget chronology and forgive incompleteness, and accept my excuse that this is how the memories stack up and highlight themselves in my head.

On the other hand, I'm fully aware that many readers will skip most of what follows to get straight to the juicy bits, where I bring the story up-to-date with the events that led to my disappearance. Some will certainly question why I've bothered to delve so far back and include so much that seems irrelevant, when all that matters right now is the truth behind this unexplained tragedy. Where are my priorities, as a writer and as a human being? Besides, didn't I publish a memoir just two-and-a-half years ago? Shouldn't this stuff have been in there?

Well, it wasn't. I left it all out last time round. This is precisely a record of the absences in that story. And as for why I take so long to build up to my part in recent events, I can only repeat my excuse – that this is how the memories stack up and make any sense in my head. The way I've reacted on this occasion is in line with things that have happened before. A pattern seems discernible, and is what forms the principle behind these chapters. What follows is as much about other people as it is about me – those who have loved me, such as my great-aunt, my mother, my ex-wife and our son, and some, like Sharon Pereira or Vera Howard, who passed through all too briefly. What they have in common appears to be this: they all escaped my attention when they could have used it most.

Two Old Women

(London, July 1975)

Two old women died when I was twenty-two and lived in Paddington (yes, to those of you who remember the memoir: my French restaurant and Sylvie-the-waitress period, but I repeat, none of what follows has been made public before). One of them lived on my corridor while the other died in our house in Calcutta; they both only ever existed on the fringes of my concerns, but what they had in common was that neither of them seemed to realize that. I spent about ten hours in total with the lady down the hall in Paddington – out of which only once did I invite her in for a cup of coffee. The other times all occurred in scraps, ten minutes here and five minutes there.

Her name was Vera Howard and she'd lived in that flat since she was seven. That would have been 1919, from just after the war. She waited with her ear to the door and waylaid me on my return from work. Sometimes she would push into my hands something she had baked – reheated fish and chips, or a small bowl of stew. Based on just that much acquaintance, I heard that mine was the only name she kept repeating as she lay dying in hospital. 'Won't Raj visit me? Can you not call and inform him?' But I was beyond contact that evening, since it was my weekend off at the restaurant.

Our other neighbour Bryan said her husband had been similar: he would hail people on the stairs – strangers even, not just neighbours – and refuse to let them continue until he had off-loaded his stories. The Ancient Mariner of St Michael's Street. And each person brought forth a particular set of stories – for example, recalled Bryan, knowing I was from India would have led Mr Howard to reminisce about his wartime imprisonment in Malaya; he'd only ever collared Bryan about his late father the doctor, and so on. He had been dead seven years, but his name, Albert Howard, remained on the letter box downstairs as well as on her door. In fact, Vera had added another name – of a sister who never existed. Bryan explained it was because she didn't want strangers to know that she lived alone. That was ironic, considering what happened.

Vera often hushed her voice and tried to warn me about Bryan, but she liked me enough not to make a point of it. I never believed he was any more than harmless. Even the time I brought over some of the guys from the restaurant didn't convince me. We were at my place on a Saturday night after work, finishing off some beers. Bryan heard the noise, walked in, sat for a while and then insisted that we join him. He said he'd put on some records and that he had more liquor. So we were sitting around, Aretha Franklin was booming, I'd pointed out Bryan's huge porn collection (actually I didn't need to point anything out, Paul had to move a stack off his chair to sit down), and as usual the conversation turned to Sylvie. Her tits, how tightly they sat in her blouse, what they would be like to grab from behind, or to have them brush down all over you, teasing you with little touches; how well her skirt showed off her ass. This was a month before I started seeing her, so I didn't yet mind anyone leching. Paul brought up the subject of her ever-pouting partially open mouth, and listed all the things he had dreamt of putting inside it. I described how I wanted to use my mouth on various parts of her. After three whiskies, even Francois contributed: he confessed he'd once taken a break in the toilet because of Sylvie. He said that evening he just had to – she looked so edible.

For a while Bryan sat there listening; he'd never met her. The next thing someone noticed was that he was openly masturbating. The others were too surprised to say anything: I knew him better, so I could shout at him to stop it.

'I can't help it,' he exhaled, eyes closed, facing forward, still continuing. 'When you guys talk like that, I can't help it.'

'Well, stop it, Bryan, it's disgusting. Put it back in NOW, or we are leaving.'

'I can see her in front of my eyes, Raj, doing everything just like you're describing it.'

'WILL YOU FUCKING STOP IT?'

My raised voice managed to force open his eyes. He gaped around and reluctantly folded himself back inside. Things turned quiet for a few minutes; then I walked the others to the door downstairs. I didn't feel like apologizing for anybody and anyway, they should have been too drunk to care. Everyone had confessed filthy things that night, so what if Bryan took things a little further?

Ok, he was a mess, but I still insisted he was harmless. 'He never washes, and he remains indoors for days, and then you can hear him crying, and he throws his things about. He got expelled from medical school for that, you know, for being peculiar. He was asked to leave. I think he often has fits. He's very unstable. Have you noticed how fat he gets and then sometimes he emerges so skinny? How could such a person be a doctor? He must have concealed his condition from them during admissions. And once I spoke to a charwoman his mother sent, and she complained his rooms were filthy. Even she refused to clean his toilet. That's where she drew the line, she said.'

'Why doesn't his mother take him home?' I interrupted Mrs Howard.

'They moved to Hertfordshire after she remarried, because this place was getting too small, they claimed. Between you and me, I think his stepfather wanted no part of Bryan. But he stayed on to study. They promised us, any problem and we just had to telephone them. Now no one ever calls on him, and our new porter keeps insisting they've changed their number. Personally,' she whispered, 'I believe they pay him to clean up after Bryan and ignore all the complaints.'

They couldn't have been more different, Bryan Duff and Vera Howard. She worked at a florist's down the road in Bayswater, six days a week every morning, and she had impeccable standards. I never saw her without her characteristic touches of rouge, her lightly outlined eyes, shadowed cheekbones, and a mouth painted just to the point of fullness. She rarely stepped out in the daytime without large sunglasses over her brow and a scarf to frame her face. Each of her long dresses accentuated and extended her body that still flowed flawlessly through everything. Even her short kimono nightwear, with no one but me to admire it in that dark carpetless hallway, befitted a movie goddess in its boldness and confidence. And the first thing you noticed when she asked you in was a pin-up of her in a swimsuit, right leg drawn up, left arm thrown out, blonde, with flashing teeth, perfectly Aryan arms, calves and thighs, all framed by photographically heightened contrasts of sunlight and shadow. It was from a visit to Germany in the 1930s, she told me, on a north coast island called Rügen, by a photographer who spotted her in a café in Hamburg and insisted on following her everywhere during her holiday.

Once I was presented with an album full of his other pictures – Vera lying down facing the camera, breasts pouring out of her swimsuit, dusted with sand; and others of her in sunglasses in the centre of an open square, pigeons and pedestrians in the distance.

'Albert loved these pictures,' she recounted, 'he often said they decided his mind to marry me. Make no mistake, it was his idea to enlarge that one. And right at the end, one of the reasons he refused to go to hospital initially was that he couldn't take it with him. Even so, I had to carry the album back and forth every time I visited him, because of course it was too embarrassing to leave it there. Before I left, and before the nurses returned, he would always ask to look at it. And each time he would pause at a different picture, indefinitely, absent-mindedly, until my eyes filled with tears.'

They couldn't have been more different, Bryan and Mrs Howard, and nothing she alleged about him was false. Now I know from repeated experience this was precisely why I liked getting on with both of them – because of their differences and because I too was a different third. I liked the range of qualities captured in our little corridor, such differences compressed so closely with myself at their centre, like a conjuror or a tightrope artist, a ringmaster or a juggler. Today I would use much humbler images – a chameleon, or even a catalyst is how I would describe my role, something itself invisible. That is what I am actually good at, drawing someone out and then gradually becoming invisible, so that they speak and act in front of me as though they are alone. I also didn't see in those days that I wasn't at the centre of any scene, that never did my knowledge of various life-stories extend to any sort of control over their unfolding, so that far from being a ringmaster, I was often just a clueless clown.

And what incomplete, ill-developed, mishandled 'knowledge'. I would love to be able to share more stories from Vera's glamour decades, more about Albert, and more about their years together. What kind of English girl would have holidayed alone through Germany in the 1930s? What were things like in Albert's absence? But the truth is, I never asked. In the days before I met Sylvie, I kept myself stifled inside a strange cloud-chamber of melancholy where I could not bear my own company in stillness for any length of time, nor could I endure anyone else's. So everything remained half-baked, my solitude as well as my relationships. Today I can't imagine or recall what my concerns could have been but as I said, everything real around me seems to have been on the fringes. Thus, what I have set down about Bryan is also pretty close to the sum of what I know about him, although in those months I realized I was his only visitor: there were days when I moved about noiselessly in my own room, and even then he would knock – seven, eight times within two hours, at one or two in the morning.

And so when it came about that they took Bryan away for the assault and rape of Vera, which led to her death in hospital after seventy-two hours of bleeding, it would be accurate in every sense to say that I was absent from the event. Not just physically on the day itself, and not just in the sense that I could never have anticipated it, though it's the least you would expect from a self-proclaimed 'ringmaster' of life-stories. I was, and had always been, absent from both the lives that ended that day, even though both of them had offered me every welcome – despite their mutual differences, despite knowing I would continue seeing the other.

In fact, one reason I often stayed away from beginning to end on holidays was that Bryan had figured out what my off-days were, and sometimes he wouldn't relent until I had answered his knocking.

I was still living in the same room (the flats on either side of me had remained vacant: they hadn't even been cleared out yet) when a few months later my father wrote to inform me that my eldest great-aunt had died. Now a letter from my father was itself an exceptional event – it was his first that year – so I could imagine the matter had moved him deeply, even though he confined himself to the indignities of the physical details. She had been found dead a few hours, lying in bed on her side, right arm reaching out for something on the table. When Baba called on her as usual in the morning, the door had to be broken down; rigor mortis had set in, and since her arm refused to submit to ordinary strength, that was how they laid her on the pyre (I could imagine him standing by alone as the flames gathered force).

The other detail in common between these two incidents, that I shared with Sylvie as we walked home from watching the second *Godfather*, was that on the night before – the last time anyone saw my great-aunt alive – she'd remarked to my father that she missed me. She was talking about a boy of fifteen whom she hadn't seen in seven years and had barely known, but (like Vera in the hospital) she missed me. And what's more, wrote Baba, such mentions of me had not been unusual. She always inquired how I was and when I planned to return. She asked about my studies, my work, my eating and living arrangements. She asked about my impressions of London. She encouraged him to write to me. She asked him if I was writing.

'She was a tiny lady,' I said to Sylvie in a café on Edgware Road, 'with whom I spent a tiny portion of my childhood. She always lived with us, but it was a huge house, and I've told you about my family before. None of my uncles spoke to her: their wives, their children, even the servants were all similarly instructed. Her room had its own exit, she cooked on a stove on the floor, and her only visitor was my father. Sometimes, just occasionally, I would go in and fiddle with something while they were talking. Or sit on her high bed, reading my comics, with my legs dangling beside hers. By the time I was eight I was already as tall as she was.

'I heard her say some odd things, but the things I heard the others say about her! I heard cousins younger than me wonder aloud why she wasn't dying, and long discussions about it between my aunts and uncles, some of whom had stopped speaking to one another for years except on this subject. Her only crime was that she wasn't married, so there was no one to protect her. And that her father, my great-grandfather, had specified that his unmarried daughter would inherit the house after the death of her older brother, a wish my grandfather had duly respected. For this offence, barring my father, each of her nephews and nieces hated her. Even though she voluntarily confined herself to a room with its own backdoor, went out into the world invisibly and earned her keep until retirement as a headmistress, and for two decades had been effectively dead to everyone. They hated her for refusing to make out a fresh will while she was alive, and for refusing stubbornly to die.

'There was an incident my mother told me about when I was older, years after she'd left my father. My great-aunt had had one loyal servant, an elderly man from Bihar, who had been with them since they were children. He cleaned her room, cooked for her, went each day to the market, things like that. He'd spent his entire life with the family, had held my grandfather's kite as a boy and bowled cricket balls at him, and he moved with them to Calcutta.

'One day he was found hanging from a beam in his room. My uncles unanimously declared that he'd been caught with a hoard of household money and had killed himself the same night. They also spread another slander – that he broke down and confessed when they grilled him about the nature of his relations with my great-aunt.

'But Ma said there was never any kind of police inquiry, even though there had been a post-mortem. My uncles must have taken care of it. What I remember is that my mother was furious at Baba one whole night, and for weeks afterwards refused to speak to him. Of course you're aware no one else in the house ever spoke to us, although my cousins were still permitted to play with me. A year later, when I was ten, Ma left the house and I was taken with her. Baba still lives there, in the same room where I grew up. When I was younger Ma made me go over and spend nights with him, but afterwards I myself stopped visiting. We had less and less to say to each other, and the older I got, the more I despised the house itself.

'In fact, sometimes we had so little to say, Baba and I, that we would go to my great-aunt's room and leave her to do the talking. She had a gramophone; she'd put on scratchy old music and question me in detail about school, my friends and my games. She often said things that embarrassed me at the time, like how I was to come over to her school one day without telling my mother and she'd point out some girls from Class Nine who were extremely pretty. She confided that she'd extended the same favour in his time to my father, and boy, was I more handsome! "To make them even say hello to your father, I literally had to threaten them with beatings and dire results in exams." Obviously none of it was true, but that part always had the three of us laughing.'

By now we were outside and Sylvie was crying, and I held her close on the pavement. We returned to my place in silence, and I reflected how I had run out of stories to recall about this old woman too.

BOOK TWO

The Perfect Worker

(The Unusual Career of Charles Robert Pereira)

No One Else Saw Anything

Every year I used to commit a murder. I'll recount it briefly because I'm impatient to get to my real story. The first time was ten years ago, in a common, when I drew a knife and drove it into a complete stranger. The idea had occurred to me as an image two weeks earlier, walking home above Hampstead Heath at three in the morning. If it was unpremeditated, I was unconnected to my victim, and I never discussed it with anyone before or after, then who could ever out me?

You grasp the pattern. In repeating it for the next four years, my randomness remained my trump card – randomness, and the fact that I never crowed about it to anyone. I felt no urge to deliver anonymous letters, leave calling cards, taunt detectives or give interviews. It wasn't sexual, so that left nothing for forensics. In fact, never did it require any more than the most rapid of thrusts, and I had never dropped anything or been spotted. There was no particular common I frequented or any sort of signature victim that I picked. Darkness, emptiness, the certainty that there weren't any witnesses, the first person walking along that looked likely, and I'd strike: once from the front, and then through the throat to be sure. No other touching, no lingering or gloating (I made it a point to avoid staring into a face), a hike through a few neighbourhoods, and I'd be on the night bus home. Even now detectives are divided: some discerned a pattern emerging, others declared it the work of copycats, and there are still a few obtuse enough to insist they might be unrelated. And of course they were obliged to investigate the victim's biography, which led them all over the place and occasionally made for interesting reading when I discovered who they had been after having murdered them for no reason.

For example, there was an idea I had after reading about the chequered history of one of my casualties (I obviously cannot divulge anything more specific). What the police uncovered in that instance led me to question the entire concept of 'innocent' victims, such as newspaper headlines commonly proclaim after a bombing or a hijack – 'fifty innocent bystanders were killed'; 'they have heinously taken the lives of innocent people'. I started wondering whether everyone, no matter how randomly selected, is only relatively innocent, or rather, contextually innocent, which simply means there was no reason for them to be capitally punished at that particular time or place. Yet each accident, each outrage, mine included, freezes criminals in their tracks: wife-beaters, sex-offenders, people with rapes and theft and religious rioting in their history, yes, as well as bigots, arms-dealers, white-collar criminals and their slime-ball lawyers. This is strictly by-the-by, a mere observation – I've no wish to formulate an ideology by which to defend my actions. Death snapshots the living in the full flow of life, which is never as pure and sacred as they claim. And anyhow, one thing you can be certain of: I never maintained a file of newspaper clippings.

I wish to begin with a strange story, one that has gripped my entire adult life. It dates from long before I embarked on this career, from the time decades ago when I was a young man still living in India, yet perhaps there are underlying connections. I loved a woman once who was normal in every way except she could turn into a cat. That, and the fact that she too once committed a murder. It was out of love for me, and there was no other way she could have done it. Her cat identity I had been aware of – it was always ginger with a bushy tail and bigger than you'd have imagined, because she had black hair and was tiny. She waited a whole year before confiding in me, to be certain we were absolutely in love first. But during that year she couldn't resist playing a few tricks on me. I'd leave the room and when I returned she would be nowhere. I would search every corner of the flat, call out her name, even look out of the sixth-floor window at the ledges below, and she had me sitting down in worry and bafflement before she rang the bell and entered. Of course she'd slipped out as a cat, changed back in an alley and calmly taken the lift up. The night she finally told me, she changed in front of my eyes. The first few weeks after that I kept requesting her to transform, but then it just became one of those things and almost never came up again between us.

Until the day of the murder. It was her uncle she disposed of, her father's only brother. For some years now he had been an irritant. He disappeared in his twenties after quarrelling with everyone, and nothing was heard from him for four decades. It was her father who went and sought him out – one of the many ill-planned actions he undertook during the excess of sentimentality that overcame him after his first heart attack, in the six months that he lived until the second. Now her uncle was claiming that one of the last things his brother had promised him was his rightful share of the family fortune, and he produced a written agreement to prove it. We were certain it was a forgery, but he brought out numerous witnesses who swore their presence on the emotion-soaked evening that the document was drawn up. His position was that his contrite brother had contacted him for no other purpose and would surely have redrafted his will as his very next action. He hired some lawyers of average skill, which was enough to keep the case simmering for two years, two years during which no one else, not even the dead man's only daughter, could touch any of his assets.

So she grew impatient. She stole up to his room one night and fixed his nightly medication. She told me how she'd watched his habits for two weeks, and practised entering and leaving his room and garden. She had pinched samples of his medicines to find out what combinations would prove lethal. That night, she slipped into his garden as a cat, climbed up to his room, changed in the dark once she was certain of being alone, placed the altered tablets at his bedside, then changed back and retreated into the veranda until she was sure he'd swallowed them. She watched him convulse and collapse. She knew from her 'research' that his heart would stop in another half-hour. All this she told me she'd accomplished just forty-five minutes ago: she was still breathless with excitement and tension.

'Of course they will have an enquiry, and even a post-mortem, but they'll be bound to conclude it was an accident. What else can they say even if one of them suspects how convenient it's proved for me? There's no poison to be found, no signs of any struggle or weapons. There are no prints of any kind. No one saw anybody enter or leave the compound; no one could even claim to have noticed anyone familiar in the entire neighbourhood. Anyhow, he had made enough enemies during his long and charming life to send them off on numerous false trails. And finally we can be married. We'll have our home back, and we can flee on the longest of honeymoons.'

What looms large of her from those moments and keeps returning in my memory are her eyes: at first wild while telling her story, then brimming over with tears, of relief as much as anticipation, then suspended in uncertainty, wondering why I wasn't reacting. After that they probably screwed themselves into expressions of disbelief and terror, but I can't really be sure, because by then I had lost myself.

My first words were silly: 'But that means you have killed him!' I exclaimed, to which she didn't reply. The tears had stopped forming and she had run out of justifications. What more could she have said, after all: she had meant it to be a huge surprise, she expected me to understand instantly. I had been with her from two years before her father died. She took a few steps towards me and was possibly going to say something when she realized I was shrinking away, moving back around the bed on which I'd been sitting. Neither of us knew then that we had already touched each other for the last time.

Anyone would have reasonably expected me to be startled, even shocked, and afraid immediately, like any law-abiding middle-minded type, of the crime not being perfect after all and somehow being traced back to us. Perhaps even an instinctive recoil, a lightning reconsideration of the person before me, seeing what she'd proved herself capable of. But I have never understood myself what next overcame me, what extremely powerful feelings of revulsion, what absolutely blind terror. With my back to the wall and my hands guiding me against it,

I crept as far away from her as possible and, in a voice that kept rising, commanded her to stop approaching. She continued ahead with outstretched arms, asking me what had happened, asking me to let her come near, eventually begging me merely to recognize her. But by then hysteria had transformed me and wiped away every faculty until it was I who had become an animal.

Holding a vase in my left hand I started screaming for help, and that there had been a murder. I screamed continually; then to make some extra noise I hurled the vase at the mirror. She was living at the time in a single room along a corridor that went around an inner courtyard, and I knew the neighbours on either side would have heard me. She was still trying to comfort and stop me – 'Darling, what are you doing? What are you afraid of? It's only me, don't you see? Everything is done already. Just let me come close to you, let me come and hold you, let me explain how I did it' – even though she must have started to realize something utterly unforeseen had occurred, that I had snapped out of shock and fear.

But until the minute I sprang to the door to answer the knocking, she could never have understood that we were no longer in this together – that not only was she alone, but from now on I was actively against her. 'There's been a killing and she's the one that did it. I know, because she just confessed to me,' I announced to the three men who were outside, one of whom was her neighbour, 'so shut the door and spread out if you want to get her.'

Finally she reacted, in the only way left to her. It must have been a moment's decision, because no one even had time to shut the door before she'd turned into a cat again. Or perhaps everyone was so transfixed from not quite knowing what was expected that it bought her a precious few seconds. After all, there was no one else in the room, just me shouting, until they noticed a cat. Only, and I realized this later – at the time I thought it further evidence of her cunning – she was so transformed by terror at the prospect of being cornered that she went straight to being a kitten, less than a fifth of her usual size.

It was I who broke the silence as she dashed into a corner. 'Don't stand there like that, don't be fooled. It's a trick of hers, I know it well. That's how she committed the murder. Grab the cat and you've got her.' I pushed the man nearest to me towards her. He knelt forward uncertainly and she seized the chance to make for the door. I shouted at the others to close their legs and bunch together. But by the time they reacted, she was outside and scurrying down the veranda.

The neighbours were proving useless; if anyone was going to achieve anything it would have to be me with my first-hand knowledge of her wiles. I chased her down one side, we circled once and once again, the others merely watching. By the time we finished our second round, I could tell that she was tiring. I was gaining upon her, and in a flash of quick thinking, I shut the door leading to the staircase. Now I would get her; now in one smooth motion I would bend while still running and grab her.

Except, once again she outwitted me: she leapt up and stood on the railing. And as I drew nearer, preparing to lunge, still with no sign of recognition or understanding of what she would do next, of what she would have to do next, I fancy I saw her eyes flash – her eyes, not the kitten's – and that was the last time I saw her.

Everything crashed in upon me in the few seconds it took the little ginger ball to shoot down seven storeys: who was actually falling down, what I had lost forever. I screamed her name in terror and my heart stopped for an entire lifetime before I realized she hadn't quite fallen. There was no smashed mess in the courtyard; somehow she was lying suspended just above it.

Someone else shouted 'the spider', and then I noticed. A giant black creature was hanging right in the middle of the emptiness, and it had spun an invisible web to every corner of the second-floor veranda. It was large even from where I stood, twice as large as the kitten which was lying still a few feet away from it. I shouted her name again and begged her to wait, that I was coming, I was sorry, I had now understood everything. Just to wait until I ran down, just hold on and trust me, and we would see this through together. We would run away the moment I picked her up and never return to the area. She was right, I shouted, even now no one else had seen anything.

I don't know how much she heard of my reassurances, or how much she believed me, because I was speeding down the stairs as I screamed. Perhaps she would have held on if she'd heard everything; perhaps she thought it was all a ploy. But it wasn't: my whole life had been about to shatter before me, I had myself pushed it over the edge and now only a miracle had saved it. I was running down flooded by tenderness; I was running down in absolute terror; I was running down full of love. Just her eyes kept pulsing before me, as she had stood on the railing. That, and the picture of her in the corner, so cowed she could only turn into a kitten. Now all I wanted was to hold that kitten – it seemed that even if I never saw her again, all I needed to be happy was in that kitten.

The web gave way around the time I reached the second floor; I saw her last paw letting go when I looked out of the little window. She didn't land on her feet as cats are supposed to do, perhaps because this time she was only a kitten. There was no blood on the courtyard floor when I reached her, and for a second I continued hoping. But my hands felt wet the moment I picked her up, and then they both turned red.

I still don't know whether the web collapsed from the strain of holding her, whether she fell through one of its holes, or whether she let go out of fear of my approaching. I don't know if she heard those last words, if she realized I had changed completely, that I was ready to see us through anything, that I only and unconditionally loved her. I don't know. What I can tell you is that the incident didn't even go to the police, because no one had seen anything besides a raving man chasing a kitten. Everyone shunned me afterwards; they thought I had lost it out of worry for my missing woman.

Yes, the police did pay me a visit, but there wasn't a single question about her uncle. That case was closed without any fuss, as a pure and provable accident. The only case that remains open is the one about my missing woman.

The Writer of Rare Fictions

Early Errors

(North India, June 1974)

The biographical note at the back of every book phrases it thus: 'After university, he remained in England...', and I have never contradicted that. The memoir follows the same arc. But they omit four months in India, during the rains of '74, when I returned to be closer to my mother. Although the job I'd found was far away from Calcutta, in the Garhwal hills, we could spend my holidays together, and she would always have a lovely spot to visit, and perhaps even consider moving to one day. That was how I persuaded myself on the eve of my flight home. I was going to deliver us both once and forever from the disturbances of our family.

My 'career' at St M.'s College lasted a month, but it telescopes in worthwhile memory into the night of my arrival, followed right after by the day of my leaving, so that is how I'll tell the story. The school rose high up on a cliff that would have been impossible to climb, a deep chasm away from the village where the train deposited me. As I stood on the hanging bridge to regain my breath and gather myself for the steeper walk that lay ahead, the building with its lit windows, towers and turrets resembled one of those ominous backdrops from an early horror movie. The sky above it was a wash of orange and purple-yellow, and there poured down a haze of sunset mist that swathed the school rapidly as I watched, until it felt even more unattainable and dimensionless than it already was.

I had put my suitcase down in the middle of the bridge, and was trying to estimate how much time the light would leave me to make it to the front gate in case there weren't street lamps all the way up. My arms were aching and I realized I'd have to hurry if I wasn't to be one of those infuriatingly unsuspecting heroes who is forever being caught out on the road by sudden nightfall, after which every hint – from the ominous cellos wailing in the background to the sinister cackling of the coachman in the deepening mist – is intended for the viewer to grasp that he is doomed. I was occupied in these thoughts, and that is why I failed to hear what the man said as he emerged behind me, opened my left fist, and entrusted it with the rope of his cow. All I could catch were his last words as he turned back towards the village – that I would find his brother right outside the school gate, waiting to take charge of the animal from me, and how it would save him the long trip down in the darkness.

Thank goodness the animal was pliant and knew exactly how to be led, because otherwise I would never have managed, even though I kept switching arms to give my freezing fingers some respite. In fact, she kept quite easily in a straight line and it was I who had to remember not to expend myself by zigzagging too broadly across the road. Darkness fell over the woods to both sides of me as I climbed, until I could not even discern the forest floor below the leaves, but belying my worst worries, there were street lights to help me make my way. I stopped and put my case down three times in the next hour, but just when I feared that the final steep hill was going to prove beyond me, a man who'd been sitting on his haunches under a lamppost arrived running to take the cow. He also insisted on carrying my suitcase all the way to the school gate. I thanked him as he left, looking around in the meantime for a gatekeeper to show me inside. That was when I remembered the map I had folded away in my wallet, which had been sent as part of my appointment package. The letter had estimated that I would probably not find anyone on the grounds if I arrived on the afternoon train on the last day of the holidays. That was why they were enclosing a detailed map to guide me to my room through the corridors and stairways of the building.

The map was as precise as I could have asked for. I found my way to the right front door, then up the stairway exactly as it predicted, past the recommended number of floors, and when I made the correct turn and left the prescribed count of doors on either side, I faced one on the right that had to be mine. Describing the exhaustion this involved would be as tedious as the climb itself, but let me just point out that I was on the top floor of that huge fortress; the roof above me sloped down each way over the rooms. And let me remind you how high above and far away the building had seemed from my place of rest at the centre of that bridge, just before the cow was handed to me.

Of course I turned the door knob and walked straight in – I'd taken for granted that I'd have a room to myself. And though the guy in his bed moved fast enough, what he'd been doing was clear. Besides, his magazine had fallen to the floor. He had whipped the covers over himself as soon as he heard the door opening, but hadn't managed to take his source of stimulation underneath in the same sweeping move. I tried to act as if I hadn't noticed but the images on the page made clear that it was gay pornography, and obviously foreign.

My first thought was that here was a student who used the room because it was empty, but as I looked around in the dark (he'd been operating under a bedside lamp), I realized these were digs for more than one person, and that more than one person already lived here. In fact, there were three beds with corresponding sets of furniture and things strewn over all of them. So in the last analysis I hadn't used the map as well as I'd imagined. Had I gone wrong in my count of floors, or was it just the door number I misread? It must have been the floor because the number was correct. In which case this was a student performing his business perfectly legitimately under the sanctity of his own sheets, which made it an embarrassment I would find hard to live down.

A bit old to be a student, though, probably in his final year, I was thinking as I turned to head back out, when he called out my name; we were now in darkness as he'd switched off his bedside lamp. 'I didn't realize you were arriving today. The last train left ages ago, and when you didn't show up for hours afterwards, we assumed you would be here first thing in the morning. What took you so long? I know the train was on time – the students and some other fellows who were on it came in and ate more than two hours ago.'

I explained how I had walked from the station when I heard the village was only a few hundred yards away, and that I hadn't known until I reached the market that the school was in fact high above the village. Then there was nothing to do but continue, stranded like that between the station and the school. I omitted to mention the further delay caused by the cow. As I spoke I could make out Rakesh was dressing himself while still in bed, and suddenly he sat up, threw off the covers, switched on his lamp once more, and came over and introduced himself. I had missed dinner, he said, and he was sorry about the state of the room. While I was replying that all I wanted was to fall asleep, he rapidly took off the clothes and towels lying on one of the beds and thus cleared out my corner for me. Sandeep was our other roommate, but he was away playing bridge, as he did every evening. After picking up and throwing things away item by item onto whichever of the beds they belonged, Rakesh showed me the room screens, which were folding wooden partitions that the roommates could use for privacy. He shook my hand outside the bathroom two doors away on the corridor and said we would talk tomorrow, because I didn't look like I was registering much tonight. The last thing I remember is returning to a darkened room from the freezing bathroom where I brushed my teeth in the moonlight, and noticing Rakesh was already behind his screen, and the lamp glow was back on again.

Most unusually for me, I dreamt of settings and events referring to that very day. I was on one side of the chasm on a ledge making my way upwards, with the hanging bridge high above and the school not even visible beyond the crest of the opposite cliff, when suddenly it started raining horses behind me. Horse after horse fell off the bridge as I turned to find out where they were dropping from. In the night they made no noise but just plummeted white into the darkness beneath. But they never landed and I couldn't see who or what was pushing them over. Had they been racing across the countryside until they crashed down this opening in the earth? All I could make out as I leaned over were their white shapes plunging, and more plunging in front of me, legs firmly in line, as if they were stiff and dead. Perhaps that is what they were, dead, which would explain the lack of screaming, and the chasm was a natural graveyard, an ancient resting ground. But there must have been some epidemic to finish off so many at the same time. I was going to continue climbing when suddenly I understood it was pointless. A huge grinding sound of wheels erupted, the bridge folded up high above me, lifted and stood straight up, and then someone switched off its lights. It must have been the shock and the sudden darkness, but I realized with my next move that I had missed my step and that I too was falling, falling, shouting, screaming but not landing. No horses fell beside me now, and that is when I woke up, into a room I had forgotten and where I couldn't see a thing.

My final evening. There isn't really much to tell except perhaps that I had a premonition, and that's why I carried my resignation letter ready in my pocket. I wouldn't stand for anything untoward today: one word out of line and I would express my disdain and leave. As in the last two weekly staff meetings, I was overlooked each time I raised my hand to respond to anyone else's point. This happened as a matter of course with other junior teachers as well, and I had learnt by then not to take such misbehaviour personally. It was the way they treated my specific suggestion that eventually forced my hand.

To begin with, it was unlawfully pushed down to the last item on the morning's agenda, which in itself showed me my place. Without so much as an apology I was thrust behind an impromptu presentation by the gardener who complained about local goats lunching on the premises because of deliberate breaches made in the fencing, and a kitchen staff representative responding to a proposal on whether the faculty could be served different meals from the students.

The choice of Class Three's wall colours was my issue. The school was being repainted that year, classroom by classroom, and I had first preference in picking the shade for my boys. Which sounds like an entrusting of responsibility, but I soon grasped it was a ploy to set me up. The master of every other class was summoned before me, which didn't make sense any way you looked at it – neither alphabetically nor chronologically – so you had to believe they were out to provoke and inflame. It was also clear to me by now that my proposal was going to be unique, but that seemed no reason to back out. So what if everyone else had merely picked a colour of paint? Besides, what would I have to show if I didn't bring out my wallpaper?

As I rolled out my sample sheet over the large conference table, the very first reactions from the senior staff conveyed everything I was half-prepared to hear – just the sounds they made, the drawing-in of breath, the clucks and sighs. And as it lay there between us and the motion was opened for discussion, the censure gushed out thick and fast, in simple stabs that weren't even sentences, as well as through longer reasoned disquisitions. To Mrs Kejriwal it was 'in awful taste', and Mr Chaudhuri thought it 'frivolous and shallow'. Mr Myers thundered unstoppably for five minutes on how we were allowing the Americanization of our children, of an entire generation, with all the consequent lapses in standards.

'Are students not even to be certain any more which is their playroom and which the classroom? And make no mistake, schools such as this are the last bastions of resistance, where at least some of the shadows of the principles the British have left behind are enshrined and transmitted – discipline, application, manliness. Why, if we are going to let them be infected as early as Class Three, we might as well pack up and go the distance. Let the seniors grow their hair; let music and film posters be allowed in the rooms. We could sell cigarettes on the premises and even dispense with uniforms.' This wasn't just a generation gap, he reiterated every few lines. This was a question of the very future of the school, a crisis in its fabric, of the direction it would take and the values it vowed to preserve.

I didn't deign to defend myself, but my hands were shaking as I pulled out my resignation. I flung it on the table, on top of the wallpaper, which led to at least one person sighing sharply from the shock. Then followed an unfortunate moment of comedy that spoiled the whole effect, but such incidents always crop up at exactly these junctures. Just as someone reached for the envelope to pass it on to the Headmaster, I pulled at the wallpaper underneath it, upsetting three cups of tea that overflowed their saucers. As if that wasn't enough, I then found it almost impossible with my still-shaking hands to fold the sheet back like a newspaper, because part of it was now soggy from the tea. So for some time I stood there with no one venturing to help me, the paper outstretched in my arms, trying in vain to find the right creases. But it just wouldn't happen, and all that the table could see of me was a face peering out over the paper, and my fingers on either side.

Finally I realized I didn't care: I mean, why fold it back when it had been refused anyway? The newfound irreverence and freedom I'd earned from my as-yet unopened resignation letter enabled me to spring another surprise. I threw the wet paper on the floor, rose and wished the assembly 'Good Morning', told them they would find all explanations when they opened the letter, announced how glad I was to be taking their leave, and turned around and marched out of the room. It was only when I was outside and walking away that I realized there were tea stains all over my white shirt-front, and that the resignation letter might now be blurred and unreadable, in which case I wouldn't have the pleasure of the last laugh because they wouldn't even be able to make out the punch-line. But that couldn't mar my triumph, how suddenly I had snatched the pleasure from them of seeing me grovel in deference.

There was one last surprise before I left, but this time it was on me. I had always doubted that Sandeep really left each evening to 'play bridge' with such unflagging enthusiasm, and that day I discovered the true import of the euphemism. His screen was up when I entered, but it was obvious there was activity in his bed. He was probably not expecting anyone back until after the meeting was over. I went straight to my corner, informing him of my resignation and immediate departure, when I noticed the screen didn't shield him from this side at all. So his 'bridge' partner had been Miss Choksi, whose attention I'd been trying to earn that entire month. They were covered up to their necks but she was above him, I could see. I hadn't suspected a thing, nor had my roommates – whom I'd considered my only friends in the place – trusted me enough to share their secrets. And every day I'd postponed making a move on Miss Choksi, warning myself I must not seem too eager.

There was nothing for me to do except set up my screen and cover them from this angle, and then get on with my packing. At least they cared enough about what I'd announced not to immediately continue, and asked me all the usual questions about what had happened and what I thought lay ahead for me, but for a while my dominant feeling as I answered was not of triumph or failure, or even of remorse and doubt, but an utterly incongruous arousal that didn't go at all with the hot tears I kept trying to squeeze back into my eyes. Why was I the only one who failed to belong anywhere when everyone else found a way to stay warm beneath their sheets and someone to keep them company?

As I gave up folding my things and started pushing them in so I could clear out as effectively and as soon as possible, I realized I had no idea where I could go next. If I could be in Delhi by the following day, and somehow find a berth on a train to Calcutta, I would have to provide an explanation to Ma within forty-eight hours as to why I'd decided to return to England. It wouldn't be easy, so soon after my equally grandiose (and unilateral) decision to move back here and 'make arrangements' for both of us, especially since she had cautioned me repeatedly in her letter against such a sudden about-turn in my plans, and had asked me to be certain I was doing this for myself. For a moment, I even considered whether it would be easier all round if I remained in Delhi for a few days and simply explained in writing.

For now, from the tiny church-shaped window above my bed, I could see the village far below, beyond the chasm after the terraced rice fields, where I hadn't returned since the day I arrived at the station. One morning I'd lifted the glass pane and stuck my head out quite comfortably, but the drop of the cliff beneath and the size of the window left me so terrified of being trapped that I never once opened it again. I would have to walk at this time of day; nothing else could be arranged at such short notice, and the school wouldn't do me any favours. I could feel already, in the very near distance, only as far away as the road outside the gate where I would arrive in fifteen minutes, a great exhaustion approaching, which I must brave if I wasn't going to let myself collapse, as had happened so many times before – the exhaustion so familiar of knowing that I would have to begin again, and that I had no idea yet where the next starting point would be.

The Perfect Worker

Pursued!

He appeared as direct about his business as I always am about mine, which should have marked him out as all the more threatening. His first and only move was an unsigned letter under my door. 'Saturday, March the 8th,' it stated, 'I was there on Clapham Common. Since then I have thought about you, after I saw your way of working. Now I feel we must meet. Come to Shoreditch tube station at seven this Monday evening. Don't look for me, I'll find you.'

It was the middle of April and the days had started to lengthen. I'd first arrived in Britain more than twenty-five years ago, but I still hadn't stopped noticing the different phases of late-evening gold and orange, or being grateful for them – the miracle of a day extending so far beyond daytime. I stepped off the train thinking how I would rather have been left alone to go for a walk on such an evening; I would have headed westward as everything turned more golden.

It was the most unlikely-looking man who sought me out, nothing like his letter persona. I made the mistake of relaxing immediately. A Bangladeshi who barely rose to my shoulders, bald, chewing constantly and smiling, his first words were my name and then a suggestion that we repair for coffee to his friend's restaurant.

It was empty but for two customers, three waiters and his friend the manager. I was even introduced by my real name, and what followed was the most curious of exchanges. He said nothing in particular, spoke in a normal voice, and asked me generally about my years in London. Where in India did I come from; what kind of jobs had I held here; which parts of the city had I lived in? He'd only arrived seven years ago, yet in each neighbourhood I named he knew people, none of whom I'd ever encountered. After half an hour we moved outside. He shook my hand, declared it had been a pleasure and that he would be in touch again.

He would be in touch if I let him. Next morning, I awoke in a hotel in Streatham. Instead of returning north, that was where I headed from Shoreditch. It was the way I had planned it before the meeting – that no matter what happened that day, I was disappearing. So all my cash was in my pocket while I was with him, but I'd taken nothing else with me. Nor had I been in Streatham anytime since he'd first contacted me; I didn't even know about this hotel. Since randomness had always been my greatest aid, I picked Streatham randomly that morning and decided to arrive and find myself lodgings. My thinking was like a castle of calculations, one atop another. What were the odds that he was working alone, I asked myself. What were the odds he hadn't yet told anybody? What were the odds it was going to be blackmail? Because, above all, what were the odds that it was an ordinary man who had stumbled upon such an incident one night: ordinary with no experience of anything like this, ordinary and knowing no one he could trust with such a secret, ordinary no matter how opportunistic?

When I saw Faisul, I had felt my gambles would pay off completely, that my instincts had been more correct than I could ever have hoped for. He hadn't dared to meet me alone; rather, in the heart of his neighbourhood. Furthermore, he'd apparently chickened out at the last minute and not even put a price on the table. Physically I had nothing to fear from him, and he was a restaurateur by profession. It was almost like paying him an unnecessary compliment to go through with my plan after meeting him, but I have always been careful by nature.

In the next week I moved from Streatham to Ealing, and then back again to Tooting Broadway, deciding solely on impulse what I would do each time. I also watched the news and read the papers: as I'd expected, Faisul had no plans to contact the police. He must have been terrified by what he had witnessed – after all, I could murder someone from a standing start in one smooth motion. He had no way of knowing that *his* days weren't numbered, that I only killed at random. For all he knew, I might have disappeared so successfully because I was always well hidden behind him: how could he ever conceive that I spent my days on Primrose Hill and at a picnic on the Heath, walking down Highgate Village and lunching one day in East Ham? My defence systems remained what they'd always been – my casualness, because I had learnt never to step out of line if no one was calling my name, and never to seem nervous unless I was sure I was being watched. I didn't need any other precautions: my hiding place was daily life and the rhythms of simple impulsiveness, the size of the city and the walls of my skull. How could anyone figure me out or keep track of me if I only ever decided on a whim what I was going to do next, and if I never told or consulted anybody?

Of course, I imagine you exclaiming, there were so many clues. How could you have misread so many things simultaneously? He tailed you that night through all those neighbourhoods and found out where you lived without your becoming aware of him. Despite the inexperience you so easily attribute, he was cool enough to plan his next move without panicking. Despite your assurance that he would have confided in nobody, he brought you out into the open where others could see you and – no matter what they knew and whatever happened afterwards – remember your face for future reference. Besides, why would he meet you alone after seeing what you did to people you found alone with you? What you interpret so casually as his cowardice should have cautioned you even further: he had you so perfectly where he wanted you that he didn't even bother to discuss business at that first meeting. And how could you have been so certain he lacked resources even after he informed you about the friends he had in disparate places? Most of all, you silly fuck, you were in Clapham Common at two that morning and so was he. With all your experience – though you looked around before you made your move – you still didn't spot him!

For a week none of this occurred to me, but it all streamed into my head in the minute-and-a-half it took Faisul to jog up to my room from the reception desk. He entered unflustered, smiling as usual, confirming my worst fears: this guy was deadly. Despite the warm afternoon, he wore a golden silk scarf with yellow flowers. 'Mr Charles, it's my fault. I gave you the wrong impression. From my nonsense the other day, you rightly thought I was a time-waster . And of course you believed that you were free to go, that there was nothing we wanted from you.

No wonder you have seemed so relaxed this last week, as if you were on holiday.'

'I was just living my life as I usually do. I'm a freelance editor who works from home, I told you. And when I'm not busy I like to stretch my legs and take the air.'

'Yes, I remember you said so. But don't worry, today I will not stay long, nor will I waste your time. This extra week was for the best, Mr Charles. It proves you are just the man we require.'

'Require for what, and why do you keep saying we? Who's "we"?'

'Don't worry, we won't be expecting you to change your profession. It's the kind of work you handle, and handle most admirably, I might add. I observed you from start to finish, and I am a great fan of your method. Not just your professional manner, but how you conduct yourself off the job. That is what has been so splendid about this past week, watching how smoothly and calmly you approach everything, how you still live such a tension-free life even after our meeting, full of parks and walks and picnics. So in that sense this time hasn't been wasted, because it only confirms how lucky we are to have found you. And that's why I keep saying we, Mr Charles. I mean, alone, I am no match for you. It took many, many people to keep up with you. In a way it was a tribute to your qualities. In my time I have never seen an operation planned on such a scale. Perhaps that's why you are a little surprised.'

'So what do you want from me?'

'Mr Charles, you must be aware that you are unique. I mean, I realized that on the night itself, but since then I have studied you. In the beginning I wondered, how can such a man be in

London, and that too from our part of the world, without us knowing about him? Who does he work for, what other jobs has he done? Because it was clear that you had experience. But when I went home with my story, someone suggested something and someone else said oh yes and nodded his head, and then when we saw the papers we realized whom we had encountered, and that of course you worked for nobody. I mean, I have to tell you – then I felt more afraid than I had on the night itself. I felt very lucky that you hadn't seen me, because I mean, imagine if you had. Look at yourself and look at me.'

'What were you doing there? You were obviously hiding, and that too for a long time, otherwise I would have noticed you.'

'That's where you have to acknowledge fate. You're right; I was waiting there, and for the very man that you disposed of. And suddenly you emerged in front of me and it was all over.'

'So you were going to kill him.'

'Ah, it doesn't really matter now. Maybe I would have killed him. Maybe I was only there to talk to him. Maybe I was there to receive a delivery. It's of little importance. Again, I admit at first I was very confused. I had never imagined he was dealing with someone else, or that he had such dangerous enemies. But you were not his enemy, were you, Mr Charles? Even now you don't know who he was, or do you at least look at the papers after you've done it?'

'What if I say I knew him and had my reasons?'

'Yes, Mr Charles, him and all the others. They were archaeologists who once worked in Egypt where they uncovered an ancient pyramid in which your ancestors happened to be buried. They lived undercover for the rest of their lives because the tomb was cursed but you, the angry young prince who vowed revenge, are hunting them down one by one,' he said very gravely, froze for a moment, and then burst out laughing. 'Sorry, I'm so sorry, you must forgive me. That was the plot of a movie I saw last week.'

'Is your friend at that restaurant a part of your gang as well?'

'Who, Shamsul? You mean the manager. He is very young. He isn't allowed to do anything yet; on a Saturday night he can barely manage the restaurant. But I am fond of him, you know. Between you and me, I have an eye on him as my son-in-law, though before that he has to grow up. Sometimes he sits in on meetings. But that day he had no idea who you were. No, Mr Charles, your identity is not for the Shamsuls of this world. You're too rare and precious for that. Even these few guys who have been following you – they think you are some small-time debtor trying to slip away without paying. We want you just as you are; we don't want anyone outside to know that we discovered you – even very few people among ourselves. But we could have learnt that from you. Your entire method consists of being unconnected, of no kind of link being possible, between motive and crime, or the murderer and his victim. You take it even further. You learn someone has seen you. How do you respond? You go for picnics. You walk around admiring houses. I don't know how you manage. I would have been in Egypt by now.' He chuckled before he continued, 'You are a higher type, Mr Charles. You operate in complete freedom because you have found the secret of freedom. And that's the way we want you.'

'So spell out what you want me for,' I muttered sulkily but there was no abatement in his merriness.

'Right now for nothing, and perhaps nothing for months and months. I am happy to say we don't have such requirements all that often. But when we do, when it's essential, from now on you are our man.' Saying which, he looked at his watch. 'Look at the time, Mr Charles, I have to dash. The first customers come through the door at six-thirty and tonight we are fully booked. So I might have to give a hand with the waiting. Did I mention, by the way, that I own the place next to the one we met in?

'But listen, two things before I run. One, of course, you will be paid for every service: that we'll discuss later. And two, you can return home now if you like or you are free to keep moving around London. But if you leave London, you'd better note down a number where you can reach us. Because we should know if you'll be away, in case at that time we need you. So here's a card of my restaurant. It has both my mobile number and my e-mail.'

I didn't get up to escort him out. But he turned at the door and continued, 'Actually Mr Charles, why don't you visit the restaurant anyway, just for a meal sometime? Weekday evenings are usually quieter; then I can sit down and pamper you. I know they all appear the same as you walk past them, and they all claim that *Prince* Charles' (at this, he winked and raised a finger) 'has visited and praised them, but come into ours and let the food speak for itself. It would be my pleasure.'

'Are you still going to have me watched?'

'To be honest, that's not up to me and I don't know what they will decide. Perhaps things will change now that you're aware of the position. But don't let it worry you. No one either way will be told a thing. And anyway, you won't be aware of who it is or even if there is someone, so if I were you I'd just put it out of my mind and go about things as usual. As I said, our real concern from now on is professional, in case we need you and you are not in London. So Mr Charles, go on doing what you do best; go on being a free man.'

I stood at the window to watch as he crossed the street, but he surprised me by turning around and waving. My plans had begun forming before he'd even reached the reception desk. Of course they were going to tail me. Now I had to estimate the size of their outfit. Either they were huge and had a relay system, in which there were people in every part of London who were contacted in case I was approaching their area and picked up the trail when they spotted me, or there were fewer people who took it in shifts to stay with me. Or perhaps they were so large that the relay operated on a street-by-street basis with the men behind me constantly changing, so that there was never any one person for me to become aware of. Yes, that was what must have happened, because I'd certainly tried to remain alert to the possibility of being tailed, especially during the first few days.

For the first time that afternoon I grew aware of my heartbeat. Everything had happened so fast that my mind had been racing – absorbing, sifting, calculating and racing. Now I tried to recall the conversation, to boil it down in my head so I could alight firmly upon the essentials. Which of Faisul's claims could be dismissed outright as lies? Although, he'd made fewer claims than insinuations. Well then, which of his insinuations were exaggerated, intended just to intimidate me? But he hadn't insinuated so much as hinted: actually, he hadn't even hinted, he'd just not specified anything. Beyond the fact which they were taking for granted that they were hiring me as a professional killer, Faisul had managed to leave without clarifying anything. But who were 'they': how had I managed not to make him answer? They could be anybody, from a large local gang to international-scale mafia, gun-runners, terrorists, dealers in drugs or women. Jesus Christ, they could be a law-enforcement agency: he could have been talking about MI6 for all I knew. Either they had decided to try me out, and if it didn't work, to pass me on to the police, or they'd cut a deal with the cops.

Consider their scale, their degree of expertise, most of all their confidence. And why just MI6 if you paused to ponder it, why not some sub-continental or Middle Eastern government? In such matters any permutation was possible. And who could be certain of how much Faisul knew: why should I even believe that he was the one who witnessed me? Maybe he was just their face. It suited them that my mind should remain confined to Brick Lane so that I didn't make any other associations.

I had to clear my head of such rubbish, none of which was actually important. In such speculation lay ruin. I had to begin from facts. First, I couldn't work for anybody; it was impossible. I couldn't do this for hire: I was sure I could never perform if anyone else knew. And second, I would never figure out who they were. It would only paralyse me if I stopped to consider the scale of what had descended upon me. What were my options? I had already tried underestimating them. What was overestimation going to achieve? But it unthinkable that I should dangle for months waiting for their call, not knowing whether they were watching me. I would have to run. Should I fetch my passport, or should I just bolt one day in the middle of the street? Suddenly the simplicity of the second plan struck me. If I took off, someone would be forced to give chase. And even if they were working in teams posted at various street corners, the chasing would have to continue. The very fact of people running after me would confirm that I was being followed, but surprising them seemed the only way to break their dragnet. If I had my passport on me and acted fast and with sufficient unpredictability, it could be my one chance to leave the country.

It took me four days to organize myself, and in that time I had two dreams. In the first one I was assigned a job, and I watched myself beating down the subject repeatedly with a spade in the middle of a dark field, the lights of the city far beyond us. Then I buried him and headed towards the lights to report to my masters. I located Faisul at a party and shouted to him over the din that I had done it. 'But you haven't,' he smiled, then took my hand and started walking. We passed through one crowded room after another until he pointed out the man I'd just killed, the big Turk, in a corner with a drink, chatting. 'Go right now and make sure you finish it properly.' As I ran towards him with my knife in my hand, two men stepped up from behind him and held his arms for me so I could swing unimpeded into his stomach. I drove into him once and once again and turned around to Faisul for approval. 'Maestro, you're losing your touch. Look carefully and ensure you have finished.' Sure enough, the Turk was still standing, but now the tables had turned. He was moving towards me; the men behind him had disappeared. I looked again to Faisul in desperation but he had already left the room. And when I started running, the Turk followed right after.

The second dream was even stranger. Immense spaceships had landed on legs as long as thirty storeys as I stood watching from the roof of a high building. The city below was already rubble in all directions, night covered everything, and they had thrashing long whip-like arms to bring down the few buildings that remained around me. The walls crumbled like chalk but it was all peculiarly noiseless. No one else was around to be aware that the city was dying. Then the first whips struck my building. Gradually, by breaking away the edges, all they left me with was a large crumb of roof, standing on a similarly shaped section of the building. The whip seized me in its grip, lifted and turned me upside down. It slipped a plastic suit over me that fitted me perfectly and covered my face and my hands, sticking close to my skin in all places. Then they started sending bolts and charges through me. I couldn't scream because the plastic had perfectly sealed off my mouth, and I couldn't close my eyes because it was sticking to the eyeballs.

A day after I had persuaded myself to return home, I ran on Muswell Hill High Street.. At first I thought I wasn't being followed because no one began running after me. After two hundred yards I was about to slow down and reconsider when it struck me that they would have the intersections and busier streets covered. All it would require was for someone to calmly call ahead and warn their relay to expect me earlier than usual. I had no right to assume anything. The real test would be the side streets: I would have to turn into a quiet neighbourhood entirely against their expectations; only there could I expect to lose them. And I would have to do this now, because they knew I was planning to flee. So, without breaking stride I turned into a suburb and turned again, and sure enough, even though I was looking ahead, a picture emerged inside me of someone in a T-shirt and shorts beginning to run on the other pavement.

For the first time in those two months, I knew terror. I had put my foot in the water counting on being bitten, and yet without expecting it. I had still believed no one could mount anything that large: after all, I'd called the world's bluff so many times before. No one ever imagined it was the cat that killed its uncle, even after they'd seen and heard everything – that had become the lesson of a lifetime. The world was so messy, so multiple, immersed in itself, entangled at so many points. Everybody had friends and enemies, debts and indiscretions, secrets – and whatever the police might suspect, they were always obliged to investigate everything. I'd kept a clear head and let nothing ever stick to me; I had thought that was all the protection I needed. Because the world was so full of the unbelievable, yet the sheer scale of the mundane helped disguise everything, or so I had believed.

I picked up speed on the empty pavement. I knew I would have to keep turning because I couldn't leave the area; I would be 'captured' again the moment I emerged on a main street. My only chance was to tire out my pursuer before I myself had to halt, and gain a lead large enough so I could hide, maybe jump into a garden. There I would stay still until nightfall. I turned around to check the distance between us, and that's when he made his error. He never stopped running but he pulled his phone out from his pocket. I made one last effort and turned. He was just approaching the corner when I turned again. Up ahead was another street. When I reached it a few seconds later, he was a street and a turn behind me. This was my moment. I crossed, jumped a wall, ran across a garden, another wall, and crouched behind a shed.

Instantly I switched off. There were streets I could have taken in front of me but I knew he would call for reinforcements.

I didn't care how long they searched – I would remain here and outwait them. I wouldn't even listen out for them, because I might give myself away. I might take an unnecessary precaution, or they might hear my heartbeat. So I stretched out on the grass on my side, my right arm acting as a pillow. And I deliberated these things for a few minutes, in the course of which I must have dozed off.

It was already dark when I awoke, but I stayed for another hour. When I was sure I could hear nothing I crawled towards the wall, glanced around and jumped over. I had already begun striding away when I realized the street wasn't quite empty. About twenty yards from me, there was a little boy behind a lamp post on the other pavement. I turned around to look at him, but he remained where he was. When I continued walking, I could feel that he was following me. I made my first turn and waited. Sure enough, he reached the street and kept staring. It would only create trouble if I went nearer or said something, I argued to myself. He's a kid and he's seen me jump out of a garden. He's just playing cops and robbers.

But he continued all the way to the main street without ever closing the twenty-yard distance. It struck me that I hadn't really seen his face, that he might be a full-grown man, a midget or a dwarf. He might be the night-watchman they'd left behind. At the same time I realized I was on an unfamiliar road, that I had emerged the wrong way. But retracing my steps meant facing him: suddenly I didn't want to be on those dark side streets again, and I couldn't be certain of his reaction if I started walking towards him.

I broke into a light jog, believing it would be enough to lose him. But when I looked, there he was, still twenty yards behind me. I kept this up for a few more blocks and then had another idea: how would a child dare follow someone who ran down the middle of a four-lane artery? So I speeded up and crossed – there were still a few cars in either direction. Though I was going much faster and we were far away already from where we'd started, the midget – for now I was sure that's what he was, their most deceptive yet tenacious tactic – never for a minute let the distance increase between us. I was running out of options. There were no empty cabs I could hail, and turning around to face him had become an alternative I wouldn't even consider.

Nearly killing myself by not noticing a car, I crossed over to what seemed a huge open space to our right. There ran a row of street lamps in the middle but surely the darkness all around offered an opportunity for me to disappear. At first I kept to the lamps, trying to fathom where I was and to gain an impression of what the darkness concealed. It was a dirt road I was crunching on, and the spaces on both sides were immense. It seemed to be a road-widening programme but then I could discern the ruins of buildings; the rubble formed small hills going up and down in the darkness. The entire area was being redeveloped as far as I could tell, except for a complex of lights straight ahead. But there was no other horizon: there was no point except the street behind us where the city appeared to resume itself. I had no wish to continue further or even to stray from the middle, but when I looked around, there he was, a steady dot still no nearer or further away than before.

A curious déjà vu now stole over me. I had never seen, imagined or heard of such an area existing within walking distance of my home, where everything had been torn down so thoroughly, but suddenly the landscape felt familiar. Another twenty yards and I recalled where I had seen it – from the top of a high building with a spaceship towering overhead, standing alone in the middle of an already destroyed city. Without any further reflection I swerved off into the darkness, making for the lights ahead. From that point onwards I could not turn around again, and anyway, the further I went, the further the road was lost to me. Now all I cared for were the lights: I lost count of how many holes my feet fell through, how many times I scraped or knocked myself going over those hills of wreckage, how often I was on all fours.

It seemed an entire hour before I finally reached close enough to make out what the lights were. It was a huge plant of some sort – with pipes, chimneys, tanks and platforms, like an abandoned oil rig or a nuclear city. The fence around it had been torn down; I climbed over and headed for some steps. When I reached the first level, I found a space under a tank and squeezed in, and only then did I look behind me. Nothing was visible in the darkness, and nothing seemed to be moving in the lighted area beneath. I could feel myself bleeding in several places, yet I lay there vigilant because I had no doubt it would only be a few minutes before I heard him cross the fence and arrive at the bottom of the stairway. Then – I knew – I would have no idea what to try next. But when I awoke at daybreak, there was no one around, only the darkest grey of a smothered morning. By the time I'd stumbled over the ruins and started walking in the direction of the main road, a fine rain had begun to spray me.

The Writer of Rare Fictions

Early Errors

(Calcutta, January 1962)

Lifting one recollection out of obscurity invariably reveals another. Why was I in a car with my father as we drove to pick up a friend of his one night when I was nine? I had finished my dinner and was reading *The Ring O' Bells Mystery* by Enid Blyton when he asked if I wanted to go on a drive. Of course Ma was against it and said so in loudly hushed tones ('What do you think you're doing, have you gone completely crazy?'), but by then she was against most things my father suggested, big or little. 'It'll be fine, ' Baba insisted, 'don't worry. It'll be nice to have him with us. We'll be home long before his bedtime. Anyway, isn't tomorrow a holiday?'

No matter how exasperated she was, Ma never went into hysterics. Perhaps it came from years of living in a room with hostile relatives on either side of us, always maliciously eavesdropping in our imagination. And even today her objection seems thoroughly sane and reasonable, just as Baba's reasons remain obscure. The only motive I can imagine for taking me along is that he meant to throw off anyone spying through a window as he left the house: he was setting off for an evening stroll with his son. There is a shrewdness in that kind of thinking that would normally be out of character for my father, but given the wider context of what he was planning, it seems exactly the sort of muddle-headed calculation that would have appeared clever to him. Or perhaps it didn't emerge as a result of any profound deliberation, but out of an irrationality even deeper – my father simply wanted me beside him. And within some unknowable inner balance of instincts, he had decided the benefits outweighed the costs.

'Why aren't we using our own car' was my first question as we drove away. 'Who does this belong to, and why was it waiting for us near the park rather than outside our door?' My father answered nothing clearly; he kept looking over at me and smiling. 'I hope you are not feeling cold. Are you wearing a sweater inside? Look how empty the roads get by ten-thirty in winter. Look at this fog, how beautiful the trees are. If we were in the village just now, walking home through the fields, I would say it's the ideal weather to be tapped on the shoulder by a ghost.'

After about fifteen minutes, we squeezed through some very narrow roads and stopped at a corner. I knew the area because my school bus passed through it to pick up Abhilash and Vinay. I mentioned this fact to Baba while we waited. Then, just to impress him, I traced the rest of the bus route with all its diversions from here right until our doorstep, not forgetting to specify who disembarked at exactly which point. For his further edification, I had begun individual character analyses of each of these renowned personages, making sure to inform him of their status as friend or foe within the ever shifting patterns of alliance in the Machiavellian nether-zone that was our school bus, when the person we were waiting for knocked on my window. I was consigned to the back after Baba introduced me, and as we set off, he put the gentleman's surprised questions to rest with a simple reversal of the truth. The official version was that I heard he was going on a late-night spin and insisted on coming along.

Suddenly I was excited, my listlessness vanished; there seemed a point to the evening. I had no conception of what it might be – all I could tell was that Baba and I were on a mission which involved elaborate layers of deception. This strange car instead of our own, parked away from the house; the need to lie to this man whom I had no basis for trusting yet. It was obvious Baba needed me, and it was obvious there would be danger, otherwise why would Ma have been so worried? My soul rose to the challenge: the only thing I wished was that Baba had clarified my role just a little, because if this newcomer wasn't a friend, how was he going to pass me my instructions?

I kept trying to decipher clues in the movements of Baba's head as he drove, even shifting over to his side of the car so that I could catch his eye in the rear-view mirror for some coded sign of what he was planning. But both of them remained silent, which impressed me all the more. There could be no more certain indicator of secrecy or gravity. I would just have to wait and watch, and in the meantime begin adjusting rapidly to the fact that my father was nothing like he seemed.

It was in this state of mind that I found we'd arrived in Dalhousie, which I had visited only once before but recognized immediately as Baba's office area. There was no one about besides the very occasional taxi and a few people covered up and fast asleep on some of the pavements. This then was the nature of our business – three men, an empty city, a strange car under cover of fog and darkness. For just a fleeting second, I wondered if one of them was carrying a gun. By now the fog had covered the bottom of every lamppost and most of what was around us. We halted outside a doorway that I knew from my earlier visit.

Completely against what I would have predicted, it was Baba who announced he wouldn't be more than a few minutes, unlocked the front door and disappeared into his office. I was baffled, and scared for the first time that evening. Who was I being left alone with, and what should I look out for? What if he drove off with me – where would that leave Baba and where would he take me? Baba had given me no directions, no clue whose side we were on, nothing with which to protect us.

I sat there very quietly, and to occupy myself, started counting to sixty over and over. I had gone through eleven such cycles despite realizing that my time-keeping was faulty, when the man said Baba should be back any time now. He asked me if I was warm, and how my mother was, but never once did he turn around to face me.

'What is Baba doing?' I asked.

The man took a while to answer. 'Nothing. There was a paper he forgot to pick up earlier today, but he really needs it for the weekend. All he has to do is find it.'

'He should have taken a torch,' I reasoned.

'Ah, don't worry. He knows exactly where it is. It's right on his desk. He asked me to come just for company. That's why you are here too, I suppose. Who feels like going out alone on such a cold night? Tell me something, do you know the score? Is Dexter still batting?'

My heart eased its beating: everything had been restored to the realm of the mundane, and there was Baba himself now pulling open one of the giant front doors of the building. He held up a paper towards us and smiled, stepped into the car and passed it to his friend. I was just about to lose all interest in this massively anti-climactic outcome when a car drew up on our right. The driver pressed his horn and slid down his window.

'Chakraborti, na? What's up, what're you doing here?' he asked my father, 'and who's that? Isn't that Jaiswal?' as he noticed the man beside him.

'Arey, Ramesh. Are you alone? Going home?' my father replied, lowering his window so they could see each other better.

'Yeah, it's a short cut. I just dropped someone off at Howrah. But you guys tell me. What's up so late at night, right in front of the office?'

'Yaar, this is what they call a coincidence,' said Jaiswal. 'We were out on a drive to test this second-hand car I'm thinking of getting, and we decided to wait till it was a bit late so that the roads would be empty. Chakraborti's son also wanted to come along; there he is, sitting in the back. Then the bastard engine started making noises, so we pulled up and he went out to take a look. And it had to be right in front of the office. Must be the aura of the bloody place. Everything about it is inauspicious. And then who should we meet but you?'

It isn't necessary to mention that I was instantly on high alert again, all my indicators of peril fully operational. As Ramesh Uncle drove off, we had no way of being certain his suspicions had really been satisfied, so when Baba suggested that since our work was done, why not actually go for a drive before returning home, I enthusiastically seconded the idea. We couldn't take any more chances, I reasoned in furious quiet –

what if he turned the corner, reversed and followed us? We had to substantiate our story.

The silence inside the car testified to the seriousness of our situation. 'Where should I go, Jaiswal,' said my father, to which he replied, 'Drive anywhere, just drive'. We soon arrived at an extraordinarily wide street, four or five lanes wide. Of course there were buildings to either side of us, but what steadily became apparent was that they were constructed as one immense block that ran unbroken for a kilometre, permitting no exits. I had never been to this part of the city before, so I kept sliding along the seat to look out of both windows, never forgetting to check as well what cars were behind us. These buildings were not new; I remember them being five or six storeys high and miraculously awake considering the lateness and cold of the evening. Every window was open, and there were hundreds of balconies running along each floor. My glance went up and along, but there were people on each of them, sometimes one or two watching the traffic, sometimes an entire family. I could make out women picking up clothes to save them from the nightly dew, mothers knitting, even a boy studying unbelievably diligently under a lamp at his desk. The higher floors were harder to see, obscured by the fog around us.

There was nothing to do but drive straight ahead. The cars behind us remained at just such a distance, there was the fog and besides, Ramesh Uncle's black Morris was such a common model that we couldn't be sure if we were being followed until we arrived at the first opportunity to turn. And I wasn't the only one who was worried; I met Baba's eyes several times in the rear-view mirror, which proved that he must also have been checking constantly.

The lane we finally turned into could not have been more different from the main road. The buildings were just as awake and busy, but here they were barely ten feet apart, not enough for two cars to pass each other. The streets were still crowded, the paan shops were open, people were muffled up and chatting on the steps of storefronts. We'd barely crawled down a few metres and turned once more when we got stuck behind a stationary bus that presently turned out to be driverless. God would have been baffled by its business in such an alley in the first place, but someone on the street advised Baba to reverse and drive away, because a tree had fallen across the road up ahead and it wouldn't be removed until morning.

It was exactly then that I turned around and noticed a black Morris three cars behind us. Jaiswal Uncle was furious, probably out of nervousness. He said he would check if it was Ramesh. 'What will you do if it is,' objected Baba, 'you'll only confirm his suspicions. It's better to see what we can do, if we can get enough people together to deal with that tree.'

'Babu,' he said turning to me, 'stay here and we'll be back in a few minutes. Don't leave the car. You have to watch over it.'

I remember doing my best to remain alert for as long as possible. From time to time I turned around to check so that I could answer their question about whether we were being tailed. But three cars away, there was no way of being sure. After a while the cold got too much for me, so I pulled up all the windows. I began another effort to start counting in cycles of sixty, and that was the last thing I did that night: I don't even remember being carried upstairs to bed.

The next afternoon, when Ma was in the kitchen, I asked Baba what time we'd arrived home. He said various bystanders had gathered and helped but it took a while to move the tree. When I asked if it had been Ramesh Uncle pursuing us, he replied without even looking up from his paper, 'Of course not, that was all Jaiswal's unnecessary worry. Why would Ramesh chase after us on such a night? He must have been glad to get home as soon as possible. That's what we should have done too; then there would have been no misadventures. You tell me, are you feeling all right? I only hope you don't catch a cold, otherwise your Ma will never forgive me. If she asks, just say we went for a drive. Don't mention anything about Ramesh. You know how your Ma gets.'

'And listen,' added Baba in English, as I was about to go down to play, 'thank you for coming.'

I'm much older today than my father was that evening, but the reasons behind my presence in the backseat remained opaque to me long after I lost any lingering illusions about my strategic importance on that mission. I never questioned Baba about it again, just as I never asked what document had suddenly been so important. They became further facets of his invisibility, which soon afterwards was sealed forever when I left the house with my mother.

Years later, I was home for the first time from England (about to leave in a few days to take up my new position at St M.'s, but with no thought as yet of visiting my father despite a three-year absence: contact between us had withered to the point where he would learn I'd been home only after I'd returned to London), and Ma had just finished cooking. She was going to bathe and then we would sit down to lunch. In a ritual that I knew since my childhood, she took off a ring, a pencil necklace and her bangles and set them down before she went into the bathroom.

For the first time ever, I looked at them properly and then quizzed her about them while we were eating. The ring was from my grandfather. The necklace had been a gift from Baba, the very first thing he had given her. She hadn't even dared to wear it for a year until they were actually married, but carried it everywhere in her handbag. And now, though he was more than a decade behind her, and these days they rarely saw each other, she continued to carry this trace of my invisible father.

(A dream noted in my diary, from February 1976, shortly after I learnt of my great-aunt's death)

In our giant family seat, a mistress has arrived to visit me. She is much older, stately and beautiful, and married to a bedridden man. A loving and devoted carer, these are the afternoons she claims to attend the club, twice a week, to have tea with friends and renew library books. I take her hand in mine just for its incredible softness; it's a small miracle. But our shared drawing room is a much-violated space: children scamper around constantly, servants peep through the cracks in shutters when they aren't appearing with unordered tea, one by one, followed by equally unsolicited biscuits, sweets and water, while relatives wait eagerly in every adjacent room for these spies to report their findings.

We move to the room I've been assigned; since my father sold up, no part of the house belongs to us. I'm suffered, kindly enough, during this unexpected stay, and two young nephews have been cleared out for me.

Here at least there are no stares. I draw her into my arms and fill my senses with her perfume, my lips grazing hesitantly against her neck and shoulders, too anxious almost to begin the moment for fear of it concluding. She smiles and lies back; I envelop her in my embrace.

We jump startled out of bed, still fully dressed: in lying down we nearly crushed something small and moving. I lift the sheet by its corner and sweep it off in a single motion. Three kittens appear exposed and mewling, without a mother. I'm still wondering if this is a prank when my lady reacts in a fashion I would never have imagined. She leans over and lifts one of them, her long fingers pinching between its ribs, oblivious to its pitiful flailing. Without pausing she hurls it a few feet away, screaming, 'Rooms are meant for humans.'

The Perfect Worker

Inside the Whale

Because of the effects of the sedation, it took me over an hour to work out that I was in Brazil. After I realized they were speaking Portuguese I thought we might be somewhere in Africa, but then I asked the driver's friend who was very courteous and open with me, just as Faisul of Brick Lane had been. He also informed me that the local time was three o'clock on Wednesday morning. Perhaps it was the policy of their organization to put forward such a face, or else it was one of the indulgent eccentricities of absolute power. As I sat in the back of the van, shaking my head, rotating my neck, and stretching my arms and legs which were sore as though they'd been tied, it was strange to ponder how Faisul had been in my Tooting room less than a week ago, and that the Wednesday before that I'd been waiting to meet him at Shoreditch station.

There wasn't much more to recall: I'd calmly submitted to the three men waiting for me when I returned to the main road after spending the night in that demolition site. Even though I'd spotted them from some distance away and it was morning, I behaved as though I expected them there, and couldn't imagine running a second time. Without a word I had got into the back of the white van whose door they held open. Later, in a room without windows, I was injected twice in the left arm, and must have fallen asleep. I awoke in another van in Brazil.

Foolish thoughts coursed through my mind: I wondered what the landlady would decide about me. She was used to my quietness and my disappearances, but would she inform the police when I didn't show up on the third for our usual cup of tea and cake over the rent? I thought about the faces at The Three Bells and how they would respond to any inquiries. It had not taken long for me to be accepted once they'd actually approached me, and soon I felt just as easy about sitting at the bar and listening to their chat as I did about taking my drink to the conservatory area to be alone. In either case my next pint was poured and waiting whenever I was ready for it. The discussions I participated most often in were about cricket, and that was only when something reminded me of an incident or a player from the seventies or earlier. Most of the other things that occurred to me to remark on during pub conversations were to do with minor changes I'd noticed on my walks through different parts of London, and occasionally I contributed an observation I found relevant, about a new supermarket appearing or a building being demolished, a shop changing hands or new kinds of people I had noted in a particular area. What these aroused was astonishment at my habits, because I spoke in detail of neighbourhoods that were as unseen and far off to those around me as India or Brazil would have been. For a brief time this tendency even earned me the nickname of 'Postman Pat'.

I thought then of Patty: would she worry or would she swear off and dismiss me? For three years she had been the reason my pints were always ready, and it was nearly two months since I first took her home after hours. Now, as we drove in silence, I recalled images of Patty astride me, which alternated with those of her face in close-up as we kissed, and Patty as she prepared breakfast in my kitchen, standing over my cooker in her underwear with the radio on, with as much command as when she presided over her bar.

I was surprised to find myself close to tears. I realized I was drawing strength from the fact that someone who had chosen to remain friendly with me despite my silences for three years would not dismiss me immediately from her feelings. I wished I had not been so self-absorbed over the last fortnight, that I had left her with at least some indication of my plans. But what could I have revealed that didn't involve revealing more, and that wouldn't have surfaced once the police were called in?

Yet Patty was the only person who would have been satisfied with a word. She never inquired about my past, never a question about why I hadn't responded to her before (except once when she remarked happily after we made love that we could have begun doing this a lot earlier). I became aware of a pulsing that began behind my temples and plunged through the rest of me in spasms, as though my insides were caving, and soon I knew this was actually the sensation of falling away from Patty. I hadn't even been conscious for most of the time since the morning two days before when I woke up amid the rubble, but now in the van my entire loss seemed to focus itself on the loss of Patty, and I felt that if I only had her with me, I should not require anything else.

Perhaps something of my distress communicated itself to the front of the van, because the friendly Bernardo suddenly decided that I would welcome some diversion. We had been driving for fifteen minutes on a tree-fringed road that ran along the edge of a cliff. The trees made tall, coniferous silhouettes in the dark blue night as if we were many metres above sea level. In between them, to our right, were glimpses of a city that stretched far and flat in the valley below, a twinkling mirage of normality that seemed as distant from me at that moment as my memories of Muswell Hill.

A few months later, when I had a clearer picture of the situation, I wished I had behaved better that first evening with Bernardo, who might after all have been genuinely warm. I realized there was no reason to suppose he was anything more than the employee of a taxi company who knew nothing about me or the purpose of my visit. But my encounter with Faisul was still too recent, and it made Bernardo's next overture appear sinister and perverse. We turned and stopped a few minutes off the main road, outside an ornate oval four-storey building. He said it was the former Oriental Hotel that had been destroyed in a fire. It overlooked the city and he went through a long list of people who had stayed there – Marlene Dietrich, Gary Cooper, Sartre and Evita. But I couldn't see what destruction he was referring to because the curve that faced us was intact. We passed through a revolving door of prismatic glass into a grand hall, with rooms arranged all around the circular corridors, each with art nouveau railings, painted walls, elaborate pillars and false ceilings; worked frosted glass made up the door panels. The whole place was lit just by Bernardo's flashlight and a few weak bulbs. In one corner stood a grand piano, and the doors at ground level all carried signs in French and Portuguese for restaurants, the cloakrooms and the casino.

Then I understood. Uncannily, ahead of us continued the city, because there was nothing left of the hotel at its rear. It was half of a hollow shell: everything ended halfway – the roof, the corridors and their railings, even the floor on which we stood. Suddenly it felt as fragile as an egg that falls and cracks open in front of you, and good for nothing any more except as an immense amphitheatre from which to view the city below. And to be viewed in turn from down there, from one of its many balconies, roofs or crowded squares, hanging over all that bustling life as a grotesque emblem: a moth-eaten brocade, a hollow wedding cake, the distant skeleton of a giant bird unable to take to the sky.

Whatever my misgivings, Bernardo reassured me enough for me to follow him through one of the doors and up a wide teak stairway to the first floor. We walked round the crescent corridor and back again, and he pointed out a swing whose seat lay tied to the railing. He said kids used it to sail out into the sky with the hotel behind and the city below them. He showed me with his hands what a huge arc it described because it hung from hooks driven right into the main ceiling. But I refused his offer to try it, because it was at this moment that my suspicion of his dishonesty was at its peak. What a convenient way to get rid of me after flying me out so far. If it were noticed at all in Britain, it would be dismissed as a tourist accident.

Bernardo didn't insist; he just handed me the light, undid the ropes, clambered on and released himself. Out beyond the roof it appeared as though he went almost as high as the top floor and when he shot backwards I thought he would surely crash. But he was evidently well-practised, and after a few turns, when his laughter and cries of pleasure seemed true and innocent and the dusty air skimmed my face from his swinging, I felt sure that no matter what his other instructions, he had taken out a few moments just to be a child. And I was envious at his exhilaration, not only because I was much farther away from home than he was, but because I realized there was nothing childlike about my life at all, and that I couldn't even remember the last time I had felt or acted in any way resembling boyhood.

The Writer of Rare Fictions

Later Losses

(Rio de Janeiro, July 2004)

I notice, gazing upon the episodes that have emerged thus far, that I certainly am delivering on my promise to provide the missing links and puncture any myths forever. Well, just remember where you heard it first. One half of the moon has faced the world for a long time – and there never will be a better moment for me to excavate the rest of the story. The following chapters are intended to serve as an account of how I lost my way in the course of things until I didn't know which master I was following any more – my real life or my legend.

It is widely speculated (and often reported as fact and testimony) that I've 'destroyed' more than one woman who loved me. If you believe some of the trial-by-media coverage in the aftermath of Sharon's murder, there lies strewn the wreckage of several lives in my wake over the years (the connection in most of these stories, between metaphorical and actual destroying, has been left implicit, so they can stop neatly short of libel). In fact, I myself am supposed to have confessed this by writing about it from various angles and disguises. Even the unnamed female voice narrating part of the last memoir – *Down to Experience* – has by now been attributed to three different people, and the book itself is interpreted as being simultaneously my self-indictment and my apology. It's become a critical commonplace that this recurring 'trope' is derived from the autobiographical: the blameless, idealized woman whose only flaw was that she loved me absolutely.

Perhaps then, it was in a spirit of atonement that I accepted Ana's invitation to Brazil for her forty-fifth birthday two years ago, even though I persuaded myself I was looking forward to seeing Seb, our son, for the first time in over a year. But when I called at his grandmother's in Leblon, her housekeeper Clara said the two of them had left for a driving holiday in Minas. She made me coffee, and after a few minutes, went inside and returned with a book in which she had pasted pictures and clippings to do with Ana. I had put it back on the table when Clara emerged with some cake; she picked it up and turned to the pages near the end. This section was full of cuttings about me. It was not Ana's mother who had maintained the book: it was Clara.

Clara's son had been killed by mistake. He resembled someone who had got into trouble with one of their favela's gangs, for being spotted talking to a rival party. Afterwards, the leader himself showed up at the funeral to apologize. This had happened two years ago. We'd got onto the subject of children because of all the questions I asked about Seb, after she dug out the photo albums and told me the stories she knew. I asked how her son was, and if he was already married. We spoke till it was dark and as I left, I held her for a long time, promising that I would drop in again on my way back through Rio. I said truthfully that she was one of the people I had been most looking forward to seeing.

The rest of the trip was a disaster, mitigated only by a couple of days at the end with Seb. I arrived at Ana's celebrated new beach house on Ilha Grande, images of which I had come across in various magazines and the Internet, though this was my first visit. When you actually saw it, it was even more than it was made out to be, full of angles and details and proportions you could never have pieced together from photographs. Ana had designed it herself – like a great white whale of a dream, something out of Fellini. Part of it stood on stilts atop a giant cave over which flowed a waterfall into the open sea: the mouth of the cave itself released another underground river. There was a long slide that led from a first-floor veranda into a natural pool immediately before the edge of the waterfall, and you were free to let yourself be pulled along a further few feet and make the five-metre drop down into the sea, where a current picked you up and carried you out as if you were on jet-skis.

This was the focal point of the entertainment, apart from the extraordinary variety of fish, flesh and fruit laid out on the long buffet table. I regret it now but I never joined in, though people were racing down screaming in ones, twos and threes all the time. I think it was the fun they were having that put me off. Ana herself went down a few times, held by a curly-haired somebody who had his arms tightly round her middle – a rather disappointing new toyboy, I decided. What was it Larkin muttered about everyone young going down the long slide to happiness endlessly, whilst he, sad bastard, stood gazing out of a high window? 'When I see a couple of kids, and guess he's fucking her and she's taking pills or wearing a diaphragm...'

I spent the whole afternoon on a bath chair by the pool and later dozed off on a floating mattress at the shallow end. In such moods, I'm informed, I radiate my displeasure in waves, and that is the reason no one dares approach me. But there was nothing I had to share with anybody; these were Ana's friends, movie people from here and from Italy, socialites, fashionable cokeheads. No one even looked particularly good or said anything interesting the few times I did pay attention, at least not within my hearing. Ana always seemed comfortable in such company: I remembered old rows about the dull people she brought home, people who had only broken through into such circles because they were rich. I would accuse her of shallowness, of pandering to flattery and the pleasure of being effortlessly superior. She brushed me off by responding, correctly, that I was so far gone up my own ass I couldn't bear not being the centre of attention even for a few hours. And I couldn't bear the fact that *she* had brought people home, rather than I, that she spent time with people whom she hadn't met with me. So ran the course of a common sort of quarrel between us.

I awoke to the last of the sunlight. Many others were lying beside the pool but their numbers had clearly thinned. I wanted to take one last walk along the beach before I left, but I had to ask Ana if there was somewhere she could recommend in Abraão for me to stay the night. Of course her invitation had extended to that, but I couldn't stomach any more of this crowd. Even Seb had preferred church-hopping in Minas with his grandma to his mother's birthday bash. Ana changed among these people, it had always been perceptible. She grew dumber. Her standards lowered across the board.

I walked into the house and towards her room. She'd given me a quick tour when I arrived, and it was all very open-plan without many twists or corridors, so nothing was too hard to find. I could hear noises when I reached her door. That instant still offered the opportunity to sidestep a scene I knew would bring me pain. I turned the knob. He must have been deep inside her; they were both sitting up facing each other, his face hungrily between her breasts. She was making all the noises. Behind them were French windows and beyond, another view of the bay.

While biking back to Abraão in the fast-fading light, I was reminded of another visit from about fourteen years ago, shortly after Ana and Seb had moved to Lombardy. I remembered arriving at her village by the huge lake, with the train hugging the sides of the mountain as we entered. Morning mist hung in wisps close enough outside the window that you could reach out and grasp them. I could see in memory the strange network of footpaths over the water – medieval, wide ways of stone without any railings, crisscrossing the bay around which lay the village. There were so many of them meeting the shore at different points, and forming nodes and intersections far out in the open water. When I climbed the hill later that afternoon to get an overview, they lay like the strands of a giant fishnet, bobbing on the surface of the lake.

I didn't try to find Ana immediately. I spent the day walking up, down, and across those footpaths in every combination possible, spontaneously changing direction whenever I pleased: it took me all that time to ingest the wonder of being able to walk on water in this way, forming such intricate patterns. Even more, of greeting people who passed me on their day's business. Vehicles were not allowed, but I frequently stepped aside for horses – and all this was happening two hundred metres out in water. You could see the point of some of them: like bypasses, they saved one the trip through the tiny streets of the village, especially if you had a cart and wanted to get to the opposite shore quickly. But most of the smaller, more intricate connections seemed superfluous – surely one could go around the extra few metres. All I could conclude was that the designer himself had got carried away by divine visions of the combinations possible and grew determined to join all the dots, come what may, as he danced over the water in zigzags or viewed his progress from one of the hills.

That night there was a great blaze. I stood at my balcony and watched the glow growing behind the roofs of the opposite houses, and heard the screams of the village gradually awakening. I joined the crowds on the street, and can still picture the immense proportions of the cathedral-like warehouse as it stood in shrouded outlines consumed by orange. Smoke, screaming, instructions all around that no one heeded, the shrill cries of children, the migraine-like repetition of emergency sirens. I had taken dinner in the piazza just a few hours before, under a full moon, and the glow in the sky had been so icy and pale.

It had taken me two days to locate Ana on that trip, and even that was purely by chance. I had gone to visit the ruin with its empty centre and hulking, collapsed walls. She was in a car with three men, gazing at the same scene. When I went over, I could discern from a distance the familiarity with which the driver had his arm around her.

'How many of those men have you slept with?' was the very first thing I threw at her when we were alone in her flat.

Uncharacteristically for Ana, she'd snapped. 'Two, if you must know. What's your problem?'

Even after a year and a half apart, my heart beat faster at such a declaration. 'Nothing. It's just the body language that gave it away.'

'Why do you ask such things, Raj? Is it to make me feel bad, or yourself?'

'I don't know. You know how I always have to pick at scabs, open them up even if they have healed perfectly. I have to say and do the things other people don't, open the doors that frighten me. Otherwise I would think less of myself. I wouldn't be me otherwise.'

Ana didn't even turn while she readied our coffee. But I knew she was smiling. She expected me to say such things; she could probably complete them for me by now.

'Me, me, me. It always comes back to that, doesn't it? You decide everything, but even then you can't let go. No, because you have to continue to be at the centre. You have to continue to be adored. You make a decision almost as a game, you say things and string them into speeches just because it flows so easily for you. You wake up feeling one way, and decide to play the part the rest of the day. You toy with people's lives, but it's supposed to have no reality for them. They should only be waiting, frozen under your spell, for the next time you have a change of heart. People should be ready to play when you want to play, love when you need love, be serious when you need them to be serious. And let you leave when you are tired of them, always at a moment's notice. Nothing should have any consequences, any reactions.'

'I never blamed you. I just asked a question.'

'Yes, but what was the expectation behind that question? What was the accusation behind the question? Raj, only you have a god-given right to be magnetic, only you have the right to be attractive. To be multiple, as you love to say, to be "elastic". The papers might be full of pictures of you with different women, but even two years after our split, I'm supposed to be frozen and miserable. Because once every six months, your heart spills over with love and you remember me. You write me a letter saying there'll be never be anyone to replace me, that I'm your missing half, and how the months of absence have only confirmed for you that we are soul-mates. In the same breath you announce you're arriving tomorrow. But of course I should just have been waiting by the phone all this time, hoping for this moment. Just like the next woman should be waiting, and the one after that. Everyone's life on hold, waiting for the spotlight to turn on them. And god forbid they should dare to get themselves a life in the meantime, that Raj should ever be put aside even in his absence.'

'If you ever thought there was anyone to replace you... You are the one who never returned, no matter how often I asked.'

'Because I know you, apparently better than you know yourself. You arrive like an absentee landlord to confirm and count his cattle. He might know next to nothing about them; he might be bored by them; he might not even want them. But god forbid if anyone else should eye them, or if they should ever prove to have a will of their own. Plus, you've always loved the drama of these big moments, these scenes. You love taking people on these highs, you love watching yourself swoop down and lift them. After months of total silence, suddenly you're pining for us. So you spend a week adoring your son and courting me all over again. You love the chance to use your favourite words – error and loss and waste; then you rant about loyalty and continuity. Finally the big closing speech about how we'll overcome every upheaval, by which time everyone's doubts should have melted away and their lives ceased to have any other meaning because they would have realized that you, and only you, are indispensable to them. What, am I starting to remind you of someone?'

'I had a child with you, with no one else but you. And I've never stopped believing that one day we will resume a life together, because it simply has to be.'

She got up, shaking her head, and rinsed her cup at the sink. Then she turned around while putting away some of the dishes. 'You amuse me. I can't believe that you still believe yourself. You know what, you should try those exact words on someone new. Then you can riff about how your life has always lacked any stability, and how you've lost each of your homes, and all you ever wanted was to make a home in someone else's heart.'

But even this wasn't enough to sober me up. 'I still dream of the holidays we talked about, with you and me in the front seat of a Fusca, on a road somewhere in India or Brazil, our kids screaming and laughing in the back, our suitcases strapped to the top. Every time I envision this, it's always your face next to mine. Every time I imagine more children, it's still you they resemble.'

Not a trace of a crack appeared. 'No, you wanted to be a father because you wanted to "play the part". You wanted to watch the great Raj play the part of father. You couldn't let such an important role escape you. That's why you had a child, as an opportunity to put more of yourself on display.'

'I can't imagine you are so hardened, so cynical, that you think so poorly of me. How can you be so certain? I spend time with people just as you do. But you're the one who's turned away so absolutely. People who have far less than us get a second chance, give themselves a second chance, but I can never get a hearing from you. You wall me off with every word. How can I prove anything when you've closed your mind to me so completely?

'You know Ana, you represent the greatest enigma of my life. You're the only person I've ever craved. I met you at the worst time of my life, and from there you raised me higher than I'd imagined possible. You enhanced me; you extended me in so many directions. Then I lost you, and I never denied it was my fault. But now it seems there's nothing I can do to win you back. The whole world opens its heart to me, barring the one person who used to love me. Everything turns to ashes when I think that I don't have you. Do you know how much it hurts me that you make movies with all those morons, but you will never agree to direct one with me? Even though you know we'd be perfect together, we wouldn't even need to voice to each other what we want.'

And so it continued. After that visit we didn't meet for seven years, except in public at the odd ceremony or social occasion. As Seb grew older, I preferred to have him flown over to join me, so that I wouldn't cause any more upheavals in Ana's life. Because she was right: I had showed up without notice in Lombardy just as I had announced, after months of silence, that I was accepting her birthday invitation to Ilha Grande. Yes, those visits were decided unilaterally; I was intruding, and there was no one else to blame if I kept stubbing my toe upon unpleasant facts. But I always tried again with hope. I returned hoping for a miracle, some immense leap of trust and imagination over the years of waste and error (there, you see, she was right: those *are* my favourite words). I returned praying to see love in her eyes, and because I felt it was up to me to try over and over again – I had to earn my last chance after squandering so many. I had to bend my knees, dissolve all pride and posturing, and open myself as unconditionally as possible.

I have another favourite word that Ana left out mentioning – exile. Whenever the opportunity arose, I would point out to different audiences how it was such a prominent theme that the Greek and Indian epics had in common – Ram, the Pandavas, Odysseus – the experience of irreversible, long-lasting exile, where our heroes are diverted (often unjustly) from the real business of their lives. Those expecting to inherit kingdoms are banished into destitution and ignominy. Odysseus voraciously fights a war he was once reluctant to enter, but then because of an enigmatic mix of accident and character, it takes him twenty years to find his way back home. And though these lives resume their expected courses, they are all past their prime, haunted by losses and scars, and their best years have been spent either wandering further away from their destinies, or merely struggling to survive until they can come home. The lesson seems to be that such is the nature of life itself, composed solely of twists and derangements, and yet it is the only thing we have, to make the most of and call our own. If we refuse to accept it because it hasn't run according to plan, because it has got spoilt, that would be the true exile, as we would then be homeless in our own lives.

But mine should have been an exile easy to accept: its terms were extremely favourable, especially for someone as restless and curious as I. After all, Ana left me free to enter the rest of the world; the only territory denied me was the comparatively tiny space of her own heart. And how busy, how full and varied a life I have made out of this wandering. Yet secretly, I have always thought of it as banishment, a homelessness, as if I was shut out from my real destiny – an imprisonment in freedom.

Now, on the way to Abraão, cycling in total darkness, I remembered my mother admitting to me one day that our living situation in that single room within '*that* family' was the reason I was an only child. Every time Baba raised the matter she had refused him, saying he would have to first agree to leave the family. Ironically, when she found a place of her own, it was because she wasn't with my father any longer.

I had once imagined myself as the father of four children, including three daughters. And though, unlike my mother I was blessed with houses large enough and a life free from interference, they were never born, because I hadn't been lying to Ana: there was no one else I would ever have children with. There were sleepovers often, but no one else ever shared my home.

Seb surprised me with his decision to study archaeology, even though I was delighted that he planned to return to India, armed with his expertise. We were in his childhood pizzeria not far from his grandmother's house, and it was amusing to contrast his present solemnity with my memories of the strands of cheese or bits of topping that stuck somehow to the most unlikely places – his hair, his nostrils, even his earlobes in one memorable photograph. Ever the individual, from his first (upright) visit he insisted on creating his own pizza, never settling for slices from ours. The manager was a friend, and always indulged him with any combination of toppings he demanded.

'Why archaeology rather than history or anthropology?' I wondered aloud, without intending offence.

Perhaps his mother had prepared him to be defensive. He strode out lunging.

'It's what I want,' he replied, almost surly. 'No one here has any objections. It's a cool subject.'

'Sure it is. I meant nothing by asking. I'm thrilled India figures in your plans. Your other grandmother will be delighted.'

'Well, don't promise her anything. There's university first, and there's no guarantee I won't change my mind.'

'Do you know I once wrote an article on subjects like archaeology?'

'Meaning what? What are "subjects like archaeology"?'

'Well, my theory for this particular piece was that most professions fall into one of three captive relationships to power, but a subject like archaeology or say, butterfly research, is not in the service of power.'

'I don't get it.'

'I don't blame you. Let's change the subject. Why weren't you at your mother's forty-fifth?'

'You love saying forty-fifth, don't you? You think I'd pass up such an opportunity to drive? I was so honoured when Vó suggested the trip herself. She trusted her life to someone with a five-month-old licence! But tell me what you meant about archaeology?'

'It was bollocks, ok? I was young, and the classifying mania was upon me. I claimed that almost all professions legitimize, consolidate or conceal the dominant ideologies and power operations of their age. So, for instance, you have the brokers, bankers and corporate lawyers: I called their project one of active consolidation of existing capitalism. Then there are sections of the media and academia, who consolidate not directly but through legitimizing; laundering, you might say. Next you have the massive and equally essential concealment industry: advertisers are the most obvious instance, their task is to keep us distracted and addicted. Our distraction allows the powerful the tranquillity they require to function undisturbed and, of course, the economy just happens to rest upon our pointless consumption. For a kid graduating from college, I argued, it's pretty hard to resist being incorporated into one of these three streams.'

'I still don't get how archaeology fits in. Are you calling it a distraction?'

'No, archaeologists were among my saving graces. I placed them in the ranks of the "non-relevant", along with butterfly- and fern- and rock-loving people, all of whose occupations for the purposes of my article were neutral to the configurations of contemporary power. They neither enhanced nor challenged it. And, to round things off nicely for my thesis, finally there was the fifth column, people from all fields of life who choose actively to position themselves in big and small ways within movements of resistance or alternative thinking.'

'I don't think it's as easy as that. People wear different hats. Guy works in a bank by day or at Nike, he can be a decent person on his own time. He might care about the melting icecaps or the hungry.'

'True. It was a stupid piece, written out of the smugness and envy that arise from living in high-minded penury. I wouldn't build such boxes again.'

'Where would you place Mum's work?'

The kid had grown up to be a prodigy, even though it was my foolishness that had provided him with the initial opening. I wished he would actually say 'Check' at this point, so that we were both clear what game we were playing.

'W-o-o-h-h! Hang on, bro, this is a bus I think I want to jump off.'

Yeah, come on, I knew he would smile. His eyes betrayed his pleasure. This was like one of those rallies from the tennis matches we played when (we were both) younger, at his maternal grandfather's ranch.

'No, don't wriggle out,' he consolidated, 'not when it's getting interesting. You always accused Mum of being an entertainer. You thought her work was shallow.'

'Is that what she's told you?'

'Come on, Baba, don't pretend. I've heard you nag her so often, about how she should move beyond her comfort zone, challenge herself and shake people up. I'm not saying you don't respect her, I know you think she's phenomenal, but secretly, not-so-secretly, you also condescend to her for making private-eye movies and period dramas, not to mention those Peugeot ads. You believe she's letting down her own gifts, and the cause of your beloved "fifth column". And now you're afraid I'm going to do the same, to lose myself in a form of irrelevant period drama.'

'My kingdom for a pizza. Will someone please stuff this kid? Why did the Buddha take so long to hoover the sofa?'

'Ok, I'll let you off this time. Why?'

'Because he didn't have any attachments. Next question?'

'Here's one I found in a Kundera interview. A Czech walks into an emigration bureau during the early years of the Curtain. He requests a visa, to go anywhere. The destination is of no importance.

'The emigration fellow decrees he must choose a country. He pushes across a globe to help him decide. The guy spins it mournfully a couple of times, then replies, "Have you got another globe?"'

'Beckett would have loved that,' I said, struggling to keep the ball in the air. I was flailing desperately for more jokes, to joke my way out of the corner.

'And Babs,' he continued, focused like a true master, deadly as a hound. 'What is this idea you have of power anyway, and of "the powerful"? It's straight out of Batman or James Bond. Who are they? Where do they gather? Are they national or global? Is it really a them-versus-us scenario? Aren't we all part of the system in our own grubby ways, doing our darnedest to rise a little higher until our faces replace the older ones? I find it strange coming from you of all people, you who lectured me about complexity before I could even read. Jeez, I never thought you'd be so simplistic. Mum never talks like that. She knows where to draw the line.'

I made sure I inhaled before responding. I was both enjoying and wary of this joust, as proud of him as I was uncertain of his motives. I remembered how, during our games of tennis, we reached the point where I couldn't keep up with his groundstrokes any longer.

'No, bro, you're not dragging me there. Let's just say I agree with you, and move on to another subject. Two things I wanted to mention: a) thanks for recommending this Catupiry and garlic pizza, and b) where do you get your cricket fix round these parts? Do you follow it on the web? Does anyone play it at the British school?'

The final words weren't even out of my mouth when I glimpsed the hurt in his eyes. Not irritation, simply puzzled hurt, glittering at me as he spoke.

'Why do you patronize everyone so instinctively? You're the one who began this conversation by indirectly accusing me of choosing a pointless career, and then when I try to discuss stuff that interests you, you bring me back down to cricket and Catupiry. Ok, fine, I'll spare you the yawns. I forgot, you're unchallengeable. How could I have had the audacity to dispute you without having reread all your articles, in which everything I could ever say has already been anticipated and disproved?'

This was the moment when I realized that perhaps I'd misjudged the mood all along. The truth was that no matter what this boy and I spoke of, and whether we were alone or not, his mother was always present at the table. Always on his side, pressing his arm in support, or seated wordlessly in the player's box – before we kill off the tennis metaphor. Over the years, drip-by-drip, living with her, he'd been coached so thoroughly, neither of them knew it.

But I refused to allow the situation to turn grave. There was so much that was delightful to focus on, such as our presence in this pizzeria after all these years, his depth and thoughtfulness, his exquisite large eyes under Ana's thick eyebrows that faded to join in the middle, his inch-long lashes, the bow-like lips. Jesus, I was having impure thoughts about my only son. Ana, of course, would know what to term it – narcissism and nothing else. But what about all the details of *her* that I was savouring so longingly, trying not to be too obvious? How had everything about us blended so well in this boy, when his mum and dad could so easily have fucked him up?

'Son, for once I feel so blameless I can gaze down from my high horse and proclaim sincerely that you have me completely wrong. All I wanted was for our weekend to go well. But, if that demands a quick and fiery debate on who the fuck runs the world, warum nicht?

'Yes, I believe there *are* power elites that operate within every country, who these days coordinate with one another globally. In each society there exists a partnership between those with the real money, and those who frame its laws and systems. At best it's a partnership, more often it's a puppet show. That's it, that's all I want to say.'

'But Baba, isn't that a bit too clear-cut? What about forces of resistance, like the landless movement, trade unions, or the lower-caste parties in India? Or competition, like when big corporations slug it out against each other? What about those journalists and bloggers who use the Internet to spread disturbing stories and radical ideas?'

It was moving to see him care so much, and to watch his mother's spirit animate his eyes and lips. This I didn't want to stop. Yet, above all, I wanted our weekend to go smoothly.

'All of that is true. What I would argue is that our elites don't *need* to repress those struggles up to a point. In a free society, no one can smother all the voices of protest, you're right. First lesson of a capitalist democratic elite: it's costly, unpopular, and it doesn't make good PR. Leave such stupidity to the Stalinists.

'Besides, for most people, what do their dreams of liberty really add up to? A bunch of expensive lifestyle choices. That's where they'll happily charge us anyway. It turns out then that this level of "freedom" is not only economically essential, it's an important part of the idea as well, because it doubles up as the distraction of freedom.

'What a power elite cares about is far less visible than any of that. They influence the decisions of every government body, draft the unreported clauses in any trade "agreement". Plus, it helps to own the big networks and the most visited websites, because then they can shape the ways in which the rest of us read the world. Sure, a few differently-told stories will sprout like weeds within the dark wastelands of the world-wide web, but they're confident that doesn't matter, because all the resources of volume and repetition remain in their control.

'So my answer to you is yes, the world will always offer numerous possibilities, and no single cabal can contain them. But I believe the motives of the truly powerful are almost psychopathically single-minded.

'The *one* thing that has evolved, and I guess it's progress of sorts, is the code of admission to contemporary elites, compared to the ruling classes of the past. In America or Europe today, you could say they are more open to new members than ever before. Now they can even claim they aren't elitist at all. They hold out a seductive promise to the talented from all over the globe, to contribute their creativity and their loyalty and end up as well-rewarded stakeholders.'

I had fuelled a lot of the momentum for my monologue by absorbing the interest in Seb's expression, and it had helped me quell the sneaking, ignoble sensations of doubt and fatigue that arose within even as I spoke. This conversation didn't matter, it was cold and pointless, because my son was merely an interesting stranger. No, not a stranger, that was too simple. It was worse. He knew me well, especially (exclusively?) my weaknesses, and he was biased. The person dearest to me, the only living being I had any claim over, one of just two who were indispensable to my well-being – and both of them so tainted by prejudice. Irrevocable, stale, all-distorting prejudice, which

I couldn't combat since they never allowed me the time, and no one else existed to represent my corner. How could this bullshit speech change that, and yet it was all I had to keep from drowning, from falling again off the cliff down the chasm with the dead horses?

His next remark crystallized my fears. Any other messenger, and I'd have relished shooting him. Come on, Ana, who'd have believed you could be so petty? This is the crap you've drip-fed him. I felt disgusted with myself for always having regarded her as principled, and peculiarly satisfied that she was human in so banal a fashion. In future I needn't feel sullied; we could fight freely in the same mud. There was nothing exalted about her. Ugh!

'Yeah, Baba, I live in the world too,' he mouthed lazily, as if wanting me to hang on to every phrase, 'but I disagree with you even though I recognize what you're saying. I think a lot of this particular obsession has to do with the Brown Bomber, I believe he still hasn't released you. You take him, or your view of the way he works, and generalize that to everyone else, an entire class of world-dominators. It's an outdated view, if you don't mind my saying so. Besides, you give him far too much credit. He's quite foolish really, adorable and sentimental. King Lear-lite, I called him the other day. Frequently wells up with remorse about the cruel things he's done.'

There was nothing to refute. It was a charge best left undefended, if I didn't want it to stick to me. Brown Bomber, by the way, was his affectionate name for his mother's father, who adored him enough to make up for the other two absent grandparents. More about him shortly.

If I was his age I would have spat in his face and stormed out. Listen, you smug-as-fuck little prick, a few half-baked received ideas and a you-can't-teach-me-anything attitude don't add up to an original mind. If only you could see yourself through my eyes, how stupid you seem, how much the dumb herd-animal raised on the ranch of your mother and grandfather.

I felt drained, but his was so paltry an injustice. He was complacent, blind, and pleased with himself for taking me on. So unfair and so limited, just like his mother. If only he knew how cramped and insecure he appeared. What better revenge could I savour? I felt no shame at that moment.

'What shall we do tomorrow? Do you want to ride the tram up to Santa Teresa and have lunch? Or we can go to that old place in the centre where the waiters have those lovely fifties' uniforms?'

Such was the weave of that weekend with my son, scarlet threads of rage and hurt flashing unpredictably out of white, blue and green, all within me, unbetrayed by word or expression. I couldn't say why I was so quick to take offence, and certain things wounded me so: whether they were real, or phantoms that bedevilled me. There was also peace and fun and laughter, more light-hearted argument, even unmistakeable indications of love. Yet something was missing from the routine, or yes, perhaps it was routine itself that was missing, the simple taking for granted of each other in absolute familiarity. And he never threw down the bridge to me, as I would have loved him to, to the small inner circle on the other side where he lived with his mother, her parents, and even Clara in the background. I was the first person in the rest of the world to him, and we never had the time for me to practice leaping over.

(A daydream noted in my diary, from 1989, not long after Ana left with Seb.)

The strangest visions flash before me, reams of them, like movies and waking dreams. For it is only afternoon, and my eyes are open, but miraculously, there is no break in the flow. I'm transfixed, while entire stories that never were unfold, build up and conclude in this matinee of the interior, as vivid as in an alternate universe.

The Brown Bomber, the great da Lima, is visiting Calcutta, and we're at my mother's. Baba is at the window taking the sun and racing through his crossword, hoping he'll not be disturbed or asked to contribute any opinions, since he is trying to beat his new all-time best achieved only the month before. Bowls of cashew nuts and almonds, and plates of various mishti have been brought in on a tea tray, my (late) grandmother is switching back and forth from her favourite serial on TV to the chatter of her three daughters, who've gathered as usual this Saturday afternoon. I am seated in silence, struggling for the right words to explain and mediate this scene to the Dom, perhaps a phrase that would capture the essence of Indian domesticity and the lovable peculiarities of our family in one. But he seems contented, and keeps repeating how much he likes the tea.

Later in the evening we're on the long speedy highway out to the airport, because my mother suggested visiting friends of hers in Dum Dum. I see absolutely no point in taking Sr. da Lima to this god-and-municipal-corporation-forsaken part of the city, and it is becoming clear to me that my parents, especially my mother, have no idea of the stature of their guest, not to mention his legendary temper. It gets worse, when we have to park beside a country road (because a linking flyover remains incomplete, and hangs spookily well-lit over us), and walk the rest of the way along muddy paths with bamboo groves and banana saplings on either side, and some cottages lit by oil lanterns, then round a pond and through a garden, before we reach a new block of flats. I'm only grateful that I seem to have underestimated the extent of Sr. da Lima's grace and tolerance, because he follows my mother, keeping up with her talk without a single murmur of anger, and even nodding when she surmises that the countryside around his town must be similar to this. She assures us of the warmth of those we have come so far to meet: a colleague of hers from school and her husband, wonderful, loving people who'd asked repeatedly if they could host us for a meal.

Yes, they are warm, yes, they are welcoming: it is obvious from every expression how pleased they are to see us. Squash is served and we spread ourselves out in their drawing room, Sr. da Lima's cane hung up behind him on a hook in the wall, its bottom muddy, just like our shoes. The lady steps in to fetch the highlight of the evening, their fifteen-month-old, who I've been informed they adopted after years of trying unsuccessfully to conceive. It has clearly brought joy to their home, but far greater than the surprise of hosting Sr. da Lima in Calcutta is my shock at recognizing the silent child immediately. He is curious, his eyes wander, he is swaddled for warmth, but even at a distance it is evident he is disabled exactly as it had been predicted by the doctors. Even at a distance it is evident he has Ana's round eyes and the burgeoning button-version of her unique nose, and what we'd imagined would be the perfect combination of the shades of our skin and hair. And if there is any chance I am wrong, Sr. da Lima's cry within that absolutely slowed-down, silent instant seals my realization.

But Ma is smiling, even Baba seems pleased, and the pride of our hosts is boundless. So this is what happened to the child Ana bore against my wishes, the child every test had warned would be disabled. This is what my mother had in mind when she invited Ana to spend the last few months with her and deliver the baby in Calcutta. This is what happened in a dream one afternoon, in a universe where everything recombined differently, to my only son Sebastião C. da Lima.

The Perfect Worker

Inside the Whale

Perhaps the extent of my imprisonment within my new life is best evoked by describing one of my attempts to escape. One day, within a week of arriving in the city of J., I took an innocuous-seeming walk beside the six-lane avenue that bisected its centre, secretly determined to continue past its end into the countryside beyond. It was only after an hour of heading southwards along blocks that continued for half a kilometre at a time – soiled white façades four floors high, with about a thousand windows each – that the city abruptly ended: a restaurant that jutted out in a triangle formed the final corner of the very last building, and then there was a shallow muddy river that acted as a natural boundary beyond which the road petered out into red earth.

Various trails branched off in different directions, separated by dusty vegetation. I picked one of them for no particular reason and continued until nightfall. Every five hundred metres or so, the thick bush and the bamboo groves were broken briefly by four or five huts – white walls, red-tiled roofs, and woven fencing all around. The same sights repeated themselves twenty times: old men and women sitting outside their doors while children of four and five ran around me in their games on the path below. All I could do was nod or wave my hand in greeting. I had none of the language yet, and I didn't see a single car once I was outside the city, but I kept going out of some obstinacy that refused to acknowledge the hopelessness of my plan. I would possibly have continued even in the darkness if the path itself had not ended: there was nothing ahead but open, burnt, red country dotted with small outcrops of rock and scrub. And all along in a curving line from where I stood ran the verge of the forest, as if I would have arrived at this horizon no matter which path I took.

Or perhaps the true extent of my imprisonment emerges when I consider my daily life within it. I was assigned rooms a few minutes west of the main avenue in the old quarter, and was woken up late on my first afternoon by Gustavo, who introduced himself as an English teacher and thereafter became my regular point of liaison. He was short, cheerful and round where Bernardo had been strong and lissom enough to swing in huge arcs from the end of a long rope, but they both had a disarming openness in their eyes, which made them either as typically relaxed as I now expected these operatives to be, or the truly ingenuous pawns of an incalculable organization.

Gustavo had a city-map for me, a Portuguese grammar and a bilingual dictionary, two contact numbers, and a sealed letter full of instructions to the effect that there were none. I was to lead as normal a life as I was accustomed to in London: there were absolutely no restrictions on my movements or freedom of association. I was given five thousand reais with which to establish myself, but it was understood that like all immigrants I too would attempt to learn the language and find myself employment as soon as possible.

Gustavo smiled as if utterly unaware of the circumstances in which I'd been transported to Brazil, and asked me if I was an engineer. He added that he would be very happy to take me out in the evenings after work to show me around the city. In fact, that first week he called three times, always with genuine-sounding enthusiasm and mischief in his voice, and disappointment at hearing my excuses. I asked him about the letter when he visited, and he claimed it had been handed to him at school; in the past, on many occasions, he had been assigned to act as a guide for foreigners. My heart momentarily beat faster at the thought that there might be others I could contact, but he immediately clarified this was the first time someone was to stay longer than a tourist. That was why he'd asked if I was an engineer, because he had heard stories of fresh prospecting missions about to be launched not far from the city. When I asked if he knew Bernardo, describing him and mentioning that he too spoke excellent English, Gustavo grinned naughtily and said I had misunderstood him. It wasn't as though there were so few people who spoke English that they would all know each other, or meet as a club for that reason.

The first few days I kept to myself and within my own quarter, venturing no further than the main boulevard to the east. I shopped at the store on the corner where people hung around and chatted as if it was a bar, and lived off croissant-like rolls, bananas and a delicious spreadable cheese. After dinner I filled the evenings on the balcony of my flat, composing a diary for the first time in my life. But it wasn't a record of the present, not yet; instead, I jotted down pell-mell anything important that passed through my head about London – stories, people, places, with no particular care for chronology, as if they were all in some danger of being erased.

Usually when I completed an episode, I took a break by studying Gustavo's map, and my attention would return to the street-life below – mostly the motor garage and the open-air bar whose activity occupied the opposite pavement. Then, on the fifth morning, I undertook the walk I have already described. I knew I would never make it back unnoticed to the airport, which was anyhow in another city, and the remaining alternative would have been the bus-station, where someone was probably assigned to look out for me. On the last day of that first week, I had a letter ready in my hand as I entered the post-office: it was addressed to Patty, care of the Three Bells. In the first draft I had told her *everything*, inserting a sheaf of pages from my new diary – that went back even further than the annual nights on the commons, all the way to my youth in India – to explain why I had always been so impossibly sealed-off. In the version I was about to post I said merely that I'd had to move to Brazil for professional reasons – there was a sudden opening for some editing work that was likely to last a few months.

There actually arrived a moment during my second week when I decided to try and stop being miserable. I had been out by now with Gustavo, though no further than the bar opposite. By night it was easy to lie back and be overcome by all that had enveloped me – pursue wild plans or ward off wilder fears – but not in that bar or at the store. The ease and familiarity that had developed over a few months in The Three Bells seemed to be taken for granted by my third day here, even though I was as reticent as ever. I was immediately deemed 'Doutor' by everyone, and the stream and variety of questions and opinions on all matters relating to England and London were unstoppable. Besides the curiosity, there was a certain goodwill underlying every overture after Gustavo mentioned that I had come here to stay. But the moment that really sealed my status was when I unthinkingly got onto the subject of being Indian. There were a few loud and knowing exclamations, which went no further than the repetition of the word India, and people nodded their heads as if attempting to conceive the distance I had travelled to be here. Someone knowledgeable asked me if I was Hindu, to which I replied that I was born a Catholic.

'A Catholic? In India? What's your full name?'

'Charles Robert Pereira.'

'But that's a Brazilian name, Doutor. Was your family Brazilian?'

I explained about Goa and how the Portuguese had only left forty years ago. Gustavo translated for everyone else.

'So, Doutor, you speak Portuguese?'

'Not really, because I grew up in Bombay where everyone spoke English. My grandmother spoke it at home so I know a few words. But I don't understand much any more because this was thirty years ago.'

'Mas fala Doutor, fala alguma coisa em Português,' insisted Gustavo, and I could tell the others were just as curious.

So I said the few things I genuinely remembered, and a few others that had been brought back to memory during my time here and from looking into the dictionary. The roof came down; those at the table invited other people to listen, and passers-by stopped to see what was so funny. The mechanics showed up from the garage. I had to repeat my stock of expressions five times. I had never attracted such an audience before or had such an effect on anyone.

'A Hindu, from India, born a Catholic, lived in London, moved to Brazil, speaking Portuguese with a Portuguese accent' was how Gustavo summed up my curiosity value. 'God, now I've seen everything.'

That evening, and for many more to follow, whenever I was introduced to new faces, this sentence was repeated with emphasis on each of its different parts, as if the speaker paused to underline the implication of each separate link to his audience, so that the cumulative significance of the whole would register satisfactorily. It became the standard line with which to present me: *this* was the man sitting before them, such had been the arc of his life. It didn't matter that I never quite rose to those heights of charisma again, and after a while I began trying my hand at broken Portuguese in what probably resembled the local accent. Even more than the occasions when I was actually sitting in the bar, the thought of belonging there overcame me when I was alone in my room. Horizontal in the semi-darkness, I would re-experience my delight at the stir I occasionally caused when one of my risk-fraught attempts to find the mot juste – from combining (on the spot, at a furious rate of thought) what little Portuguese I had picked up with whatever I imagined could be translated from English – would take off so spectacularly that it shot over the edge of the known language itself.

One such instance was my dredging up of the little-employed word 'conseqüentemente' at the end of an argument I was making. My friend Victor asked me to repeat myself. Then he walked over to the bar and used it in another sentence. People came up and congratulated me throughout the day, for the rate of progress I was making and the choice terms I was employing along the way. 'Demais, Doutor, demais. Con-se-qüente-mente. Really, too much. The truly rare Portuguese of an Indian visitor.' How many times that week did I hear someone round off a paragraph with the flourishing, savoured use of my sonorous archaism?

I knew that the extent of my emotion was both incongruous and disproportionate the first time I heard my name being called to join them downstairs. I even dismissed perfectly legitimate suspicions about how many of them were actually paid to befriend and watch me: what could I do, how could I tell, and why should I miss out on the friendship of those who were genuinely warm, especially when I had no idea how long I was going to be kept here? Surely the professionals had to be in the minority – this was after all a real, living city going unconcernedly about its business. Any other possibility seemed too grotesque to consider.

Often I was asked questions about what they saw as my extraordinary travels, and I replied through Gustavo with discreet stories, but on the evenings when he couldn't come, I had no more to say than my pocketful of words. Yet these were the occasions when a smile or an arm around my shoulder moved me most. Sometimes I could make out that one of my stories was being retold at a nearby table. Within a few weeks the novelty would wear off, but by then my place at the bar had become permanent. For my part, I began treating it as another room in my own house: I would take what I called my 'homework' there, adding chapters to my London diary or my study of vocabulary and grammar. I regularly ate there – the pork stew, the fried chicken, the daily rice and beans and manioc chips accompanied by the occasional omelette. I would consider the changes that had crept over me when I saw myself shouting out a word to another table, asking for its meaning. I had never raised my voice for anything in a public place before.

I sometimes wondered if Bernardo would stop by again, since he knew where I lived. But he never came, and no one in that neighbourhood seemed to recognize the description. I waited to be contacted, but no one called apart from Gustavo, who knew nothing beyond his immediate duty of settling me. One day Hamilton, a regular who spent most mornings at the store and moved afterwards to the bar, asked me if I was a writer. I asked stupidly what had given him that impression. He pointed to my open diary and added that writers come to faraway places to be undisturbed. That was when I heard myself replying that actually I'd be happy to find some kind of employment. I said anything would do, as long as they understood that I was still a beginner with the language.

J. was a town full of men past their prime, either returned from long years working in the great cities of the southeast, or the fathers of children who had now moved here. There were a few young men who seemed to be employed for part of the day, but spent a lot of time idling in groups. Hamilton took me along to meet Auguste, the chef who owned the triangular restaurant that ended in a pillar and formed the southern tip of the city. He was French: I learnt later that he'd arrived here after his first divorce, only to end up staying well past his second. He needed a waiter who could work Friday and Saturday evenings because, I heard, that was the problem with young men 'everywhere': 'they all want the tips and their wages at the end of the week, but they stop coming when you tell them they have to work when everyone else is having fun.'

Well, Auguste and I hit it off from the beginning, most of all because I had no trouble working while everyone else was having fun. Efficiency was his single criterion for warming to his employees; as he never tired of repeating, 'I don't care if your team isn't winning or your wife isn't the woman she used to be two years ago, as long as you do the work I pay you for.' He led us by example – he was in the kitchen at eight-thirty on a Monday morning, when he changed into a chef's suit, and the next time anyone saw him in 'civilian' clothing was on Saturday evening after closing the restaurant. During the week he walked home down the main avenue with a jacket over his whites.

We chatted on the slow nights and in the bar opposite us after work, along with Noel, his best friend, chauffeur and imperturbable commis-chef, and Nelson, the one-time boxer (about whom more in a while) who manned the kitchen sink. Noel's previous life as a well-paid computer programmer in São Paulo (a true pioneer, he seemed, as he listed for me the number of everyday innovations he'd taken part in designing) had changed the day his first wife left him after fifteen years: one day, four years into his second marriage, he got into a car and just kept driving north. He met Auguste and liked the conditions in his kitchen, and a month had already gone by when his wife telephoned with an ultimatum: either he returned at once or the marriage was over. Noel's exact words were the Portuguese equivalent of 'Frankly, my dear, I don't give a damn'.

He carried in his wallet an old photograph of himself in which he resembled James Dean standing by a motorbike, and he still sauntered into work with the same leather jacket slung over his shoulder. Working a few feet away from the burly Nelson as he clanged and bashed the pots together, Noel the former programmer was as delicate-fingered, precise and unconscionably slow at preparing entrées and desserts when there were thirty-five people outside waiting for their supper as he was for a table of four. Sometimes Nelson turned away from his dishes and hummed the theme music from *Chariots of Fire* as he mimed in slow-motion the care with which Noel arranged five leaves of salad, oblivious in his zone of perfect calm to the growing concern on all our faces.

Nelson had grandchildren and had worked under Auguste since the time he first moved to Brazil from the royal palace of Sweden where, as we were constantly reminded, two hundred and forty kitchen staff rotated in three daily shifts of eighty. In fact, Auguste let slip no opportunity to remind us of the Olympian standards of efficiency and expertise to which he had once been accustomed. Among his favourite examples was the occasion when his services were lent to the new Russian state as a gesture of friendship, and he had assumed charge of a historic banquet in St Petersburg. But he'd steadfastly refused to serve the hors d'oeuvres because he hadn't been warned about the immense distance between the kitchen and the dining hall, that would have wreaked havoc on the eighty individual soufflés he had prepared. This was after he'd flown his entire shopping with him in a specially chilled hold from Paris, having calculated every ingredient and unforeseen requirement down to the wildest of emergency scenarios: all except the two hundred yards from kitchen to table.

No amount of pleading about the delicate demands of diplomacy and the possibility of an international incident could outweigh the threat to his hard-earned reputation; this was Auguste's breaking point – the perfect surface of each soufflé. And so Yeltsin and his new cabinet had been kept waiting with one lie after another while elite KGB men took off their shades and suits and rolled up their sleeves to hurriedly set up a chamber next to the hall as a working area.

We heard stories about the visits of Baroness Rothschild and two American presidents, and how ungratifying it was to feed

Greta Garbo who sent back course after course barely tasted. But all this crashed to a meaningless nothing when Auguste lost the custody battle after his first divorce. Between the day the appeals judge in Paris decided that he was to be allowed visiting rights once every second Sunday and could take his daughter away for just two weeks a year, and the morning he stepped off the plane in São Paulo, all Auguste remembered was wandering around the Gare du Nord and the tenth arrondissement with twenty francs in his pocket for what seemed a day and a night, thinking only if he should walk into a boulangerie and spend it on this or that. He was too low-spirited to drink. Still more twists, a wedding, and a couple of years later he was here, on the nervous opening night of the city's first French restaurant in seventy years.

But what was lost was lost forever, not just as a father, but also as a proud professional. Even though many of the province's most powerful people were our devoted clients, including the Governor, several judges on the High Court bench, two editors, and a police commissioner who saw to it that certain key supplies were flown in directly from Europe, as unhindered and under-taxed as possible, and even when they insisted on summoning Auguste out of the kitchen to shake the maestro by the hand, he would permit no one any degree of illusion. For as long as I knew him, he maintained that he could only ever operate here at about twenty per cent of his capabilities.

'Leave aside the matter of quality ingredients,' he held forth to guests standing between tables, 'to achieve anything more than this, I need a minimum of six fully-trained staff working under me, whereas what I have are basically three amateurs.' (That meant us: in this context, 'amateur' was a euphemism not far above outright abuse). 'I mean, I could surprise you one day when it was quiet, doing everything myself and preparing dishes the like of which you may never have seen before, at least not on this continent. But what happens when you bring your friend in on a Saturday night when the restaurant is full, promising him what you tasted on a Monday? Then both of you leave disappointed and I lose two clients forever. So I have to create sustainably, according to what is possible, not according to what I am capable of.'

He had similar irremediable qualms about the limitations of our wine list, because he had to order second-hand through the brochures of suppliers in São Paulo, rather than travelling himself to tasting sessions and vineyards in France. Still, even in these degraded, depleted surroundings, we had a few ongoing stories of our own, our little entertainments. For instance, there was the retired Judge who lunched over ten times a month with his mistress, but only on birthdays and anniversaries with his wife. Yet, on those rare latter occasions, it didn't matter that we'd seen him only two days ago; Auguste and I would both exclaim what a pleasure it was to host them after all these months, and make a big fuss about the unacceptable injustice of such long absences when everyone we asked informed us that they were both in town. No one was ever sure whether our productions fooled anybody, but Judge Carvalho always seemed pleased enough to leave us fifty reais under his glass of Armagnac.

Then there was Madame Grace Duvalier who had reverted to her maiden name after seeing off two husbands in fifteen years. She'd arrived from France as the Anglo-French bride of a young mining director who was still remembered with affection in these parts because of his unprecedented degree of concern for the lives and working conditions of his men. Unfortunately, it led him to be buried alive when the roof collapsed during one of his visits underground. The considerably older successor they shipped out shared nothing of his predecessor's socialistic temperament and, perhaps understandably after what had happened, resumed the time-honoured practice of keeping a healthy and disdainful distance between himself and the physical circumstances of his minions. Hence it had been deemed remarkable how rapidly the recently widowed Madame Piquaut had succumbed to the charms of someone so distinct from her ex-husband in character. Perhaps she had wanted to make certain that no spouse of hers in future would ever be tempted by any dangerous inclinations. But mosquitoes here bite the rich with as much relish as the poor and make no distinction between socialist and bourgeoisie, and after twelve happy years together, Madame had lost M de Balincourt to malaria.

All this tragedy had obviously taken its toll, and even though Madame frequently confessed that Auguste's restaurant was the only sanctuary left to her, where she could retire from the bright, hurtful light of the deadly 'tristes tropiques' into her grief and her memories, she often added in the same breath that every detail here also tormented her because of its associations with Hubert and that she frequently had nightmares set in this restaurant. To which Auguste responded, once he was back in the kitchen, that it was odd how many of *his* nightmares also featured her in the restaurant.

Her entire temperament seemed to have become confused by her losses: she visited us five times a week even though she could barely drop her guard for a moment, racked as she was by her constant worries about our hygiene. She turned the handle of every door with her own tissues, and informed us vividly that she never let herself touch the seats in the toilet with her bare skin. She didn't trust our linen or our towels and followed me around the restaurant, reporting every stain she had noticed. Careful not to wound our feelings, she often drew the significant distinction between her complete confidence in us and her general mistrust of the outside environment. Which meant, she assured us, that she would have used everything in our private kitchens without a moment's hesitation, but we had to understand this was a public establishment visited by one and twenty strangers we didn't know or control. No matter how stringent our twice-daily cleaning standards, who could ever be sure where our other clients had put their hands before they washed them? Besides, she could reel off an entire list of mutant germs that, according to her, survived the strongest detergent. Especially after Hubert's death, she insisted, she couldn't be careful enough.

She sent back plates when she claimed to have detected a tiny smudge invisible to any other naked eye, and held up each item of cutlery against the light. One day, Auguste would have stabbed her but for Nelson's extraordinary strength acquired from his boxing days, when she began a meal after unwrapping silver she'd brought with her in her handbag. It took all of my impassive diplomacy to suggest that perhaps we could save Madame the trouble of carrying these back and forth each day, by storing them in a special case behind the bar.

She often announced she was gathering her courage before making a decision to return to Europe, but one afternoon Noel fed Auguste some crazy idea that this time she was out to bury *him*. 'She's run out of directors now, because they've been scared off by her track record. And who's the only other Frenchman left in the city? I tell you, it's either you or her; both of you will never leave Brazil alive. How frequently does she enter the kitchen trying to be alone with you; how often does she stay after everyone else has left, and what about all the times she wants you to invite her home for dinner?'

At first Auguste laughed him off and concentrated on his simmering velouté, but Noel continued enumerating his evidence of Madame's intentions in so dead-pan and grave a manner that even I began turning over the possibility in my head. Auguste would have rushed straight out, grabbed the faux filet off her plate and banned her from the restaurant forever if Nelson hadn't suggested a much smoother idea, in which we only had to initiate events and then stand back and watch them unfold to their inevitable conclusion.

Senhor Dom Viceinte 'Joe Louis' Moreira da Lima lived up to all one's expectations of the gallant old-time gangster: white suits, silk ties, silk handkerchiefs, the occasional pair of two-toned shoes. He was an enormous man of quick temper and eccentric generosity who, true to form, never sat with his back to the front door and hated above all things to have a soiled plate in front of him once he'd finished a course, and then to be kept waiting for any length of time between courses.

I wasn't allowed to attend to him on the first couple of occasions he dined during my apprenticeship: I was instructed to wait at the bar and watch Auguste closely. He was always escorted by two bodyguards – who sat two tables away from him – and a lady, one out of a local pool of three companions that he maintained (who never visited the restaurant with anyone else, though they sometimes came alone); and we knew in advance since there was at least one large photograph in the papers whenever he arrived in town. His countrywide renown might have extended from Foz do Iguaçu to Manaus, but here especially he was the most famous local boy ever to have made the big time. In fact, he began as a boxer who went on to become champion of Brazil, and he got his nickname from his lifelong idolization of Joe Louis.

Apparently, in the old days, this great name alone had sufficed as his stock reply to most questions: 'Viceinte, who would you most like to fight?' 'Joe Louis.' 'Where did you learn that uppercut, Viceinte?' 'Joe Louis.' 'Who do you think can beat you?' 'Only Joe Louis.' Our restaurant had a special place in his heart for many reasons, one of which was Nelson's presence: they had been friends and sparring partners throughout his career, all the way to the championship.

Actually Auguste began the restaurant as little more than a boulangerie, with quiches, tartes, feuilletés and sandwiches, perched on the absolute edge of town because that was the only spot he could afford. Sr. da Lima was driving by in his famous, immaculately restored red-and-cream Duesenberg one morning when he recognized Nelson smoking outside with Auguste. He stopped immediately, stayed for a sandwich, returned twice in the next three days, listened to Auguste's dream of something bigger, and wrote him a cheque that allowed him to begin renovations within a week.

That was the kind of man he was: he jump-started his own post-boxing career on the back of a similar impulse. Sick with himself for having surrendered his title under threat from the boss (Sr. Saldanha) who controlled boxing bets in São Paulo, and who had placed a large amount at very profitable odds on Sr. da Lima's unfavoured challenger, he jumped off the table during his rubdown, spoke to someone on the phone, and went inside for a shower. By the time he'd towelled himself, six men belonging to a rival gang had sidled in through the back door and were waiting for him in the locker-room. He dressed, and they left together for the ringside where Sr. Saldanha was finishing his cigar and an accountant was totalling up his winnings.

Until this point Nelson claimed to have been an eyewitness, but the legend continues that young Viceinte da Silva (his birth-name) stepped up to Sr. Saldanha, who was now in an affable mood and even promised him a favourable rematch within three months, and shot him in the middle of the forehead. Before his three bodyguards could pull out their weapons, the other six men emerged holding Tommy guns, from the shadows behind the seats.

There was a rematch, and Nelson insisted it had been fair because Sr. da Lima would never accept a tainted title. But his opponent went down inside the first minute with a chop to the back of the head and ironically, that victory ended Sr. da Lima's boxing career in its prime. His dream had been to fight his way up the continent until he got a shot at Marciano whom he'd never forgiven for battering a Joe Louis long past his best, but now no one dared challenge him in Brazil, not even in an encounter he publicly guaranteed would be fair.

And it was this strange twist of fortune, more than any active desire, which had forced him to retire as champion and begin a new life in the underworld. In fact, insisted Nelson, in their frequent heart-to hearts between two old fighters Sr. da Lima still complained that he regretted the way his career had been curtailed by fate, when he should have been remembered with the same honour and matchless dignity that people associated with his hero. These melancholy sessions usually ended with a shameful invocation of Louis's holy name: 'You know what I always ask myself, Nelson? If He ever heard my story, would He want to have anything to do with me? I met him once, I went up to say hello at the ringside the first time Ali defeated Frazier. He was sitting in a wheelchair and gazing straight ahead, and I told him I was once champion of Brazil. Speaking very softly, he asked me my name, and I said people sometimes called me Joe Louis. A small smile broke out on his face and he made an effort to wink at me, then he held out his famous right hand and said, "I should charge you money for using my name".

'Whenever I picture that slow smile I think I should have remained a fighter. No matter what the provocations, no matter what the challenges, if I really wanted to live up to his name, I should have got on a boat and left for New York and started again from the bottom. That was the turning point, Nelson, my crucial mistake. But I'd been fighting for five years already; the thought of arriving in New York as an unknown and battling my way up to Madison Square Garden, I couldn't face it.

'Also, I had begun to have my own doubts. Did Zé go down because I hit him, or did he go down out of fear? No, I lost everything the day I lost my undefeated record, even though it was fixed and I was miles ahead on points when I dove in the eighth. Do you know Saldanha wanted the odds to climb even further, so he actually placed his money during the fight? He told me to fight my natural style until the eighth and hit Zé as often as I could without dropping him.'

The legend continued that the now retired fighter da Silva returned to his home city and went to pay his respects to his departed mother before embarking on his new profession. Whilst at the cemetery, he noticed a name on a gravestone that for some reason he liked and soon, as if to mark his shedding of one skin for another, he re-emerged in São Paulo as Viceinte Faria Moreira da Lima, soon to attain renown as Senhor Dom Viceinte da Lima. But people here had their own way of exonerating him of criminal associations. Though (even) they had to admit there was a long list of killings that could probably be traced to his orders, they insisted he had never killed an 'innocent' man. Nelson once summed up this fine distinction for me.

'Understand, Charlie, if Sr. da Lima needed to kill you, it means you were involved in the game in the first place. Your hands were already dirty. You had made a choice, you understood the rules, and you knew there was always the chance you would end in this way. You would obviously have done the same thing to many others in your time, and you would do the same to him if you could get to him first. The point is that no one uninvolved in such matters has ever been one of Sr. da Lima's victims, not even in any kind of accident or crossfire. Even his enemies haven't been able to accuse him of this. He belongs to a world whose rules are different, and people say all sorts of things about him because he is always the winner, just like they did when he won his fights. But the truth is that he fights his wars behind closed doors, within the walls of that world. He never brings it out into the open or harms anyone who has no dealings with him. When you know Brazil better, you'll realize what a rare thing that is.'

Of course he was a hero to Nelson, whom he treated with a unique respect that ignored all differences in their positions, and Auguste still wouldn't charge him a centavo even though he'd paid him back in full two years ago. But Noel never contributed to such discussions, except once when the restaurant was closed and the others had taken their beers to the table in between Sr. da Lima and his bodyguards.

'Brazil is a very big country, Charlie. So the north has no idea what the south is doing. You can kill a hundred people in one place and build a hospital with some of the money elsewhere, and they both tell different stories about you. There are many favelas in Rio and São Paulo where they would say something very different. Perhaps innocent people can't help dying there, it's much more crowded and desperate than here and it's not always possible to do things so cleanly. Also, not so many people love you, so you have to keep many more of them afraid.'

Anyway, following Nelson's plan it didn't prove so difficult to resolve the problem of Grace Duvalier. All it required was a tiny, almost indiscernible fingerprint I left upon the edge of her plate, another even fainter smudge visible only against the light upon the cutting end of her special knife, and a bit of strategic placement. It was a busy Saturday lunchtime, and I'd made sure to leave just one table unoccupied, specially for Madame, right in between the ones usually reserved for Sr. da Lima and his bodyguards. By the time I brought the gentleman his Ricard, he had already noticed her minutely examine and send back her cutlery. Then she refused to touch the St. Jacques I placed before her, because of the little saffron finger mark by the plate's edge. I pointed out that the sauce itself was saffron and it must have tilted slightly to the edges, to which she replied frostily that it didn't matter how busy the restaurant was, since we charged the same prices at all times, everyone had a right to expect impeccable standards. And she made it plain that I wasn't to palm her off with the same serving moved onto another dish: she expected a fresh, untouched portion.

Normally, no matter how full the restaurant was, I kept an eye on Sr. da Lima's plate so that I would be ready the second it was empty, but this time we took a few moments deliberately rearranging Madame's dish in the kitchen. In fact, if memory serves me right, we poured ourselves a kir each and clinked glasses to her imminent annihilation. I pointed out that we had to applaud her courage or at least her degree of obliviousness: no one could have failed to recognize Sr. da Lima at the next table and yet it made not the slightest difference to her behaviour. Far from being intimidated, she kept tittering little asides to him in between reprimanding me for my lapses.

We had calculated each phase of the sting to a nicety. Ten minutes later, when I walked out with her immaculately restored starter, Auguste marched behind me carrying Sr. da Lima's rack of lamb himself, and stood with his back to us profusely apologizing for having kept him waiting. Striving to satisfy 'unforeseeably particular customer demands' on what was already an extremely busy afternoon had tied him up for the last ten minutes.

Sr. da Lima was short with Auguste but his ire was clearly directed elsewhere. We kept peering through the porthole in the kitchen door to catch the frequent glares he sent in her direction, which she didn't even notice, obsessed as she was with wiping her fingers and mouth every time she set down her cutlery. Then Madame made her own displeasure evident when she refused to hear of dessert and asked instead for a Grand Marnier straightaway with her bill. I almost felt pity for her as I played our last card, leaving a single but visible thumb impression upon the glass I would normally handle so nimbly by its stem. I hadn't even returned to the bar when she shouted out my name; I turned around to find her marching towards me with her liqueur held high in front of her.

Sr. da Lima had delicacy enough to have his message delivered once she was outside the restaurant. One of his men followed her out, and that night a very shaken Madame called and asked for Auguste to inform him that she'd been banned from the restaurant whenever Sr. da Lima was dining, and so there would be no more of her daily walk-in visits; she would phone ahead in future so that we could warn her before she reserved a table. Auguste sounded mortified, and spoke with passion and sincerity for a long time about how she was one of our most treasured patrons, reiterating his regret that we had only ourselves to blame for this depreciation of her custom. But it was a well-known fact that Sr. da Lima visited the city at least twice a month, and so from that day onwards I could always reply that of course we had more than one table available, as long as she didn't mind the risk of running into Sr. da Lima, who never gave us any advance notice before arriving.

Those first months were full of happiness. We would often end up drunk at Auguste's, either straggling down the main street until we reached his door, or else we'd enter his block through one of its side doors and continue through the endless corridor. He lived at one end and this disorderly but merry trudge through his building was almost half a kilometre long, moving from patch to patch of light thrown by the high, naked hanging light bulbs. Even at one o'clock there would be many doors open to either side of us; we could see families eating behind the curtains or sitting on their beds in front of the television. Some men would have gathered to play cards in the room of a bachelor, while outside a few children ran from room to room down the corridor and old women sat darning in the poor light on some of the benches. Auguste pointed out one boy who diligently practised his keepy-uppy skills alone every night until three. We happily greeted everyone we saw.

Or there was the time we decided it would be an adventure to explore in the other direction, down the riverside, along the city's edge. In that mixture of early dawn and the last of the moonlight it was just the two of us, but we were so drunk I had to hold on to Auguste to stay upright while he never let go of the railings. Then, a little distance away we noticed a stripped-down double-decker bus standing forlornly in a lane. Despite its rusty condition with no seats, or glass in any of its windows, it reminded me with a sharp twinge of London and I vaguely (with some embarrassment) recall a lot of sobbing. Not quite knowing how to calm me, Auguste must have suggested we climb aboard. Like a true friend he pushed me up each of the steps and all the way to the front of the upper deck where we remained for a long time, while he revealed a side of himself I'd never have imagined before. He was a sculptor once, he told me, and he carried around numerous ideas in his head, all to be hewn out of stone.

'I must leave something, Charlie, somewhere, just as a mark that I too inhabited this earth. Once I believed it would be a book of recipes, and that people would remember my dishes. But I lost that opportunity, and perhaps it's for the best. Memory is fickle, anyway. It's better if it's something made of stone.'

I didn't know how to respond to this, so I encouraged him and praised his cooking, and he tightly held my arm as I descended ahead of him one step at a time.

All I wanted after that was to lie down in my bed and grieve, perhaps read some treasured pages from my diary, but we reached a large field beside which were parked a lot of taxis waiting for the crowds inside the bars and nightclubs. Somehow Auguste got into an argument with one of the taxi drivers. My next memory is of being chased, or believing that we were being chased, by a host of vindictive cabbies, who frightened us so much by their numbers that we fled right over the railing and knee-deep into the river. We would never have drowned if we were sober but the fast-flowing muddy currents kept pushing us over. Thankfully some of the more humane cabbies took mercy on us, and three of them waded in and helped us out. Before we left we promised them all a free lunch at the restaurant that Sunday; ten of them took us at our word, and it was a marvellous success.

The Writer of Rare Fictions

Later Losses

(Rio de Janeiro, July 2004)

'Your grandfather rarely wrote, but I grew to dread the letters from Ma. It was obvious she was ashamed to bother me, that she loathed those people as much as I did, and felt no kinship with them at all, but it was a peculiarly interlocked entrapment. She had no one else to share these occurrences with, and my father had no one to share them with besides her, even after the separation. I still have the letters: the incidents they describe are extraordinarily repetitive. Often they verge on the surreal, not in terms of the events which were without exception nauseatingly petty, but surreal for the degree of malice evident in those plots, surreal for the sickness of the minds that cooked them up. Surreal that he could even inhale in that atmosphere, this most criminally inoffensive of men, who never raised his voice to defend his own wife, not even from the filthiest of charges, some of which I only learnt about a few years ago. It shamed my mother even then to repeat them.'

'And all this was why?' asked Seb.

'Once again, because of the curse of the will. My great-aunt had transferred the title-deed of the house to my father, something she skilfully managed to conceal during her lifetime: otherwise she would simply have been murdered. They wouldn't even have hired a killer – my younger uncles would have chopped her up themselves. But this curse landed squarely on Baba's head after she died, and of course in their fury and shock they turned all their heavy artillery upon him. Without sparing my mother, who'd lived apart for many years. Now the separation itself proved their goldmine. What tales they minted from it: why Ma left Baba, what she did now in her empty house to support herself.'

Seb had led me down this path, by asking about the present status of the Calcutta house, a long-running row that rumbled beneath the surface at a court hearing every couple of years, even though the guns rattled from within the trenches numerous times each day, since all the warring parties continued to live alongside one another on the disputed property. Thankfully, we'd washed our hands off it twenty years ago. The united front of his brothers and their families had collapsed the morning after my father wrote away his inheritance to one of them and moved out: now it was just plain schadenfreude to watch them rip chunks out of one another. Ma took little interest, but I can unashamedly confess to receiving reports of said behaviour with great relish from another cousin.

'Once, Baba was accused of having vilified the family at length to his fishmonger, and the proof they presented was the apparent "testimony" of the guy who sat with his back to Baba's man and overheard the entire tirade. One of my uncles happened to be his regular customer, and the story was that he faithfully reported everything verbatim.

'Now you won't recall meeting your grandfather, so you'll just have to accept my word as to the unlikelihood of this story, its sheer incompatibility with his personality. If only he'd been feisty enough to complain at least to the maachchwala. But you know our neighbourhood: can you imagine a fish-market scene in Lake Market on a Saturday morning, the crowds with all the screaming, the scaling, the gutting and weighing, the top-of-your-voice contests for customers, the discarded gills, the intestines and the mud underfoot, the dogs, the boys who slice and pack everything swarming around, and my father with his whispery voice competing with that cacophony to slander the family? After my great-aunt's death, when her servant was found hanged, there was no one to shop and cook separately for Baba. It was only the conscience of this same fishmonger that kept him from being swindled each week. And even if Baba had said anything, it's a ludicrous idea that all of this would be duly recalled and reported by the other chap who sold fish to my uncle.

'Of course, the question of truth didn't enter into it. Charges of that sort, and there were numerous other equally insane legends, like weekly episodes of some wild soap, spread like a pox down the corridors of the house from bedroom to bedroom, carried by servants and my youngest cousins. Nor did truth or its utter absence affect how much it tore up my father. It would silence him for weeks. He gave up eating in the dining room. It wouldn't occur to him to spread a few words of self-defence in retaliation, let alone some form of counter-propaganda. He would attempt to soak up the insupportable until it finally proved impossible to swallow, and then arrive a few weeks later on my mother's doorstep. No doubt Ma realized immediately the purpose of his visit, since no one came from that house with good news; yet it would take the third cup of tea for him to slowly unspool his story.'

It was the evening after our night at the pizzeria. We were traipsing round Lagoa for the second time, and the sun had just moved behind the humpbacked hills, some of which I'd always envisioned as gigantic whales run aground. As we talked, I was being reminded with renewed delight how many sides there were to Seb: he had his mother's gift for listening, but also for diverting a situation, especially as he sensed how much these recollections still wounded me. It made me feel even more embarrassed about my over-reaction the previous evening to our harmless little difference of opinion. I'd been directing the frustration I felt at Ana towards poor, unsuspecting Seb.

A girl promenaded towards us, chattering on her phone, wearing enough colours for a harlequin. She seemed wealthy and English, very West London, as if she were walking in Chiswick on Boat Race day along a different body of water: faux pink Pashmina, lime-green peasant skirt, brown suede boots, big beady fuchsia necklace, Chanel sunglasses hiding her eyes. As soon as we passed her, Seb pulled out his phone and dialled.

'Hello, hello, is that Emergency?' he hollered. 'I wish to report a brutal crime that has just occurred here in only slightly narrowing daylight. Yes, I'm the victim, and the assailant is sauntering away casually even as we speak.'

After a brief pause, he continued as I watched, probably gaping. 'This evening at six-thirty my fashion sense was savagely assaulted in an entirely unprovoked attack, that too by a foreigner, a gringa, a guest of our country. The initial diagnosis isn't promising, and I advise that you send an ambulance straight behind the police. It is very urgent, especially as she looks like a serial offender, and I have almost no doubt she will strike again tonight, possibly within the next few minutes.'

Seb pulled things like that with a straight face, without breaking stride. Afterwards I realized he'd dialled his mother: it was a comfort and counselling service they provided each other, the two queens, to help them through the first, most traumatic moments of shock.

Yet the same boy never flinched from anything difficult. In fact, he was hungry for every story I shared from my Calcutta life, especially if it involved his grandparents. He adored his Thamma. She was some sort of paragon for him.

'You know, when I first met your mother I would often secretly compare our backgrounds. She was exactly the person she remains, already fully formed, and I wondered from where she derived that unassailable cheerfulness, that unerring instinct for handling everything just so, with precisely the right detachment. She never appeared to carry any excess weight on her shoulders: she just didn't give the impression of being subject to the law of gravity. Everything seemed possible for her, and by extension everything seemed possible around her, within her aura. I adored her too much to envy her, but it was as though she never had any doubts about her entitlements, and no scars of disappointment or loss. The next thing she wanted would invariably be there, at exactly the right moment. When we spoke about childhood, and our families, initially I was ashamed. It seemed to me that all her confidence was founded upon the successes of her father – the imperiously benevolent master of the glorious fazenda I could only imagine, the provider of those idyllic holidays she described, and the trips to New York and Europe.

'So I'd conceal my real feelings, my abhorrence of falling victim to what I'd already grown to privately term the curse of the Chakrabortis. I never mentioned the sensation that I couldn't have escaped far enough to feel safe, safe from the infection of the ill-luck stories that arrived from home in a relentless fount, long before the era of ISD, stories solely of disease, malice, greed, desperation and failure. Which ignored great-uncle is languishing from an incurable illness because he can't afford the treatment; which cousin has been cheated out of some measly amount by his brother; which aging uncle has lost his job as a petty clerk and is now begging my mother to shelter his entire family in her tiny flat. And worse, much worse, suspicions of incest, allegations hurled at one another of the most twisted sexual connections, all within the fold of the mythic Indian family, whose embrace I couldn't escape even in England. No letters ever brought news of any special achievements, or of someone who'd attempted something beautiful and unusual, or simply of someone who was happy. And every last character in that cast, both the oppressors and the victims, was an acquaintance or a relative.

'Some of those episodes are so sordid and frankly unrealistic, I never used them in any of my novels. Did you know you have an uncle who is so fixated upon his daughter, your cousin, two years older than you, that he follows her to college to make sure that's where she really goes, and then spies upon her after classes to see which boys she speaks to? He takes half-days off from work at random to do this, he monitors her mobile, decides what she should wear, everything. His wife, a cousin of mine, confided in my mother. She's desperate to send her daughter to another city to study.

'It wasn't as though there was no one decent at home, or generous, or loving. But I was too young and insecure myself not to equate character and circumstance, not to blame everyone for their miserable condition, and to see that sometimes survival, in some recognizably human form, is the only possible success story. Or perhaps everything was too close to the skin: I feared succumbing to identical weaknesses in myself, the same excuses for lifelong mediocrity, or worse, a reactive impulse to bully and oppress if I ever had the chance.

'Because all these tales were topped by that of my father's, a man who had completely surrendered control over his own fate, whose example I feared as much as it repelled me, even though we never once came near to discussing it. Sometimes, standing beside Ana, especially in my darker moments, I felt like a fool running on a stairway, forever struggling to keep pace with her as she effortlessly sailed upwards on an escalator.'

'You never gave her the chance to empathize.' Seb spoke calmly, unsurprised, as if he was familiar with these stories and justifications, though I had never shared them with him before.

'That's true. I honestly feared I would scare her off. You see, from everything I heard I believed home for Ana was actually the ideal that the Christmas industry defines it to be: the escape from the trials of the world, the sanctuary from all its pressures. How could I explain that for me and Ma it had always symbolized the opposite: the most demanding test, the focal point of our repeated violation?

'In fact, I went further. Despite numerous pleas, I kept Ana from visiting India with one excuse after another until well after the success of my first novel, which meant we could stay at the Grand, invite Baba over every other day by telephone, and take Ma on a holiday to Himachal. Instead we visited Brazil thrice, at my insistence, and each time I was more certain this was where I was meant to be, where I should have been born. It had so many of the things I loved about home – the light, the trees, the warmth and the chatter – but it was two continents away from everyone I hated.'

'And it didn't bother you what the Bomber did, in order to provide this paradise?'

'Sweetheart, when one is a tourist, one gratefully accepts the luxury of not interpreting, of not taking responsibility for one's surroundings, and so it proved with me. Whatever is wrong with Brazil, it's not my country. Of course, my early visits were during the dictatorship, yet I emphasized everything that was beautiful, and allowed my brain a holiday, both in the house and when we walked around in the city. This happy approach continued almost until you were born, when we decided to move back, and this became my home.'

'Did you never feel you'd abandoned Thamma? What about missing out on all those years with her? You could have shielded her from so much. Or at least, you could have brought her to live abroad with you. I know Mum would have welcomed her.'

'Hey, that's a lot of explanation being demanded for one evening. You remind me of your mother's lawyer, only you're far better looking. Ana will tell you how many times we invited your Thamma to join us in London, and then here in Rio, long before you were born. She always refused because her friends were in Calcutta. She loved her teaching job, and felt she'd be unemployable in Britain at fifty. And if she didn't work, how would she make friends? Overnight she'd turn into an old lady, she insisted, and then steadily become a burden, because she'd depend on us for everything – money, conversation, company.

In Calcutta she had her own circle, even though it included the crap Baba brought in periodically with him.

'As for moving back, that's the hard part to answer. The truth is, I was always too afraid of being swallowed up again, and not even the thought of living alongside Ma could outweigh that terror. Your mother was an enchanted article for me; she was a magic carpet, but also a simple life-belt. I saw her as a sign, a gift, an opportunity to begin again in Brazil, unencumbered by my past. I just couldn't let go.'

'Yes, you could, you let go just a few years later,' he pointed out, looking straight ahead, walking beside me. We were returning to the beach through Ipanema. For some reason, the lights on this particular street weren't working, yet I'd recognized it immediately.

'Do you remember your baby-sitter Beatriz? She lived here, and I used to drop her off in the evenings.'

'Yup, right down there, after the next crossing. She's in London now, working in a primary school. She published a book, co-written with a friend: an exchange of letters between them. She wrote from London and her friend replied from here. It's called *Os Fósforos: A Box of Matches*.'

'Her parents still live here though,' he continued as we passed the house. 'You should drop in. They'd recognize you. It would please them.'

'Seb, why archaeology?' I asked after a pause, as we emerged from the neighbourhood a few blocks later and crossed the avenue to the beach.

'It turns me on, Babs. It really does. You know how Mum likes recreating cities from the twenties and thirties for her movies, and you'd show me all that film noir when I was younger? Why was that? Because you liked inhabiting that world, even though there was no real connection to the present. You and Mum taught me it's cool to move to new places. Well, I think it's equally okay to move to other times. Just be wherever you feel at home, right?'

'Of course, bro. I'm just thinking I'm going to have to read up some to make conversation when we meet. I confess it's not been an area of priority thus far. But I'll tell you something odd. The unlikeliest of people once confessed a secret to me, that when he was young he'd yearned to be a pilot, although there was no opportunity for an Indian in those days. And his second preference would have been archaeology. But his father swept all such fancies out of his head, threatened to write him off without an allowance, and forced him into a degree in banking.'

'I know who you're referring to.'

'You do? Well, he would have been proud of you. I tell you, he was my own Discovery channel. Everything – Egypt, the Indus Valley, Mexico, Peru, he just lapped it up. He kept clippings from the newspapers. He relished the essays my mother brought home, even though she only taught Class Six. The few things I ever saw him indignant about were errors, factual or presentational, in my history textbook. He once ordered a set of world mythologies as a birthday present when I was eight.'

'Well, maybe these things do flow through the genes. Look, I'm making no promises. A big part of this is wanting to live once more in New York. I don't really care what subject I pick. We'll see how it goes, Babs, where the hottest chicks are. Maybe you'll see me tempted out of my otherworldly digs by some Gisele or Gwyneth in English Lit.'

'Well, if you ever swing the other way, just walk over to law school or the MBA programme, because that's where the biggest pricks are.'

Through all this, an earlier remark of his had remained in the air between us, about my letting go of them when he was young, and I responded when we had found a table at a beach-side kiosk.

'Seb, has your mother mentioned that I've regretted that ever since? Perhaps I began regretting it the morning after. You see, I suffered in those days from a rare condition that afflicts one in many millions. Thankfully it's curable, but it's debilitating while it lasts. It's the illness of ideas. There are milder versions, but I caught the severest form. I sold myself this damn-fool theory that I'd outgrown the limits of individual life, that there was much more potential within me than ordinary human ties, to family, friends and children, could ever satisfy. I took it further. Not only did domesticity have no outlet for my energies, I believed – and even wrote the stupidest pieces about it – that overselling our bonds to the bourgeois family might be seen as an active corporate ruse, to fill our heads with the mundane whilst they carved up the world unnoticed, to turn us into addicted consumers and nail our asses to our loans and mortgages. And finally to saturate our hearts with the narrowest possible definition of caring, focused entirely upon the nuclear family, so that we never reflected upon our connections to each other as a wider society.

'In a nutshell, I transformed what never demanded to be an either-or into a crossroads for myself, with calamitous consequences. All because of the disease of ideas, because Gandhi said, you have to be the changes you want to see in the world. That is how I took it.'

'Wow, living Marxism, huh. But in your defence, let it be noted you hardly had any experiences of family worth embracing.'

'Thanks, bro, very decent of you to mention that. Apart from Ana and Ma, that's true. And yet somehow I chucked out the baby too, meaning you. I managed to lose all of you along the way.'

'Is the Ovomaltine place still open back there?' I asked, watching the bathers in the distance, and making a mental note to wake up early and challenge Seb to a game of Frescobol. Since, unlike tennis, there were no ground-strokes to chase down, I believed I could still give him a keen run. The last time had been desperately close, about two years before: I'd been let down by some terrifically biased refereeing – Seb's home advantage – by Clara and his grandfather.

'Yeah, of course, still outselling McDonalds by a mile. Are you thinking of retracing your steps?'

'Perhaps, perhaps. I wasn't a lot older than you when I first came to Rio. In those days I sneaked down here almost daily, just to gawk. Can you imagine the effect this beach had on a poor starved boy from Calcutta? And many years later, when someone first took us to that Ovomaltine place, I experienced the same craving once more.'

'Yes, it's there, and so are the omelette places and the padarias and the juice shops. How big a Sunday breakfast are you up for? We could do a brunch crawl?'

'Well, I will need to celebrate, since by then I will have kicked your ass definitively in our morning title-round of Frescobol,' I replied.

'The glint of contest gleams in his eye. The insult will not go un-avenged. Same referees as last time?'

'I think not. How about someone neutral, someone who'll officiate for the pleasure of watching the old master carve up the young stud? Like some passing gostosa we can charm tomorrow morning?'

'Oh, Babs, I hate to think of demolishing you twice in one morning. Why do you want to shatter your heart as well as your pride? How will you continue living without either of your vital organs?'

'Did you know J-Lo only has coffee that's been stirred counter-clockwise?' I replied, unable to raise the bar on the trash-talk.

'Do I dare believe the evidence of my own ears? Are you trying to get down with me? You old humbug, you. I always suspected this was your secret vice: last time I even caught you flipping back to VH1 to catch that Destiny's Child video. I gotta tell you, Mum thought that was hilarious.'

'Well, I'm not sheepish at all. I would stand up for Beyoncé any day. It would be criminal to be embarrassed about it.'

'Hmm, she has power thighs. I prefer her waist upwards.'

He knew exactly how to rile me. The argument raged all the way to the long queue at Bob's the Ovomaltine geniuses, though it soon metamorphosed into an even more passionate defence (by me) of Test cricket, when he confessed he never felt the urge to catch up with India's doings on cable. I compared the unfolding of a five-day match to the manifold rhythms of life itself, and to the descriptive passages in Proust that only someone crazy for constant climax would skip ('What will you be, Seb, a skipper or a savourer?') and finally, in that vein, I stretched the analogy to tantric coitus, at which point Seb reminded me to curb my enthusiasm, since there was a group of evidently American teenagers in line before us, staring and eavesdropping.

The Perfect Worker

London Diary: Martina's Story

As soon as she'd been poured her Jack Daniels with Coke, she'd head straight for any available table for two and settle down to text on her phone, but rarely was she left alone. Some smart-ass who fancied his chances would inevitably walk over to try, not so much the regulars but the punks who strode in from fixing the road, each of them succumbing to the enticement of the unspoken contest, as if in pre-arranged turns. She always refused to look up from her mobile after the initial brush-off, four or five of them within half an hour at peak-times when they all poured in to wet their beaks, and I think this was what attracted Patty's attention and then her sympathy. Because the second week onwards, she glared down anyone who gave any hint of sidling in that direction, becoming Martina's unpaid guardian angel, her self-installed filter of spam. A month later and Martina was history, but for those three weeks between being a constant novelty and disappearing without warning, she became, how do I put it, a feature of the afternoon that reliably marked the passage of time. Noted with silent satisfaction, like anything peaceful.

It wasn't long before Martina grew aware of this favour and repaid it by remaining at the bar for a few minutes after receiving her drink, her attention devoted solely to Patty. Just small talk, but a small talk laced with mutual respect, which somehow made itself apparent even to me, though I was too far away to eavesdrop. They resembled each other in some peculiar inner way, nothing to do with their discrete physical qualities. Martina was tall and looked like she scored a lot of coke. Brown hair, small mouth, very urban and frail, not someone who'd usually visit our kind of pub. She would never be in *The Sun* with her top off, she wasn't someone any of us ordinarily fantasized about, yet that is what made her compelling. No one would have glanced at her in Chelsea, she would have even seemed shabby there. But she baffled us by returning daily, five times a week, materializing and disappearing without any context.

It was Patty who introduced us one slow afternoon, perhaps as the one male of novelty value who would never consider bothering her. This obliged me to acknowledge her the next few days with a greeting, and culminated in her joining me in the conservatory that Thursday even though it was obvious I was reading the paper. I was startled, but pleased despite myself. Sure, the pub was full, and all her usual tables had been taken, but she could have just stayed talking to Patty. We didn't have much of a conversation: a nod, an offer by me to hand her a section of the newspaper, Martina declining with a smile so she could text. After half an hour she left. The only outcome of that afternoon was that I too started showing up daily instead of thrice a week, though it wasn't for anything specific. I couldn't have told you what I hoped for: I wouldn't have owned up to the word 'hope'. Yet I had also noticed that I now added a small smile to my greeting. But no words. Believe it or not, there were never any words.

And out of nothing more, I decided to follow her the next Wednesday. I left the pub two minutes behind her, before drawing closer on the sidewalk, assuring myself I would go no further than the tube station. When she boarded a double-decker, I followed her in but remained downstairs, face firmly in my paper, afraid she'd get off any minute. We continued eastwards for half an hour, and eventually I would have nearly missed her because I began reading again, but managed to alight just in time, concealed behind a small crowd on Stoke Newington High Street. I watched her march decisively down a side street, then another, and enter a house, while remaining at the corner myself: the road was empty and I'd surely have been spotted.

The next time, I left the bar minutes after she'd arrived – so as not to arouse suspicion that we were regularly leaving after each other – and took up position in a kebab shop with a grilled haloumi sandwich and a perfect view of the bus stop. It was more than likely that she would use another route, or that she had only been visiting a friend. But my guess was proved right: that was Martina's home. Now, all I had to do was confirm another suspicion.

Four days later I was back on her street, during the hour I knew she'd be at the pub. I had to be quick, in order to be out of there before she returned. It was a large three-storey row house, which she must have shared with friends and compatriots. For half an hour I walked around the neighbourhood in a random fashion to remain inconspicuous to any observers, while always heading back to the same corner. In that period I watched two girls leave, dressed very similarly to Martina in high boots and skirts, and five lone men knock and enter. There was no other significant activity on the street, apart from a trickle of schoolchildren trudging homewards in ones and twos.

I soon ascertained that the male visitors weren't boyfriends (or mates), but 'lovers' of a lesser sort, and very nearly caused myself harm. The roughneck who opened the door didn't believe the story about my buddy Pablo who'd promised to rendezvous here, and went straight for my collar when I turned around to leave. I could have been a plain-clothes detective for all he knew, but he didn't seem like much of a thinker. I evaded his first punch and blocked his second before kneeing him in the groin and then again flush in the face as he kneeled to clutch himself. That was all the violence it took to free myself from his grip, and I took off for the high street before he could groan for help.

I couldn't return to the area in case they were waiting. Anyhow, Martina's life was none of my business, and for the next week I suspended all adventures, my purposeless curiosity satisfied. I remained in my corner throughout her visits, greeted her amiably and savoured the warmth of her response, although there was never an opportunity to share tables again.

Perhaps she had touched a nerve, and I reacted oddly because I hadn't felt anything like it in over twenty years. Or else, possibly, I'd recognized what she did right away, and that is why I was moved. Until a few years ago, I used to visit such places often, though lately these requirements had somehow vanished. Anyway, I should confess that after the one dramatic accident of my youth in India, I'd never touched a woman without paying for it. Close friendship with Patty was still a couple of years away.

The last time Martina visited, she had a prominent black eye and a cut across her forehead, inadequately dressed. She was also wearing a coat although it was June. She told Patty it was the price you paid for having a big Bulgarian boyfriend; they came with Balkan tempers. She seemed to want to behave normally after her brief explanation, and Patty respected this by not fussing. Martina found a seat and pulled out her phone, but everything was wrong about the tempo that afternoon. She drank too fast, frequently placed the phone on the table, brought out some tissues but didn't cry, and once buried her face in her arms. I watched everything from my barstool. When she left after ten minutes, I took my drink through into the empty conservatory.

It was a stroke of fortune. Five minutes later, my oversized but not over-bright contender strode in, apparently eager for an immediate rematch, grasping Martina's arm, growling in what I now supposed to be Bulgarian. I was far away, to the left at the rear of the pub, next to the garden door, with a partial view of the main area. It was a normal afternoon, and conversation had ceased abruptly with this interruption. I realized Patty had reacted, possibly by stepping out from behind the bar, when I heard Martina's voice: 'It's all right, Patty, I promise. Don't worry. We're just taking a look.'

How had he linked his attacker to Martina, and traced me down to this pub? Had he followed her just like I did, and suspected she was meeting a (quixotic) admirer? But this wasn't the moment for reflection, and I soundlessly gulped down my drink (because an unfinished pint would have been a clue), and let myself out through the garden. It was an unusual exit, but not unprecedented. People did leave through the back if, for instance, there was a game on TV and you didn't fancy shoving through a roaring crowd. No one would suspect a connection.

Luckily, new assignments kept pouring in during the next few months, for short films and commercials, and I had ready excuses to avoid visiting the Three Bells. Sometimes in the studio, to give my brain and my eyes and ears a break, I'd switch off the light and retreat underwater into recalling Martina. There was no doubt by now that I felt something for her: in fact, if I didn't know her story and believed she was just an ordinary girl, I would certainly have returned to ask her out.

It was longing I felt, and it steadily jumbled my brain. In my isolation, with no one to trust for advice, I couldn't keep the various cards between my fingers, the conflicting variables to consider. What about the pimp recognizing me, should things go any further? How would I explain following her? How could there be anything between us? We hadn't even spoken yet. What else would emerge if I drew any sort of attention to myself? How much of my life could I share?

I would have returned much sooner had I not repeatedly been thwarted by the idea of having to reckon with the pimp, once I decided to approach Martina. Buying out the Bulgarian wasn't an option, though for one shining moment it seemed appropriately chivalrous. I didn't have any such amount to hand, and anyway, would it even earn us a final resolution?

For a while one afternoon I actively considered the option of being frank with her, and very nearly reached the pub before my resolve dissipated. I would take her out to dinner and confess about my trip to her house. It could even be my trump-card, my willingness to address the issue before we began anything ourselves. I wouldn't for a moment divulge my real plan, the nasty, anonymous end that would soon befall her Bulgarian: I'd just speak about running away together. Yet soon I modified the idea, wondering if the Bulgarian should make his exit in an unrelated *previous* accident, thus freeing Martina even before I entered her life?

The choice turned upon the crux of connection. I had got away with two murders solely because they were arbitrary. I could not risk being a quiet regular in a pub that the dead pimp's girl visited, way across town. Why did she get a drink so far away: she must have been meeting a co-plotter. If the link had occurred to that gorilla, a detective would surely sniff it out. A few routine questions, and someone would connect the murder and our sudden disappearance. From there it was one step too close to exposing everything else, everything I would put behind me anyway during my future happiness with Martina.

But Martina might link me to her dead 'boyfriend' herself, if I showed up with my proposal directly afterwards, and that would frighten her even more than her present entrapment. Would she be willing to run away with a stranger who'd proved himself to be a murderer?

It would all be resolved with the correct blend of sincerity and discretion, I'd worked out by the time I finally reached the pub. As always, I must only reveal things to her on a need-to-know basis. For the foreseeable future I should just be the older man chancing his heart one last time, a sentimentalist whose silence had concealed his desperation, even something of a fool.

Roger, Steve and Gerard were pleased to see me back, and in my happiness at being welcomed I stood them all a couple of rounds. I was also chattier than usual with Patty, which seemed to surprise her, and I casually raised four or five subjects as decoys before I dropped in a question about Martina.

'I would love to know myself where that poor girl is,' she said, 'seeing as she hasn't returned since the day that ape slapped her around. I wish I'd asked her where she lived, so at least we could make some inquiries. So many times I've said to Gerard, perhaps we should have a word with the police. But he's right, we've got no leg to stand on. No name, no address, no charge, what would we give them? Sometimes I catch myself pursuing terrible thoughts, and I really fear for her safety. But the boys here say it's just an average case of domestic jealousy, and they're probably right. You get an ape like that and he's bound to use his fists before his brains, especially when he doesn't speak the language. It's happened so many times in front of my eyes, even right here in this pub, without mentioning any names and present company excepted. And each time you wonder, what's a girl like her doing with a beast like that? But all you can do is stand by and watch people make their mistakes, though there are some mistakes they can't even run away from.'

Martina was obviously far from forgotten, although no one had any idea how to trace her. They'd spent a lot of the intervening weeks puzzling over the events of that afternoon, and I was glad to realize my absence had gone unnoticed. In fact, Roger mentioned it in passing, saying, 'If I remember correctly, you narrowly missed the fun, Charlie. You were here, and then you left. A few minutes later, Beauty and the Beast, the North London debut, right here in humble old Three Bells.'

The rest can be sketched in fairly quickly. From the top of the road, there was an unmistakeable 'To Let' sign visible above the small hedge in front of their steps, though I walked to the door to be sure. There seemed no danger in visiting the estate agent handling the property. They were nearby on the high street, and were evidently pleased to receive my inquiry. They would be candid with me, the agent promised – they were having trouble shifting the place. Frankly, the previous tenants (selected personally by the landlord) had left it requiring a few major repairs. The owner didn't have the cash upfront to spare, so for now, if the tenant didn't mind a few breakages that would each be imminently addressed, it was actually, pardon the expression, something of a legalized steal for a fully furnished Victorian terrace. I could view it an hour later and be laughing all the way home by four o'clock, the entire, outrageous transaction conducted in broad daylight.

I prised myself from his enthusiastic clutches with a couple of false promises and a request for some thinking time. In the greasy-spoon a few doors down, I attempted to dismantle the matter over my coffee. There would be ample opportunity later to feel remorse over losing her because of my delay. I blocked that pounding regret from view, and gazed wholly upon the option facing me. Should I contact the landlord or not, to inquire about his ill-chosen tenants? But there rose again the spectre of connections. I imagined locating Martina and the Bulgarian, and finishing him off before I reappeared in her life. In the best-case scenario, she would agree to my offer of beginning afresh elsewhere, although she might certainly choose to employ her freedom towards some more attractive end than eloping with a middle-aged loner. Or perhaps I'd have hurled her into the fire, because of course there would be other cronies and pimps: they would assign her to someone worse, assuming she wasn't suspected of complicity. On the other hand, to repeat my most persuasive objection, wouldn't any investigator visit the landlord to ask him if he knew his property had been used as a brothel?

At which point he would remember my visit, and my questions about where the Bulgarians had gone.

What else remains to be spelt out? I sank helplessly for the next many months, and never stepped outdoors except to buy bread every few days. I turned down all new offers of work, and didn't go near the Bells (they had no contact number for me). There was no sequel to the Martina story; she had disappeared as if she never was. And really, wasn't that what truly transpired? In what way could I claim we had existed for each other?

It grew worse when I acknowledged that I'd begun planning possible solutions very early, deep within, almost as soon as I'd suspected her profession, long before I tailed her. Those weeks of inaction had proved fatal, and I now suffocated from the recognition of my selfishness. Yes, committing murder for a cause as unlikely and far-flung as this would have been an insane option. But that hadn't been my reason. I had already killed twice: there were no boundaries to overcome. It was no more than self-preservation, the terror of exposing myself to connections. Although, this time someone else's fate could have been transformed, even if she didn't feel anything for me.

It wasn't until six weeks later that I resumed my afternoons at the pub, and for the first time allowed myself to freely chat with Patty. In the interim however lay another incident, the death of a Greek professor jogging along just after dark in Putney Heath.

The Writer of Rare Fictions

Self-Evidence

(London, Late February, 2006)

I misread Sharon at the start. I mistook her toughness for an act, and responded by trying to patronize, charm, awe and muscle her, sometimes in succession, frequently all together. I construed her as a punk reporter: she showed up to bust some myths, spar with a legend, punching hard straight from the bell, and by the evening she was flat on her back, completely under my spell. I remember inwardly congratulating myself at pulling it off yet again, and even outlined my 'method' to her in one of my responses, which I knew to be an explicit underlining of my triumph.

'You see, getting through has always been paramount. Reaching as deep as possible inside the widest range of people. Because I have always believed you can, without any trade-off or compromise. In movies and in politics they manage to sway millions by reducing everything to the lowest denominator. The flip side of that same cynicism is those who believe complexity must necessarily be exclusive, since most of humanity is too coarse for things like truth and beauty.

'But I've always found that individuals fill whatever vessel you provide them. They calibrate themselves to whatever level you meet them at. What it does take on your part is a basic faith in such potential, the capacity to imagine that despite appearances, each other person is as deep and mysterious as you consider yourself to be. Added to this, you require the suppleness of soul to re-tune your register each time.

'I remember once telling a gathering that fluent communication requires a very simple instinct: the ability to talk less than someone who is naturally inclined to be more voluble than yourself, and to speak more than someone who is inclined to be quiet.'

She was recording everything, so she sat through this with crossed legs and pursed lips, fingers curled around the handle of the coffee mug, all of which for some reason irked me immensely. She didn't have the same rights my son had, to be sarcastic or familiar. Besides, you had to earn the right to be provocative by, for instance, having thoroughly boned up on your subject's works as preparation. Did this woman seem that diligent?

'So you're telling me that what I, and many others, have long considered a simple hunger for publicity is actually something deeper than that, that it is a symptom of this "suppleness" you're talking about? Is that why you let yourself be photographed indiscriminately at nightclub openings and London parties, as well as at demonstrations and refugee camps, or alongside known criminals, some of whom assume the right to call you their friend?'

'W-o-o-o-h, hold on a minute and first put down that weapon. You're among friends here; you might hurt somebody. Is this the way you interview all your subjects?'

'No, only the ones who seem to get away with murder, the ones who never get asked the questions we all want them to answer. So tell me, is it another way of remaining in the news, since you haven't published a serious novel in what, five years, nor have you begun any of those movies you announced you were planning in collaboration with your ex-wife?'

You can say what you like about me, but you can't deny I love a challenge. I've given you a taste of what I was up against so that you appreciate my sense of achievement when four hours later Sharon and I were lying together, pillows propped up so we could gaze out through the French windows at the garden below. It was five o'clock, and the glass of Lagavulin in my hand only enhanced the self-satisfaction I felt within. Under the sheets our legs were entwined, and from where I lay with my face near her hair I inhaled her scent frequently. Sometimes I would kiss her softly on her cheeks and next to her eyes. What can I say: I actually liked her. I liked her style. I liked her smell, her voice, her length inside her one-piece dark blue dress. I liked the way she made me work to please her. I liked her legs, her knees, her jaw-line and her cheekbones, and the way her lipstick filled out her mouth. When I undressed her I liked the way her tits pointed sideways as if they were well-experienced, as if they were used to being handled and providing pleasure. I liked the thought of her teeth, and the lines of her back. In fact, most things I could have liked about a woman, I liked about Sharon.

The detail that seems most comical to me now is when I first went down on her, and she said it wasn't worth the effort since no one had ever made her come that way; as a matter of fact, she never could see what all the fuss was about. So of course even at my age I strove, and how idiotically pleased I was by her responses. The other odd thing, odd given the context of everything else, was that I liked her because she reminded me of my son. Seb acted tough with me in the same way as Sharon: ever since he'd grown into his teens he considered it part of his filial duty to hit me with the really difficult questions, to be merciless with my bullshit and unsparingly critical of any flab I might have gathered (of course, needless to add, he inherited some of this instinct from his mother). And I enjoyed the challenge, almost as if I was taking on a much younger opponent to prove I was still a worthy champion, that my relevance and commitment still rang true, that I remained as cool as ever.

'There was this line I came across in one of your interviews, that I wanted you to clarify. You were asked what your overall body of work added up to, and replied that in the final analysis, beauty was always your "only argument". What did you mean by that – the beauty of your work, or the beauty of the way you lead your life? You think it's beautiful to embody contradictions and reach out to everyone – which to you means being friends with gang-lords and warmongers and the occasional dictator? Speaking of which, since you were there just a few weeks ago, have you ever glanced at the beautiful CVs of some of your Davos drinking buddies?'

Getting up to refill my glass, I had to laugh. This was from someone who'd been yelping for pleasure less than twenty minutes ago with my hands cupping her ass, her legs tightly around my centre, and her tongue almost down my throat. But I liked her for her spirit.

'You make me sound like Walt Whitman. You know, my son hurls the same accusations, and in the same tone of disgust. He says, Baba, doesn't it ever disturb you that you are friends with everyone, people who hate each other, people hated by everyone else? I tell him I am simply a curious guy, curious about investigating everything human beings are capable of, everything they've done and are doing on this planet. And when you make that your objective, it must necessarily imply associating with people many would deem unpalatable. Because the world is what it is, right, and yet we all have to make a go of it together. We're past the whole business of sending our opponents off to Siberia.'

'Yes, now we like to meet our close chums over skiing in Davos. I'm sorry, that was snide, but you and I do have very different ideas of "investigation".'

'You know, those air-quotes would work a lot better if you weren't still naked under the sheets of the guy you're supposed to be grilling.' Those were my words, but my smile never dropped.

In response she gave me the finger. I got back into bed beside her and started up a chat about Lord Krishna.

'Look, I don't think even those who've hated my work from the first day for its lack of a consistent "morality", would dare argue the proposition that I spend time near the rich, the powerful and the notorious in order to launder their actions. Yes, I am interested in their humanity, I wonder what qualities it requires to be successful in those spheres of remote-control power. I want to learn how it is they view the show and how they run it, those people whom Rushdie calls "the never encountered but ever present kings of the world".

'You know, I have often spoken about Lord Krishna and his importance in my thinking. Look at Vishnu, of whom Krishna was an incarnation. Vishnu is meant to be the preserver of Creation. Yet, each time the earth was threatened by a different crisis, with remarkable flexibility this most important of deities assumed exactly the form best suited to deal with that particular threat. It's not like he descended only as a Brahmin or a Kshatriya, or even as a human being for that matter. It wasn't beneath his dignity to show up as a fish when he had to, or a turtle, a boar, a dwarf, or even a half-man half-lion because that was what the situation demanded! When the mission was the perpetuation of existence itself, no form could be too lowly.

'And even when he appeared as Krishna, he never allowed himself the luxury of being entirely divine. There are numerous instances of Krishna's possible fallibility, where we can question his judgement as if he was almost human. That is one of the two things I love most about him. He even allowed himself to be cursed with the destruction of his own clan, and the most anonymous of deaths. That is what I have always taken my inspiration from: that is what I mean by openness to the fullness of life.'

Far from elevating the level of exchange, I seemed to be giving Sharon's mischief more fuel. 'Ah, so now you're an avatar of Vishnu. This must be a world-exclusive. Can that go on the record?'

'It can if this can,' I said, pointing to her still lazing under my sheets, and barely restrained myself from launching a major pillow fight. Oral sex was one thing, but pillow war would be too much on a first date. Instead, I cleared my throat and retained the high tenor of my musings.

'All I meant was, I've aimed to create as plastic and as flexible a soul as I can. A soul as slithery as an eel, a thoroughly amphibious soul. But you know something else I learnt, souls are made slithery only through exercise. You've got to exercise those joints if you want them supple. That is where the writing comes from; that is what it's always been about.'

'How would you rate our soul-exercise this afternoon, on a scale of slug to Nirvana?'

What I did was, I turned the irresistible urge to launch a surprise pillow strike into an admirably tender post-coital kiss.

'What is the second thing?' Sharon rejoined after a while, sitting up under the covers.

'What second thing?'

'You said there were two things you love about Krishna.'

'Oh, the second thing isn't moral. It's his unashamed capacity for pleasure, of kinda doing what we just did. But definitely don't quote me on that.'

We didn't even get to discussing my new book until dinner, although she'd informed me it was the focus of the interview. I set out risotto cooked in red wine, with cream, peppers and aubergines, whatever was in the fridge: she did all the chopping. It was incongruous, and for me, quite unprecedented. No critic had ever chopped for me before.

'I hoped I would befriend you,' she said. 'It would add so much to the piece.'

'Come on,' I laughed, 'there's no way any of this is going into your article, though you can mention I went to the trouble of preparing you a snack. For the rest, you'd be fired and someone would probably contrive some grounds to nail me. It would just about finish me off. How long will it be anyway?'

'There will be two versions, one for the weekend review and one online that will include the entire conversation. But it won't be a transcript. It'll be in first person, impressionistic.'

'I just want to remind you that we're going to share a meal together. You've come, showered and broken bread in my flat. Be merciful, even if you can't be a friend!'

'Hey, you backed up your big talk. You *are* open. You are trusting. So you've got nothing to worry about.'

She took care of the salad dressing – again with anything at hand, which today was olive oil, soya sauce and honey – and told me something about herself. Her father was from Goa, but she'd been raised in London by her mum, who was a well-known newsreader on the BBC. I knew the lady from numerous parties, but hadn't made the connection myself. We also had acquaintances in common in India.

'So how did you manage,' she continued, returning from the kitchen, 'to piss everyone off within a month? You even lost the friends you made through the pro-capitalism book with the post-7/7 article. I mean, they're creeps, let's not pretend any false objectivity here, but at least for that brief interlude they courted you, since you went to the trouble of making them appear respectable. Think of it: your first well-reviewed work in the *Wall Street Journal*. They were willing to forgive you a lot, and then you went and spoilt it all by saying something stupid like I love you, to the 7/7 boys! Huh! Go figure?'

'Don't talk with your mouth full. The risotto will taste better with a little more salt. Is your recorder on?'

'No to all three. Don't change the subject. This is the business end of the interview. This is your chance to share your soul-shattering insights with us. Remember, we lefties don't do fatwas, but there's always the risk of the lone loony. Have you Googled yourself lately?'

'No. Is it heart-breaking?'

'Let me tell you, on this one matter we've all gleefully joined forces – the moral police, the eco-warriors, the World Social Forum people. Just before I left the office this morning, someone compared your private life to Meursault's, you know, *The Outside*r, for your neglect of your mother and son. Then he admitted he's never met you, but went on to conclude that he wasn't certain whether you should be committed or plain imprisoned. Still, he's sure you're a pest, sane or not.'

'And in Delhi, they tell me a recent review of my political about-turns turned into a sexual charge-sheet, hinting at many who would only be too happy to recall their experiences of loving, being used, and discarded by me.'

'Ah, so you have Googled yourself,' she grinned. I refilled her wine.

'Yeah, this was hilarious. The woman mentions interviewing an unnamed someone I once dismissed within a couple of nights after cruelly listing her physical shortcomings – because she'd dared to utter the word love. My memory isn't so great, forgive me if I can't recall *every* cruel thing I've said, but I'm thinking if anyone comes close to filling that someone's description, it's most likely the writer herself.'

'But of course. None of this is new. I've done my research. Your biography makes clear that you were an ambitious climber lacking all scruples, and ruthlessly ditching those who provided you succour during your penniless years.'

'Shall we get through the interview before I start to get cruel with you?'

'Oh, yeah, you want to get started on physical shortcomings? Don't forget, it's been twenty years since you shot those birds down. I'd be generous with my compliments if I were you.'

'This was the unkindest cut of all. Blow, winds, and crack your cheeks! Rage! Blow! You cataracts and hurricanoes... blah blah blah, I tax you not with unkindness, I never gave you head, made you come, you owe me no subscription.'

It was the sort of silliness Seb loved. Again, impermissible and peculiar thoughts, but I regretted this lovely creature's age, inconveniently equidistant between me and my son. He was too young to be of interest to her yet; I was too busy to seek more beyond this afternoon. I realized then how much I looked forward to his growing up for all sorts of reasons. Still, New York abounded in spirits like hers, and I had no doubt Seb would be introducing me presently to a selection of them. Perhaps female, perhaps not always. When I look at certain details – the kathak (?) lessons he briefly took while staying with my mother in Calcutta three summers ago, the intense awareness of women's fashion – I honestly am not sure. Maybe I could ask Ana what she thought, if I raised the subject at the right moment.

Back to the present. We were both cosy under rugs on opposite couches when for the umpteenth time I began my explanations, still hoping someone would actually discuss the paragraphs in between the sound-bites. Sharon was right: everybody had snipped off only what suited them, the "friends" as well as the implacable foes of my poor little book. There were the baffled literary guys, and the even more bemused *Wall Street Journal* people (not to forget the incandescent lefties), none of whom could quite fathom this socio-spiritual macro-economic tract they were compelled to review. Yet it was plainly argued, and ordinary readers seemed to have no problem comprehending the point in its entirety.

'Sharon, you know it was a simple book, essentially non-serious, a few suggestions by a non-specialist. Perhaps that's the best way to leave things.'

She was obviously annoyed by my last-minute coyness, and even placed her glass of wine on the side-table, so that her outburst wouldn't stain my sofa.

'Don't go soft on me after all I've been through to arrive at this point, no slight intended. It was a serious book because you took the trouble of having it published. And I agree with you that the argument has been misrepresented, numerous times, ok? Happy? But I'm your best chance for a full-on hearing, followed, I guarantee, by an all-inclusive rendering, on this, on the terrorists, and on any sundry matter you've put your foot into recently.'

She was so amusing I wanted to give her a chance. I was already looking forward to being let down by her full-length 'impressionistic' article.

'All right, here goes, keep in touch. I'm not even sure I agree with myself any more. I actually regret making it seem like a thesis.

'Anyhow, there were a few points at the heart of it. First, and most categorically, it was not "pro-capitalist", though that has become the standard tagline for it. On the contrary, the opening chapters do nothing but attack the false claims, inconsistencies and hypocrisies of contemporary capitalism that many better qualified writers have made me aware of. It's a simple book, a human book, perhaps exactly the wrong-headed sort of economic and political book you'd expect from a flaky novelist.'

'Then why did you write it?'

'I don't know. I suppose I wanted to challenge that very idea, that artists are too dopey to offer anything specific or useful to society's other debates and preoccupations. I guess that's an original aspiration, huh? I merely added another gravestone to an already crowded cemetery.'

Sharon was biting her upper lip to hold back a smile, her head tilted away from me. 'There is another way to interpret this trajectory. After all the charges of being a sucker for hype and celebrity, you wanted to recapture your social credentials, prove you were still politically engaged? Run with me: it's more fun if I play the d's a.'

'It wasn't anything as grand as that, so I'm simply going to ignore your bait. You know what I was really attempting? I wanted to ask in a new way what a novelist's options are if he's interested in exploring structures and systems along with the stories of individuals.'

'Then what made you defend giant corporations of all things?' She disappointingly parroted the same stale charge every reviewer had picked up on during the past six months.

'This is the hilarious bit. *Power and the Person* was an essay in eight parts, three of which raised these issues. Less than half the book, yet that's what everyone has chosen to highlight out of context. But I'm too long-suffering to mind. I am a powerless person. I will valiantly restate the rather more subtle point I was making. First, there was no defence of contemporary capitalist practices intended in my book. Will you please please please quote that, and then at least a bit of what I'm about to say?

'Once we accept – and by now only loonies on the extreme left and right don't – that a six-billion-strong integrated society is here to stay, inter-related in most things, with amazing benefits as well as victims, we also must concede that vast quantities of capital are required to fund the goods, services and projects this population demands. And whoever controls the strings administering that capital, be they private investors or government departments, automatically gather power to themselves. Mass societies need huge flows and pools of money to get things off the ground, and this inevitably creates hierarchies of power.

'Not for a moment am I holding this up to praise. What I would ask my anti-globalization friends to contemplate, before they shut the door on me, are the energies and the inventiveness represented by capitalism. Have these really achieved nothing other than to make certain classes rich and powerful? Have there been no comparable benefits to offset the tremendous costs?

'Capitalism embodies an onrush not just of colossal waves of desire but also of creativity and dynamism. The money never stands still, unlike the era of our inbreeding forefathers on their feudal estates, who could only think of using it to preserve stagnant hierarchies, or to wage senseless wars. Today they've come up with so many angles for multiplying money, that they don't even need to build factories or produce things any more. The markets generate money on the promise of money backed up by the distant mirage of money, none of which has come into being yet. There's a lot wrong with that model. Who is it set up to serve? How much of that loot ever really "trickles down"? What about the volume of legal "leakage" that disappears each year into the world's various tax havens?

'Nevertheless, even acknowledging its crazy history and all its ongoing excesses, I feel there's an energy there that should be harnessed as fuel, because what are you going to have instead? Are you foolish enough to make an enemy out of such inventiveness rather than dam and channel it to new ends?

Because it's not just money: it's ideas, and people. Aren't *we* entrepreneurs of a sort, you and I, having this fiery conversation in London, far from where we were supposed to vegetate and die, precisely because we were allowed to make the most of our minds? To me, one kind of dynamism is bound up with another, and to watch them sizzle together is wonderful. The problem arises with the fundamentalist notion that we can have no collective objectives other than the short-term profit-centred fulfilment of such energies, and when you hold the survival of the planet hostage to these singular aims.'

Despite the recorder, I realized she'd been scribbling. Perhaps objections, perhaps questions. It really pleased me, the flare in her eyes as she responded.

'And this is all you implied: harness the energy but inspire it to new ends. This beautiful, simple message.'

'Pretty much. I confessed to a shameful vice, that actually I deeply admire some of the achievements of advanced capitalism, whilst being aware of their tremendous cost. Have you ever been to a major port and watched the containers being offloaded? What about the freeways and their beautiful spaghetti intersections, and those long trucks that can transport twenty cars at a time? Or even the bear-pit itself: have you visited an old-fashioned trading floor, shaking up billions all around the world? Is there nothing to marvel at in these feats?'

She raised her eyebrows in exasperation. 'Considering I worked for the *Financial Times* for five years, it'd be highly irregular if I wasn't familiar with these places. Don't forget, I'm not and never have been a literary critic. I only own two of your novels, and one of those was a birthday present.'

'Wow, you really clarified things there. I'm sorry, all of a sudden I realize how irrelevant most of the afternoon has been for you. I didn't read your card and never asked for a background check. Nor did I Google you when you called. That is why I wasted so much time pronouncing on the soul.'

'Hey, easy on the insults. I thought we financial types also embodied immense creaturely potential. Finance isn't the dictionary antonym for feeling, you know. And I told you, this interview is intended to be personal.'

'Yes, I recall your exact word. Impressionistic, you said. I thought it odd at the time. Now I see it was your soul peeping through.'

She stuck out her tongue at me before resuming. 'So explain to me – because I'm slightly baffled, and beginning to believe that the *Wall Street Journal* understood you correctly after all – how any of this is different from what the hard-right is saying. Leave all solutions to the market. Trust our genius. Let's treat this century as a Hollywood cliff-hanger, a race between those melting icecaps you bleeding-hearts blather endlessly about, and our ability to invent miraculous new technological solutions. That would be the way of *real* men.'

This had been the pre-eminent accusation against the book, and I raised my hands in weary surrender. 'Look, all I pointed out was that it's been amply demonstrated that entrepreneurialism works reasonably to exceptionally well in many areas and for certain purposes. At the same time, how can a society premised upon a fundamentalist conception of pure capitalism ever achieve any of the broader objectives we might share as human beings rather than as profit-psychopaths?

'And there were two final points I wanted to leave people arguing about. The first is an obvious truth that's worth restating: we are a monopoly planet. There are no other producers or consumers in the solar system. If we get together and resolve not to undercut our neighbour in a race to the bottom to attract investment at any price, then the guys holding our Third World balls right now will have to wake up to the painful fact that there's no other planet to do business on. The denominator will be raised around the globe. Of course, for this to happen, the class that controls the government in each country has to somehow refrain from betraying its own population in favour of colluding with its counterparts worldwide in narrow self-interest, and my dishonourable presence at places like Davos is solely intended to work towards persuading them of this bigger picture.

'Second, wherever we go, let us preserve the best of modernity to assist us in our challenges. I believe that money and education have been the great secular fuels of the modern world. It is education that keeps money from pooling in a few hands, by generating new ideas, new possibilities, players, products, and markets.'

As I spoke, I noticed she wasn't looking combative any more, but seemed strangely relaxed and yet alert and taut. The recorder lay on the table between us: she was sitting on the couch opposite, rug flung off, legs curled underneath her, leaning slightly forward, hands by her side, not unlike a starter's crouch before a sprint. But she didn't seem aware of her body at all. At this point it was all words, fast and flashing, heat and light, in the air between us.

'And especially for us in the global South, despite our mistrust of Western history and its dreadful track-record of violation, let's not lose sight of that original emancipating potential Adam Smith was excited about, because wherever money and learning show up, they set the static world in motion. You can hope to die differently from the way you were born. In between you can think different, want different, make and buy different. Others who cling to older convictions, about the primacy of place, birth, blood, race, or faith, remain baffled, desperate and angry. This was the real legacy of the industrial revolution, not that they abolished elites, but that the rules for entering elites were altered forever. Of course things aren't....'

'You know,' she interrupted as if finally at the end of her tolerance, 'it surprised me to hear you deliver that oration in the book and it surprises me all over again – coming from you, an Indian, a child of the unwilling – is there a better word for it? – anus of early capitalism, jolly-rogered for two hundred years, with the famines and the opium and everything else.

'Anyway,' she continued, slumping suddenly, as if the effort had been excessive (it was also quite late, she'd been here since early afternoon), or was it from some subtle disappointment? 'I must leave soon, and I have more than enough material on *Power and the Person*. If I could quickly get a few clarifications about the 7/7 article – was that written out of sympathy for those you just mentioned, the ones with convictions about faith and blood and race, who have nothing now but their desperation and bafflement?'

'I don't know where that emerged from. I was powered by an instinctive anger. About everything, from the lies they told us about Jean Charles de Menezes to the new laws that redefine our right to public debate: which actions we can approve of, and which ones it is unacceptable to "glorify". It's all in the piece, but I admit my anger might have confused some about its sympathies.

'Once when there was a war, this city endured a five-year blitz. That was expected. Today we're taken aback at the smallest sign of retaliation that disrupts our daily life, even though there are aggressions being prosecuted in our name in countries around the world. All I wanted to ask was: people who are more aware of these actions than we are – because it is their homes that are flattened, their oil that is stolen, their despots upheld and relatives murdered – do they have a right to a response? Are they more heinous because they didn't come at us in uniform with warnings? Doesn't it speak of their desperation that they wage war in such hopeless ways?'

'How does that last argument apply to British Muslims? Raj, someone in your position can't afford to be angry when writing. It's counter-productive, and you confuse the issues.'

'Ok, fair point, but it was one piece. It amazes me that people have forgotten everything else I've written over the years. But then, journalistic memories are expediently short, unless you go on to surprise me.'

She picked up her recorder and switched it off, and started looking around for her bag. I offered her one for the road, but she declined. She gathered her stuff and went to the bathroom to fix herself up. I realized how drained I felt myself, and acutely dehydrated.

When she returned, she had some more to say, but the recorder remained off.

'I feel this session has come full circle. We began with your refusal of commitment, and everything you said just now confirms that. Don't worry, none of it will go into the essay, but I wonder how one can retain the right to express any real-world opinions they like, publicly, even ones that shift from week to week, and yet have no particular loyalties to a place or movement? I've read my share of novels to agree with you about the freedom of the writer to explore different perspectives. Yet, when he puts on his non-fiction hat, I wonder what the point is if not consistency or commitment. Otherwise who is he trying to reach?'

The very thought of extending my defence wearied me. In any case, the answer seemed obvious. 'I've never claimed to be an activist. I agree that political action is slow and requires deep roots and daily involvement. I'm just a disorderly source of ideas. I don't possess any truths, nor do I seek votes. I throw out ideas that might be useful to various people, and I believe that conflicting voices are, at the very least, worth hearing.'

Still she refused to leave, and it was I who moved towards the front door as a hint. But she didn't seem to register this.

'So what does it take to make the leap from weekly opinion-hopping to acting out some of your real beliefs? And what does it cost: are you saying anyone who lives by their ideals is necessarily less open-minded than you are?'

I was unduly brusque, and the night closed on a tart note. 'We're at the end, and you're still not letting go. I sensed earlier on that I might have disappointed you with some of my responses. But now, you run the risk of doing the same. There's a faint undercurrent I'm getting that this will develop into a boring old gas about belonging and responsibility and eventually, as ever, about my son and/or mother. I've thoroughly enjoyed your company, and want to leave things that way. You have my email: any little details that need brushing up, I'm always available. Good night, my sweet Ed Murrow, and good luck.'

I believed it would be the first of many encounters with this extraordinary, vivacious young writer. I emerged pleased from that evening at having initiated what I was sure would evolve into lasting friendship, despite the apparent friction. But six days later, Sharon lay dead in her own doorway, on the eve of a trip to New York.

I didn't register anything for hours after hearing the news. Then my numbness broke, and the first of the aftershocks reached me.

Very early in the police inquiry it would emerge that she'd visited me twice in the week before her murder.

Also, there was the other side, her killers, and the likelihood of their attention.

What will follow presently is the public version of my testimony, while I am still able to record it.

The Perfect Worker

London Diary: Asif's Story

I first encountered Asif at Hira Mandi, one of my regular joints in Tooting. No matter where I chose to ramble in South West London – Richmond Park, Putney Heath, Wimbledon Common – I usually caught a bus afterwards that snaked me to the Broadway for a meal. There were similar appointed places throughout the city, on Green Street, in Southall, Bayswater, Edgware Road, the West End, depending on where I was. In each of them, my habits were familiar, and I merely had to nod when one of the regular waiters confirmed whether it would be 'the usual'.

Asif was new, and walked over to my table as soon as I sat down. So we had to speak, although it was obvious he wasn't especially gregarious. He was of delicate build, in his early forties, with a perpetually concerned expression (at least while he worked) and an unusual gait – he swayed faintly from side to side, as if in the flow of some imperceptible breeze. There was nothing exceptionable about his service manners: he was efficient and polite, and seemed experienced, but for some reason my eyes followed him around the room, although no other waiter had ever held my attention in this way. I couldn't formulate it, but he was different, even as he stood with the others during a quiet spell. He didn't seem to belong among his compatriots, although I could tell his Urdu was perfect.

At some point he grew aware of me, and we locked eyes inadvertently a few times. I felt embarrassed and looked away as he dealt with my bill. Nothing further happened, and over the next few months we grew accustomed to each other, and the need for words vaporized beyond the initial greeting. Yet I never lost my sense of his slight incongruity, and for this reason there was an unremarked connection between us. I felt everyone there treated us both warily, though not coldly, as though we weren't really Asian under the skin. Perhaps we were too aloof for them, and in their eyes we had both gone native.

Outside of these occasional musings when I was in the restaurant, I never thought of him. And it was further evidence of the similarity in our temperaments that he didn't make any unnecessary overtures either. At that point I hadn't even asked him his name.

One evening, I was about to enter Hampstead station when I realized I was missing my travel-card. I had spent the afternoon rambling round the heath, from Parliament Hill to Kenwood House, and it would normally have been impossible to trace it. Also, it was early November, the clocks had just gone back, and dusk was rapidly giving way to darkness. There was only one spot worth chancing, under the bench I had briefly rested on, and fortunately I recalled exactly where that was.

When I entered the park, already the strollers, prams and duck-feeders had departed to be replaced by a different crowd, young men slowly growing in numbers, just off the paths. My bench was about ten minutes away, and my card was exactly where I'd pictured it: it had slipped out of my back pocket and through the gap between the boards. I was briskly on my way out again, when I recognized a familiar gait, approaching from the street.

It was impossible to ignore each other. 'Hello,' I ventured.

'Hello. Are you leaving?' He was still somewhat diffident, but appeared more at ease here in the open, than he did in his waistcoat and uniform amid all that Asian noise. He didn't seem in any hurry to continue, and it was I who pressed on the pedal.

'Yes, I have a train to catch. See you sometime.'

'See you at the restaurant.' He nodded, smiling.

I returned there on Sunday, and learnt something more about Asif when he invited me to attend a recital of fusion music at a converted church in Tufnell Park, where he would be playing the tabla. He seemed to me remarkably self-assured during the various jugalbandis, no matter how complex the improvising grew. Yet he wasn't any more expansive in person, and this made his musical confidence more apparent, since he matched everyone else for audacity, rhetoric, and even the occasional passage of pure, joyful, talent-soaked cheek. This was also the evening I learnt his name, from the stage announcer.

He asked me if I enjoyed walks on holidays, and we discovered we had parks and heaths in common. Neither of us felt the need to clarify anything about the Hampstead evening, and the issue settled itself naturally because it was never mentioned. Ours were long, silent rambles: we didn't grow into great conversationalists. But I was surprised how pleasant it was to have company each Sunday, and somehow we never found each other's choice of venue disagreeable. In our pace, our silences, even in the intervals when we required a rest, we were well-matched. We bought each other rounds, and I often read the paper with my pint. He didn't seem to mind.

Once he suggested a matinee at the cinema, and I agreed. It was a film I'd noticed myself among the reviews and later, after our drinks, he asked if I wanted to stay out for dinner. We went to a Turkish restaurant, where he'd worked before. The food was above average, but the live belly-dancing wasn't for me. So the next week I recommended a small French place in Islington, and that integrated itself into our routine. Once a month we saw a film, and afterwards shared a meal. Although now we also met during the week, because he played often on the town-hall, library and converted-church circuit of cabaret and world music. I enjoyed watching him perform: he was still recognizably Asif, but enhanced beyond his frame in his gestures and expressions. He emanated himself through his playing, and for me it was as vivid as if he were speaking. I would shut my eyes and still feel his presence close by.

After a few evenings out, I had grown to consider him a friend. It had occurred to me to invite him to the Bells sometime, and introduce him to Patty and the boys, but I decided against it. Patty would understand, but it seemed likely the guys would see me in a new light. They would misinterpret my silence and my habits, and the Bells would cease to be a sanctuary.

I surprised myself by raising the subject of Martina with him one evening, the Sunday after I'd confirmed her house was a brothel. 'Asif, I think I fancy a woman who is working as a hooker.'

'That's an odd vein of humour, coming from you,' he smiled.

'I'm not joking.'

He gazed at me as if not recognizing this newly revealed leg-puller. Why was I attempting such a weird gag? 'Well then, I have to say you're a hidden diamond. You're the last person I would have expected to associate with such people.'

'She is very nice. I don't think she chose this line of work.'

Now he appeared more startled by my sharing a confidence than by the words themselves. 'Is that where you met her?' he asked.

'No, she comes to my pub quite often, I suppose between shifts. We greet each other with a smile, but I've not yet spoken to her.'

'Did someone tell you that's what she does?'

'No, somehow you can guess. She's eastern European, and dresses in a certain way. I'm pretty confident of my suspicions.'

'Well, if I were you I'd confirm them first, since it's very important to be sure. It would change everything if she isn't. On the other hand, she'll have a most unpleasant crowd behind her if she is working in that line.'

'You're right,' I replied. 'That's why I've held off speaking to her. I'm not sure what I would initiate.'

'Have you ever been married?' he asked after a brief pause, apropos of nothing.

'I came very near it once,' I said readily, 'but it didn't work out at the last minute. I'm talking about way back, when I still lived in India.'

'Did you not agree with your family's choice of bride?'

'It wasn't like that. She was a love-affair. And it wasn't I who backed out.'

'I'm sorry.'

'No, it's fine. It's not a painful memory. Anyway, I soon moved to London, and since then there hasn't been anyone even close.'

'Did you guess that I'm married,' he then ventured, even more uncharacteristically. 'I'm a father of three, you know.'

'That's truly amazing,' I responded. 'How old are they? Are you separated? Surely you don't live together. I'm asking since you spend most of your Sundays with me.'

'No, we're still happily married. Her name is Razia, and she lives in my village, in Rawalpindi district. We were paired off at eighteen, so believe it or not, my oldest has just turned twenty. The middle one is thirteen, and then there's Laila, my baby of four.'

'And you never thought of bringing them over. Wouldn't it be better if they studied here?'

'They love their grandparents too much, and everyone there dotes on them. I couldn't afford to support them here, but in Rawalpindi they get an excellent education. Salman does political science, and Khurram wants to be a pilot, for PIA, I hope. I wouldn't want my son dreaming of bombing you guys.'

'How frequently can you visit your family?' I smiled.

'Annually. In fact, I'm leaving in two weeks. There's also the sale of a few fields that I've been interested in for many years. We'll knock the walls down and put two of my nephews to work there.'

'Do you have plans to return permanently?'

'Yes, when I'm older. There are no opportunities for my kind of music in that district, not even in Pindi or Islamabad. People don't want to stage it, although I'm sure there would be audiences. It's not Islamic enough for them. But return I will, definitely. I must. I've missed out on the growing up of both my sons. I need to spend time with Laila before we have to give her away.'

'Do you miss your wife?'

'Razia is my best friend. I speak to her almost everyday. She has been to London a few times. She even moved here to live once. I enrolled her on a computer course, while teaching her English at home. But we couldn't keep it up, though it was just the two of us. And it would be impossible being a father of three on my salary.'

'So you make this big sacrifice just for the sake of your music?' I regretted the question as soon as I uttered it. Its insinuations didn't reflect my nature at all, and certainly not my feelings about Asif. I valued his company, and considered him a decent, gifted man. It actually enhanced my respect that he had raised a family, and I could easily imagine him as a compassionate father.

'I'm sorry if that came out wrong,' I mumbled before he had a chance to reply. 'Your decisions are none of my business.'

'It's all right. It's a valid question. Everyone who knows my circumstances looks at me strangely. All I can say in response is that London is full of people like us, who are here for mysterious reasons. You take the weather, the distance, the expenses, and yet it's full of us, and not just for the money. On every bus you hear us, from Brazil, from Africa, from the Middle East and Pakistan. So there must be something we receive in return for everything we give up. I believe that is what we all have in common, something as important as home and family, even though it is often invisible on the outside and we all have a different name for it. I think of it as my music.'

'That's a good way to express it. I know what you're talking about. I recognize myself in your description, except perhaps my purpose isn't as clear. I have no special gifts or motives.'

'Maybe you just like the parks, Charles, the long, undisturbed walks. From what I've heard about India, I doubt there are as many green spaces in Bombay. Besides, ours are not countries where one is easily left alone. That's worth coming all this way to find.'

We spoke for a while longer about my options regarding Martina. He asked about her the week after, and I replied that I'd been trying to put her out of my mind since I had confirmed what she did. He seemed sorry for me, and suggested it might still be worthwhile letting her know, since circumstances do change.

When they did, he wasn't there to find out, since he remained in Pakistan for ten weeks, sorting out family matters. He emailed me twice during that time, telling me about the walks he was taking with his sons, Laila seated like a princess on his shoulders, practising tabla on his head. And Khurram was a bit of a hothead as he'd feared, but not to worry, he was working on him to convince him once and for all to fly only for peaceful civilian purposes. Salman was much more law-abiding. He wanted to join the UN. Yet, said Asif, for all the fields and the woods, he could not walk freely with Razia. Not that there was anything wrong, but people would still stare and deem such behaviour odd, typical for a Vilayati. 'This is why we are in London, Charles,' he wrote. 'It is the best city for walks.'

The Writer of Rare Fictions

'Unknown Author Dies'

(London, Late February, 2006)

The two days after our interview, I thought about Sharon whenever I sat down to either of the unfinished projects on my table. Would she have deemed them mutually consistent or incompatible, useful or counterproductive? There was a speech to be delivered at the ICA, about the forked possibilities offered by capitalism when it came to the winning over of Middle-Eastern affections. Apparently some diplomatic phone-card had been lost, and used by a group of locals in Baghdad to call sex-lines to the tune of half a million pounds. I'd come across the anecdote in an article, and was planning to use it as a point of departure, perhaps even a form of hope.

Then there was a story long awaiting completion, about the last evening of a would-be self-detonator in Jenin, wandering through the alleys of his childhood, sitting down to one more home-cooked meal. The sentimental beginning was meant to throw the reader off guard, since the story went on to divulge the degree to which he loathed the poverty of their circumstances, all of which had accrued into a self-hate greater than anything he felt towards the occupiers.

It was a peculiar story to write, since it involved excavating so much that was autobiographical – my own detestation of my childhood home and our helpless entrapment within the family, for which I had always blamed my father. It was the secret wedge that divided us forever, and yet I never admitted it, although my mother would have required no confession. It was him I'd grown to despise, and his influence that I feared above all. Yes, I even feared the genetic taint of his passivity, and somehow in my fervour to escape, this abhorrence of my family had expanded to cloud over my memories and reflexes about India itself. Ridiculous as it sounds today, until my life in London was established on a secure footing, I dreaded constantly that 'India' would swallow me up and spit me out, after chewing me into an unrecognizable mulch. At their worst these phobias took some strange turns, which culminated in my seething privately against anyone who was weak or unfortunate. I regarded my carefree foreign friends with envy. How did it console me that three hundred years ago my civilization was as creative and glittering as theirs today, and that many forecast the turning of the wheel once more? I would be an old man by then, with nothing but deprivation and anxiety to recall from my youth.

From such unlikely origins, I relocated and drew out the implications of a similar twisted rage, and a futile desperation to escape, that burned within my West Bank protagonist. But these are shaming sentiments that he cannot fully admit even to himself, and somehow he is led by an awful mix of guilt and pain, and sheer hatred of the very sensation of being in his own skin, to volunteer for this particular mode of reprisal.

Sharon showed up without calling on Saturday morning, the twenty-fifth. I'd woken up early to write, and my coffee was still brewing. Hence I misunderstood her intention at first, and wearily began rehearsing a shrug-off speech. She was calm and bright, although palpably excited. She waited for me to down half my coffee before she announced her decision. That was how she announced it: 'my decision'.

'Based on our meeting the other day, I have reached a decision,' she declared, as if it was eight in the evening.

Oh god, was my unexpressed sentiment, oh, god.

My expression must have betrayed me. 'Are you interested at all?' she asked. 'I'm sorry, I just assumed you would be interested. I've been inexcusably wrapped up in myself the past few days.'

It gets worse and worse, I feared, still wordless. Then I spoke. 'Sharon, it's a bit early, and to tell you the truth, I feel somewhat assaulted. I promise I ascend the rungs of evolution quite rapidly after my second cup of coffee, and I suppose it's an impressive sight, but right now you've caught me on the verge of the Homo Erectus stage. Also, I didn't realize we'd grown close enough in one session for such impromptu displays of warmth. If you needed a quote or a clarification, you could have just called.'

'I'm sorry. There is no decent excuse for my intrusion. But can I please stay, if I promise not to speak until you've finished your coffee? And just so you can savour it with an easy mind, I assure you it's not what you're thinking. This request has nothing to do with the other night; it'll be so left-field you could never have predicted it.'

'If that's your relaxing formula, you should consider patenting it. You know what, I'll take you up on that offer. If you remain silent until I've had two cups of coffee and look ready to spar and dazzle, I will for my part take my finger off the button beneath this armrest that opens a trapdoor under your couch. And with that, let peace prevail.'

An hour later I was frantically absorbing her calmly-delivered idea. She had respected all my rules and yet, when she spoke, there wasn't the slightest rush or hesitation. It didn't even take twenty minutes to deliver, after we'd watched *Seinfeld* together, the one where Jerry and George find themselves inadvertently posing as Aryan Nation icons after cadging a lift in a limo under false pretences. How did she sit through it?

'I have researched and put together a new book, and I'd be very grateful if you provided the foreword.'

She had sounded so disappointed in me the other night. Why would she think of me for her book? 'I've never claimed to be anything but an enthusiastic amateur when it comes to matters of serious economics. You yourself hinted as much during the interview. How could I be of any use?'

'It's a book about personalities rather than economics, although yes, in that area generally. But if you hear me out, it'll be clear why you're perfect for the job.'

'Well then, go ahead, and don't mind me while I fix some yogurt. I'll be listening all the time, even if I'm not facing you, and despite blobs of cherry yogurt on my beard. I hope you realize that everything today is off the record vis-à-vis the interview. That is an absolute condition. Should I turn down your request, you can't have a go at me with retroactive malice. Capisce?'

And so I became the first person to hear about *The Leap* or, rather, the first person its author ever confided in. This is a crucial distinction, I insist, as important (for the police) as discovering how many others learnt of its blueprint, legitimately or otherwise. No one among you will know anything about it, not yet, and now I'm certain, not ever. It is a book that never had the chance to exist, about which only the sketchiest outline remains (in one fugitive mind). Nonetheless – I claim publicly for the first time – it is a phantom work that killed its author. There is no other explanation.

The very silence surrounding it clinches my case. It could not have gone unmentioned had it been found amongst Sharon's effects. Its disappearance is most eloquent, in the manner of primary witnesses who never testify in major gangster trials because they have all succumbed to purely coincidental accidents.

I can easily visualize her briefing me, striking an unaware silhouette in the morning sunshine; clear, urgent, confident, as if she knew I would not refuse. She was right. She had mapped out her territory well, and I understood this as she spoke. The interview had been a stake-out, a sizing-up. She had deliberately volunteered for the job. Perhaps the ready consent to jump her bones was part of the strategy too. But this proposal was so enticing, I didn't care. I didn't mind being "used" for such a purpose. I only felt warmer towards her, and steadily more excited myself. Excited about not having disappointed her the other night, excited about what was being demanded. The next few hours were gripping, as the implications of her project sank in.

'My book is about what I term the "quantum leap", the missing five (or less) years in the lives of several so-called self-made billionaires. It began as a commission to write a biography, about eighteen months ago, very authorized, very well-paid. I won't say whose just yet, though I have to tell you it's an Indian. The instructions were laughable. I was basically ordered by one of his vice-presidents to produce the new "New Testament": believe it or not, he told me they were planning to leave copies for guests in every room throughout their chain of hotels! Shamefully though, I coveted the money, and said yes that same afternoon.

'However, even hagiographies require a minimum of research, and I couldn't bring myself to be glib enough to work solely with the facts and "quotes" his PR team provided. I flew to Bombay, which took them by surprise, since they were quite happy for me to do most of my writing long-distance. They insisted they didn't want to disrupt my life in any way, and that their London office could provide me with any material I sought. Which should help you picture the kind of thing they had in mind.

'Still, I found a nice all-expenses room awaiting me at the Marine Drive Hilton. Actually, the first meeting was both hilarious and sinister, if you can imagine such an unsettling combination. They were at pains to guarantee they would not interfere with my authorial sovereignty. The PR vice-president even assured me that my own encounter with the "leading light" – as the boss was referred to continually, I kid you not – would make such an impression that I wouldn't need any prompting to write respectfully. It was as if we were waiting for an audience with the head of a cult.

'When we entered, I was asked by my escorts to "voluntarily" remove my shoes. I noticed the "leading light" was barefoot too. Of course I took a seat immediately, but they touched his feet, two VPs, I swear it, and then stood by the wall behind me. At some point I unthinkingly lit a fag. The "leading light" paused in his speech, which was about the importance of maintaining integrity, as if slightly startled, then continued droning. Only after we returned outside did both visibly shaken VPs – they were like Thomson and Thompson, completing each other's sentences, each naming a fresh name – stammer to me that no one had ever lit a cigarette in the presence of the "leading light", not the prime minister, not the country's most important businessmen, cricketers or film-stars, nobody. And yet, he had once more demonstrated his magnanimity by overlooking my blunder. Needless to add, *they'd* touched his feet before escorting me out, as if additionally requesting forgiveness for my sins.

'Perhaps it's just the way things are done in saffron India, but spurred on by this encounter, I set out to dig some more on my own, fully aware that I would be vetted chapter by chapter, and nothing remotely controversial would be allowed. Our meeting had amply clarified that, no matter what they said. Still, being an ambitious girl who has trouble meeting her own stringent moral demands, I sold it to myself as a win-win situation. I'd pocket the money for now, and enjoy the fringe benefits to follow. And if I unearthed any real nuggets, I would wait poker-faced until I was independent once more. Then who was to stop me dropping them here and there in different articles, and sitting back and watching the fun?

'Within a few months my entire project had changed, although officially I remained engaged solely on the biography. Just the first five weeks of proper follow-up had yielded so much, I went a bit crazy from everything I was discovering. I first had to wade through the usual flood from both sides, paeans of worship as well as the most scurrilous of rumours. Everything: they whispered he once ran girls, gold, arms, slaves, insurgents, drugs, whatever you care to chuck into the mix. You realize why I'm not yet naming anyone. This very conversation would be a non-bailable offence. But such slander is common currency about most of these overnight badshahs of the bazaar, and so completely unusable. There is in each such life a murky period in which someone offstage suddenly shakes her wand, the miracle happens, and our Cinderella emerges one starry night with a horde of capital and a shiny new carriage, although until that morning he was a judicious little grocer or owned a tiny lottery-ticket kiosk. Yet, after the initial whispers, no one in his new circle mentions this discrepancy, at least not in public.'

I made my only interruption. 'Couldn't it be the judiciousness though that is the true source of their capital, the dal, rice and the lottery-ticket rupees squirreled away one by one?' But it barely disrupted her flow.

'Yes, a natural enough objection, only the numbers don't add up, not in his case, not in anyone's. I commissioned a young economist to compile some forecasts for me. From my research we came up with certain best-case scenarios of earnings and savings from their old lives, and I'd like to challenge anyone to buy their first petrochemical plant or textile factory with the profits from retailing perfumes. That is why it is a quantum leap: it's a different realm of operation, many zeros higher, in a galaxy far, far away. No official loan, no phenomenally tax-dodged under-the-mattress savings account, could ever have covered it. It would be like believing in a helicopter that promised a round-trip to Mars.

'So, from some perverse instinct to strike dirt, I decided to follow up some of these baseless, irresponsible, malicious allegations thrown around by small-time brokers, former neighbours, fellow traders, as well as other chronically mean-spirited friends from my own line of work. Decided isn't the right word, I found myself doing so; one day I was in Dubai, then following a few leads in Egypt, finally tying things up in the Canary Islands.

'It was actually on the flight home from Tenerife that I developed the idea for the bigger book, the one you will hopefully introduce. What if I continued with this line of inquiry until I had a new work devoted not to any particular business luminary, but to this *specific phase* in the lives of several, hand-picked leading lights, the secret five-year-plan behind this crazy lift-off into the ranks of gigantic capital? What if I picked ten household names from three or four continents? What patterns would that reveal? Would they all have a grey period in their past, and each leave behind that same trail of unproven yet persistent rumours?

'From then on, the idea was like a fever. Once I had my glittering short-list of six, suddenly I was flying all over to meet aging, forgotten little-leaguers: hoods, pensioned-off concierges of front-companies in the Caribbean, dealers, old sea-captains, harbour-masters, and even resentful ex-buddies and discarded partners, anyone whose name cropped up in a paper or a chat and who responded to my overtures. As the scope of my book grew, my interviewees included diplomats, civil servants, customs officers, aristocrats, oil executives and, right here in London, retired accountants, tax-avoidance specialists, wealth-management lawyers, even art collectors and estate agents. Always off the record, especially when things turned interesting, always working through an extensive list of decoy questions. In many cases they still wouldn't commit a name to words when I asked, but merely nodded or lifted an eyebrow, as if they half-suspected I was taping them. I tell you, the amount of name-dropping I had to do to earn those interviews, and the goodwill I had to encash. I also know, if I ever want to work again as a financial reporter on this planet, I'll have to deep-throat almost all of those sources.

'Yet each one of them added a piece to the story. Not strictly evidence, but a new layer or a missing link. Perhaps fictional for the most part – and most of it I binned – but gradually certain shapes emerged. Someone who could not have known someone else, because I was looking them up in a different country on the track of a completely distinct rumour, would unwittingly corroborate another trumped-up, boozy slander. This was the thrilling part, especially as it became too frequent an occurrence to be dismissed. Sometimes it was heart-stopping to the point where I could barely maintain my mask of casual neutrality. Of course there was no way they'd speak in sight of a pad, but I was sneakily building up a nice little archive, all with that trusted recorder you saw the other day, nestled cosily next to my delicates.'

'Stop, slow down. You're turning me on, and I don't mean the bit about your delicates.'

She giggled. It was the only break in her self-assurance, when her energy and anticipation overcame her.

'Raj, the things I have discovered, focusing just on that five-year period in each life, ignoring any leads to the time after they were famous. Three out of the six names are dead. So it's not just contemporary; some of this material adds up to an unofficial history of the world going back to '45, or even before, including dodgy dealings with Axis forces. In fact, I began with the departed and moved on to the aged, because the witnesses you want to unspool feel less threatened that way. I took a sabbatical, cashed my advance, and today my passport is full of stamps. Cyprus, Argentina, Brazil, Angola, Lebanon, Bulgaria, Moscow, D.C., Grand Cayman, Johannesburg, Israel. Also, incidentally, before you ask, I have nothing left in the bank, in none of my accounts.'

It was I who kept rising and sitting down idiotically as she spoke, as if I were stifling an urge to pee. She couldn't expound rapidly enough for me, yet I noticed she never even leaned forward. Her composure was something to marvel at, considering, I was about to learn, this was the world-première revelation of her stupendous project.

'I had three meetings lined up this week. If you're on board, this afternoon I see my lawyer. It'll be the second time ever that I pitch this spiel. So I hope you feel slightly honoured. We discuss the material I have, and he informs me by next week what would be outright impermissible, no matter if it's on tape. Then I fly out Wednesday, and dump it all on the desk of a friend in New York. We'll probably boil it down together to the stories backed by some form of supplementary evidence – documents, records, the little I could actually turn up in court archives and newspaper morgues and public record offices wherever they were cooperative. It'll break my heart to keep back the rest, but I'm mentally prepared. I have to pick my battles. You see, I had no authorization, apart from the alibi of my biography, which I claimed was about some of the world's great entrepreneurs. So all access was severely restricted, because I didn't want the purpose of the snooping to become evident at any point. Most of the red-hot stuff was earned through charm and chatter, unfortunately, and remains inadmissible as evidence.

'But diligent cross-checking even among official balance-sheets and reports and yearbooks, of outstanding lawsuits and incomplete, long-buried news-stories – though they are the dullest, blandest, falsest versions of most such subterranean shadow-play, assuming any records are kept at all – turns up a surprising number of incongruities, if you're unrelenting enough. I tell you, if forty per cent of what has been suggested, repeated and substantiated over the past fifteen months is published, I would formally be rechristened Pandora Pereira. Not even forty, twenty per cent would be enough to fill a few more *Fahrenheit 9/11*s. Contra arms deals, A.Q. Khan's sales reps, Central Asian pipelines, East European women, Ecuadorean oil concessions, Iranian plane downings, Australian uranium, Filipino slave-girls, coups in Africa over oil and in Central America over the Panama Canal, deals with the generals of Argentina and Indonesia, and each of my living legends crops up somewhere or the other, furiously networking, lobbying, hosting, dining, midwifing, middle-manning, skulking.

'Different incidents, different insurgencies, contracts at stake for projects and treasures on five continents. The Indonesian flies to Saudi Arabia to meet the American, the Israeli sells to the South African when he's not dealing with the Iranian, the Indian goes prospecting in Southern Sudan with the blessings of the Islamic government. Everything is financed through front companies, contacts are established with the highest ranks in intelligence or business, with *both* rebel army and government, and it's all pimped by one or more of my six lover-boys, each in the springtime of his life, handing out and pocketing the most stratospheric commissions for various inconceivable services.'

My voice must have been almost disappointed. 'And my role is just to provide a measly foreword? Consider it done. It would be a privilege to ride piggy-back on board such an effort.'

For the first time she leaned forward. 'I'll be brazen with you. I need more than the foreword. I need everything you can bring to this book, heft, publicity, credibility, hype. This friend I have in mind in New York would personally set type in the old-fashioned way for the pleasure of detonating such a bomb, but I need your profile. At the right time, not now, but soon, I want you to stand by me and bring everyone else on board who can shine upon us the right sort of attention.'

Nothing in her voice shook or crumpled. It wasn't incongruous to either of us that seventy-two hours ago, we were strangers. It never once occurred to me not to trust her, just as I didn't pause to ponder the consequences of my intervention. She left soon afterwards, promising to call me on Monday after hearing from the lawyer. I embraced her at the door out of sheer admiration, and she glanced back at me warmly.

'You've been very gallant today. There is nothing you owed me. Our acquaintance is two days old, not to mention arranged and contrived as I confessed, and I haven't told you anything about the project. I haven't even named anyone yet. I promise you, all that will follow next week. We'll have a much clearer picture of what form the book will take. Part of me wants to advise you to seek counsel yourself before stepping on board. If this gets nasty, it's best you're forewarned. I won't hold this morning as binding if you decide to decline afterwards.'

'I would never decline. I trust you. Of course I want to hear more. But I wouldn't turn you down for the world. Your book was taking shape before my eyes as you spoke. It promises everything such a work should have: detail, character, thrill, magnitude, and the crazy part is, it'll all be true.'

She fluttered her eyelids and left. No work was possible the rest of that day. For a few hours, I scribbled on the phone pad to try and second-guess her by anticipating her list of names, from the titbits of places and events she'd hinted at in her sneak-preview. Then I Googled everyone on my list to see what I could unearth. It was already evident there was no one I could call to share the story with. Thankfully on Sunday I had a date for lunch, with friends who never let me leave until early the next morning. So I could return home and crash, and keep at bay the butterflies for another day.

Sharon texted as promised on Monday afternoon to suggest dinner the following night, at a little Sri Lankan place in Tooting (her suggestion). It seemed appropriately out-of-the-way, and we agreed to meet there directly, in front of the Broadway station.

However, I was saved the trip purely by chance when I turned the dial onto Radio 3 while getting dressed the next evening, and the brief hourly bulletin between concerts announced her murder. As is well known, it was her mother who found the body, lying in the hallway just behind the door. Sharon had invited her over for tea impromptu earlier that afternoon. They decided she was killed about an hour after that call. She had answered the doorbell to someone who'd raised a silenced handgun and shot her through the forehead. Then he pulled the door shut, and disappeared.

Having arrived at this point, although I've been prepared for it throughout the writing of this book (perhaps every other chapter has been a deferment of this moment), I realize it isn't possible to justify my inaction of the next few days. My reluctance baffled me at first, in how it physically pinned me down. I went for a run in the park the morning after as a deliberate measure to reassure myself and restore a more balanced picture of the world outside, but then remained indoors for the next seventy-two hours. Somehow, gradually, it grew impossible to leave the house. I lay in the bath all morning, reheating the water occasionally, before moving to the large sofa under a duvet. The rest of the time I searched for information online, and read everything Sharon had ever posted. I didn't switch off the radio after that initial bulletin, and listened to all the updates. I saw pictures of her street and watched her neighbours give testimony on TV.

I expected to be contacted at any moment. Thankfully, no one visited during that time, but I expected each phone call to be from the police. I was one of the last people to have spent a significant amount of time with her, and either her lawyer or someone at her magazine would surely be aware of this. Hell, who was I kidding? From there on things might take quite an uncomfortable turn for me, if they discovered unfamiliar DNA on her person, and then matched it with mine.

But there was no point at which any of the reports hinted at specific leads, although very early on, after an initial examination of the house, the police dismissed the possibility that it was an ordinary burglary gone wrong. They focused on the meaning of the randomness: was it someone alone and deranged, or someone unknown yet organized, with a reason, or a contract, to finish Sharon?

What I was most interested in was the imminent discovery of Sharon's notes, and the draft manuscript of *The Leap*, and whether such a finding would be announced, since the implications would be obvious as soon as its subjects were named. The tabloids in particular would leap all over it, unless some of their mogul-proprietors were among those investigated. Statistically the killer could have been a stranger with little or no personal connection to Sharon, but I had long since fixed upon her book as the objective of the crime. In fact, isolated as I was from any means of sharing this secret, at least until events had clarified themselves, my fears distilled themselves into one peculiar sentence that increasingly became a mantra I couldn't help repeating: 'The bastards issued a fatwa. The bastards issued a fatwa.'

Perhaps I feared implication, perhaps retaliation. I reiterated each day that the next morning I would make myself presentable and head straight for Scotland Yard. Of course they would appreciate the reason for my delay: I was evidently in shock. Tomorrow, tomorrow – over and over. I also knew that coming clean was the best way of securing protection against whatever it was I apprehended.

On Saturday morning I told the police everything. In fact, I spent Friday preparing a much more concise version of this statement, and took it with me. (It included no chapters of fiction, nor was it a résumé of my lifelong regrets). It is due to investigation following on from that statement that I've since been acquitted, although the official position remains that they would prefer me to resurface. I asked them to respect my cover until I should choose to return to public life. They consented, on condition that I would keep myself readily available to them, especially if someone was brought to trial.

You, who've read so patiently thus far, endured so much circumlocution and delay, deserve some more of the facts. I assure you, as I have repeated countless times to the detectives, I don't know where *The Leap* is. I cannot even be sure how much of it existed, beyond the research. I know from the police that the lawyer in question, who is protected from being named, claimed to have been contacted for a meeting the following weekend, since he'd been unavailable on Saturday afternoon. Crucially, the CCTV footage from his office backs him on this score. There were no images of Sharon passing through reception. So it follows that he wasn't yet aware of her plans: one dead end so far.

The other is the location of the notes. The police conceded an outside likelihood to my story since all the books lying around Sharon's house seemed relevant to such an undertaking, although then again, she was by trade a financial reporter. What deflated my assertion was the lack of meaningful content on her computer. There was nothing on the desktop hard drive, no diary, no drafts, no obviously relevant downloaded material. Of course, they have to buy my suggestion that she worked on a laptop, and the trail of her eighteen-month-long itinerary is simple enough to pick up. But where is the laptop? In the same numbered vault as the rest of her notes? People do travel for all sorts of reasons, they argue, though it is evident they're not convinced by their own counter-premise. They remind me that every gap-year student is not a corporate whistle-blower.

Sharon's voice-recorder was located soon enough, with the full evidence of our first interview, but without any of its earlier mini-discs. It was as though she hadn't used it before. The detectives reasonably concede that authors, especially of inflammatory material, might choose to hide their work somewhere at a distance from themselves, and they would scour every last possibility, from the houses of Sharon's friends, to all the bank safes they could unearth. Since she spoke of meeting a lawyer and a publisher in the same week, there was a good chance everything was near at hand in London. But where, Mr Chakraborti, where?

Most of all I sensed from their visits that I had provided them with something that jammed rather prominently in their throats. Neither acceptance nor outright rejection came easy. My suggestion wasn't outlandish by any means, even though despite overt pressure, I stuck to insisting that I didn't know any specific names. She'd only met me twice, for Christ's sake. Perhaps she needed more time to trust me, although from her sketch, I could start them off with an estimate as to the initial Indian big-shot. Besides, didn't my information about Sharon calling her lawyer check out? Although they never found a ticket to New York, where I claimed she was headed soon after, I argued she was probably going to pick one up at the last minute. Her friend over there, whose name I mercifully remembered, confirmed she had texted to announce she was flying over on the Wednesday, but couldn't substantiate the more crucial part of my story. He said Sharon had used exclamation points and xxx-es, and had asked him to keep Thursday morning open.

But their retorts weren't unfair either. 'There are hundreds of sensational authors, Mr Chakraborti, from Mr Rushdie to Bob Woodward to Michael Moore,' the rather well-informed detective objected, 'who are all thriving openly. There are conspiracy theorists all over the bestseller lists and the Internet, writing about Bin Laden, the US President, the CIA, Mary Magdalene, yet no one is putting a hit on them.'

All I could do was to persevere with my contention: 'Send people out with her photo to some of the countries she visited.

Speak to those she interviewed, compare your testimonies. You can probably retrieve much of what she uncovered. Perhaps you'll be able to guess some of the names she was pursuing. Then you have already reached another stage of inquiry. You have some specific people to examine.'

I threw my own objection in their faces. 'Don't you see you've got a book-shaped hole in this case? Have you unearthed a sounder premise? What, a burglar, a stalker, a crazed hater of her columns, an ex-lover? How come you've got nothing and yet refuse the ten per cent of something I'm offering? Even if you cannot trace anything all the way up to the big dudes themselves, you can be certain of one thing. If it was the book that killed her, then the leak would be from one or more of those small fry from her travels. Whether in the Cayman, or Dubai or Cyprus, isn't it amply plausible that one of them found her questions disconcerting and called someone else by way of caution? Who's this girl that's been snooping around? More and more reports start to come in from all over the place, the trickle turns into a flood, one big boss phones another, and they put a watch on her. Soon it becomes clear she's not law-enforcement; what can she be up to? They don't buy her cover-story for a minute. Then they begin to connect things, one by one, from the pattern of her questions and journeys, and realize just who is being fingered and why.

'You know the official story, right? You check her flights and her bank statements, and tell me what any of that has to do with writing an admiring, authorized biography of a business giant who has rarely left India in the past decade? Her advance was ample, she was encouraged to write the book ensconced in her flat in London; yet she emphatically told me she had

/ance from just any publisher for this othe
e been too risky.

' I added, 'it's only a theory, but it covers
nt – the window of time after the assassina
vho'd been watching her for a while, pro
ed bugs planted inside the house, would kr
ze right after the shooting. Which room t
laptop and the voice recorder were kep
ıf her notes are still out there somewhere,
on would have done herself a disservice, e
a vault under a false name. There is no v
ık their client to this murder. That's the
ıancial crimes people to track down, I sup
etectives didn't appreciate my offering sı
f they seriously considered my story, I dc
uaded them that I wasn't withholding so
t would shed more light on Sharon's (
fact, I can tell they don't respect me be
out to save my ass. But they leave me alo
ı't come up with anything more. After a
ııtted to leave the country, as long as I co
. I thought about that for a day, then tol
ew York, to see if I could get anything out
riend myself, even though the police h
d him fruitlessly at my insistence.

The Perfect Worker

The Turn

You must be amazed at how I appeared to have accepted everything about my life in Brazil at face value, having apparently forgotten within a few months the circumstances in which I was brought there. What happened to him, I hear you asking. Is he some sort of idiot who manages to misunderstand or underestimate things precisely when it is most urgent that he doesn't? Or was he so terrified by the sheer scale of his imprisonment and the number of appearances he would have to unravel – faces, allegiances, motives – that he chose to put up his hands instead and meekly embrace his destiny? 'And finally, you psychopathic undeserving sonofabitch, what about Patty?' I imagine the more romantic among you screaming, 'Didn't you feel you owed her anything?'

Well, all of you are probably right, though I still find your questions impossible to answer. The same objections occurred to me frequently during those early months, and I realized that yes, I do tune out of the most pressing situations; perhaps the voices and urgencies that sound inside other heads fail to speak out in my own. I also noticed upon thinking back that I often forget things: the examples came to me unbidden. Remember how I went for a picnic in the heath while I was being followed, or fell asleep in the garden the moment I thought I was safe. I concluded that this arose from an ability to ignore the bigger picture. Perhaps it is founded upon a lack of imagination, or else an unwillingness to imagine. I remember how rapidly I would skim the newspapers in the weeks after one of my murders. I was looking for reports on the progress of the police inquiries, in the course of which I might glance at the photograph of the victim or go over a few paragraphs of his story. No more. I would then finish my coffee, fold the day's paper and plan out a walk to some area I hadn't visited in a few months.

What would it have availed me to discover that Auguste, Noel, Gustavo, or Nelson were fakes? Or that Sr. da Lima was the one entrusted with my maintenance? How would I have found out without giving myself away? What if they turned hostile and finished me off? Or, they could simply have sent me down to some dungeon without a window to be released only as per requirements. In any case, my life between the bar and the restaurant would have been ruined.

There was nowhere I could go. I would have probably been stopped if I tried to flee in a car. I couldn't call anyone since they would trace it back to me, and there was no one I could write to: how could I have even e-mailed Patty without taking a step towards telling her the truth?

I wish I could claim I encountered electrified fencing at the perimeter of a gigantic estate, or some other evidence of all-enclosing surveillance that would at least have proved I was desperately unfree, perhaps along with numerous others! That would have been something indeed, to try and spot some of them, hear their stories, and collaborate to plot the great escape. It would have catalyzed some sort of action: I couldn't easily have ignored its implications. Or, if I could have believed that my condition resembled a movie I once saw, in which a man's entire life was a television show from the second of his birth, and everyone – his parents, wife and best friend, and every single person in his town – was an actor playing a part; the town itself was a giant set he was never allowed to leave.

But it always seemed as though I was 'free' under an open sky, with real people in a genuine city that was in turn surrounded by wide-open spaces and even visited by tourists. The only detail I had to overlook was that I wasn't allowed to leave. And hypothetically speaking, where would I have gone? Where would I have begun a new life without money or papers or acquaintances? Where in the world would they not have found me?

I reassured my sceptical half by arguing that nobody in the grip of this organization seemed to know more than the required minimum, which was what always made their warmth both incongruous and genuine. Why should I have assumed they were all perverse and sinister when it could be that each of them – Gustavo, Bernardo, even Auguste – made up their own stories about me in the absence of the truth: that I was a visitor, a refugee, maybe even a fugitive who had been working for Sr. da Lima in another country and had his own reasons for keeping mum? That could be why I chose to accept the appearances of camaraderie, and a life that felt more real and full than anything I had known in London, barring the few short weeks with Patty.

Yes, this must have been my primary consideration. Why otherwise have I spent so many pages these last few days fondly recalling the characters and routines of my new life, whilst I pause to debate the question of their sincerity in just a couple of cursory paragraphs, as though I still don't wish to consider too closely other versions of those events? More than believing in them, it must be that I want them to be true. From very early on, I wanted to believe in the truth of that life and my place within it so much that I chose not to think too deeply about Sr. da Lima's reputation or his power. I preferred to ignore how I was led to a job in that restaurant, and argued instead that Auguste always seemed to believe me when every three months or so I couldn't come to work for five days (my excuse being I would be away for a quick trip to the interior, or a break by the coast).

Because these were the dates of my 'missions', the reason I was kept in their employ. I was flown out by night – sometimes for a few hours, sometimes across oceans – landed and housed, handed a plan to memorize from which was subtracted all purpose and background. Only my role was highlighted, and I was given two days to prepare myself. The appointed place could be the toilet of a restaurant or a hotel room, a make-up studio, a bank vault, a locker-room scenario once for which I was 'disguised' in nothing but a towel, and even the deep end of a swimming pool. Twice, we were inside rented limos: I had been made up as a chauffeur and only had to turn around, fire, then park and walk away. Most recently, I simply shot a young lady on her doorstep.

Though there was no pattern of locations, it was always arranged so that I could strike at close range, and afterwards I'd be in a private aeroplane within two hours. I have as little idea of who my victims were as I have of my employers, whether I was putting away the same man's enemies or being maintained by an entrepreneur who rented out my services to various parties. There was a phase when I was sure of being the instrument of a government agency. After five years, I have no such certainty any more.

I wish I knew all the cities I visited, if not some of the stories. Only once, just weeks ago, I was taken back to London for the first time since my capture (for the assignment involving the lady). It was strange, the moment I understood this, and in my sudden euphoria I even considered asking to visit my old flat, if not the pub or Patty, to see what had become of my stuff, especially my studio equipment. But I stayed quiet, because it was obviously impossible. Besides, although I sometimes dipped into my London diary at bedtime with as much pleasure as before, I realized I was no longer certain that I wished to return to my earlier life.

But things have changed very suddenly, and I'm writing this in the present. I am in New York at the moment, arrived two days before a job. The target is a middle-aged man. His face appeared somewhat familiar, but as usual I refrained from asking, or pursuing the question in my own mind (it would only have complicated matters for everyone). We were to get him around ten the next day on the street outside his flat, since he usually goes out for dinner. Or at least that was the plan.

This morning, the man who called himself Fred apprised me of some unusual circumstances. Apparently, things are suddenly "hot", and everyone is disappearing for a while. They claim they won't even be able to use the airstrip just now to fly me home. So it's been decided to suspend the mission, and release me for the present in New York. When they need me again, as always, it'll be up to them to locate me.

It is clear to me that I lost my composure in responding to this surprise, although Fred kept insisting there was no more he could say, and that he had no idea I was from Brazil, nor had he ever spoken to anyone from there, so he wouldn't know what my bosses were thinking. When I moved aside from the door, he told me I had to leave the room in three hours. He left an envelope on the table, which turned out to be full of notes. I didn't count them, all I cared about was whether they'd left me any numbers I could call. Where could I plead my case, explain why I had to be taken back? Brazil was all I had now, and hadn't I always given them my best?

Fred has vanished when I emerge from my room, and I give up and head down the street. I could return tomorrow, although such a hope is belied by whatever little I know about my employers. A voice within me wonders if I'm being put out to pasture, and this freedom is a sign of their recognition. Immediately I realize this is what I'd dreamt of for almost a year after my capture: no matter what the city, I'd have given everything to be released. But now "capture" seems an alien word: I haven't thought of it in that way for several years. All I can visualize is Saturday evening at the restaurant, and the merry drinking afterwards. Who would stand in for me? Should I accept the company's explanation at face value? Why couldn't they retire me there? Is there enough money in that envelope to buy a regular ticket?

There probably is, but I remember I have no passport, and no way of explaining at *any* Embassy how I'm here. I know I could be pleased that after five years I have earned enough trust to be allowed to wander on my own: isn't that another reason to believe their story, that they will eventually re-hire me? Then the counter-explanation occurs – they are just confident I am aware of my lack of choices.

Anyway, it has only been a few minutes since the idea entered my head. Perhaps I'm merely light-headed, or being a fool, because I don't even have a weapon. But what better way could there be of proving that I'm an exemplary worker? I remember all the specifications precisely: 14th Street, ten o' clock, his face from the photograph. What I have to decide is what crossing the line will mean. Will they be impressed and consider it initiative, or will my disobedience infuriate them – that I jeopardized the entire organization? In that event, I could be sure I would lose much more than Brazil.

I'll tell you what I have decided: I'll find a hotel and remain horizontal till the morning. Then I'll take my cue from my own impulses. I'll trust to my old habit, my greatest strength, that no one, not even myself, ever knows what I will do next, and my ability to do it without being paralysed by any regard for the implications.

The Writer of Rare Fictions

Derangements

(New York, March 2006)

I was heading home from supper at my usual time (Ana and I still share a place on 14th Street, and I was planning to stay there till the autumn, to be near Seb when he started at Columbia after his gap-year), when I felt there was something unusual about the speed of the guy walking towards me. A moment later, I realized it was his speed as well as the line that he was following, although he was facing downwards. He didn't maintain the distance you'd expect on a broad sidewalk: instead he seemed to be making directly for me. He was still a few yards away, but based on this much evidence, I looked around quickly for anyone within dissuading distance, made up my mind, turned, and began running. As expected, no one followed me, but that didn't resolve anything. I'd sensed what I'd sensed.

There are two memories that stand out from the following week. The first is of my incessant peeping through each of the windows of our flat for any obvious signs of surveillance. Frankly – though it only transmuted my fears into something else at the time – there were none. The second is that of night, since daytime had no meaning except as emptiness I had to wade through, and all that was real happened after midnight, as I lay not daring to switch off the light because that was when the real shakes began, accompanied by the sweating and its seepage from skin into the sheets. And then the dreams of being stranded in a sinking city, and of being chased down a wide empty street with blocks on either side as long as a thousand windows, except none of them was open and I was trying to make a getaway in a cycle-rickshaw.

I gave way to prolonged fits of weeping each day, with broken breathing and high-pitched yelps, because what was beginning to sink in along with my initial, self-centred terror and shock was grief. Another exceptional woman had been lost on my watch. How could I have not warned Sharon to be more careful and hire protection, because of how deadly her adversaries could be? How did I fail to foresee that?

As I dwelt on her memory, it grew clear at last that I hadn't accepted Sharon's offer simply out of enthusiasm for the project, essential and thrilling as it had seemed. I had loved her, instantly, and had leapt at the chance to deepen our association. Yet I was not in love with her, despite the events of our first meeting. It was something else she had restored to me, from another life, a much stranger and more unforeseen form of love. I scoured the pictures on the Internet to verify these sensations, but what I sought was more ephemeral than they could capture. She brought back my son to me, or perhaps a phantom daughter I'd never had. It was in her gestures, her pitches, her rhythms and her volatility; I'd been embracing all of those. I realized I would have collaborated with her on anything when she walked in that Saturday morning. My initial misgivings now exposed themselves in an alternate light. I didn't want her to misconstrue my warmth. I hadn't wanted us to be lovers.

On the third morning when I had actually noticed daybreak before I fell asleep, it occurred to me to pick up one of the books from the shelf behind my sofa, from the Enid Blyton Five Find-Outers series. Seb had brought them over from my mother's storehouse of my things in Calcutta when he stayed with her one summer. I went through *The Mystery of the Spiteful Letters* in an hour and a half, then a Mr Meddle book, *The Magic Faraway Tree* and *Mr Galliano's Circus* all on the same day. The evening after that I began with *Just William*, moved on quickly to *Shock for the Secret Seven*, and arrived at morning chortling my way loudly and helplessly through *William's Treasure Trove*. There were so many priceless moments in every story, such as the occasion when William replaces Robert's letter to his latest flame Diana, which he has accidentally dropped into the brook, with one akin in spirit to what Robert might have written:

> Dear Dianner, I hop you are well. Thank you for asking me to cum to the sowth of france with you I will cum to the sowth of france with you. I don't think that your conseated and die your hair or that you look a site without makeup or that your harfwit and I wouldent mind being seen ded in that hat with fethers and I no weel have a jolly good time in the sowth of france. with luv, Robert Brown.

These last few tactfully phrased statements are a bunch of insults he has overheard his sister Ethel spew out about this girl, only William feels he has turned them round successfully into compliments.

I began earlier the next evening with Seb's copy of Roald Dahl's *Collected Stories*, but somehow they were too menacing and adult for my present needs and I gave up and picked instead my old *Rubadub Mystery* starring Roger, Diana, Snubby, Loony the dog, Miranda the monkey, and Barney. That was also the first night in a week when I dared to lie in the darkness afterwards and wait to fall asleep.

It is extraordinary how I still remember those nights as an oasis of safety, a refuge so incongruously innocent I wished the whole world was peopled just like that, like Peterswood policed by 'Clear-Orf' Goon or William's timeless village, or the Malgudi of Swami and Mani. I went through half of the thirty-odd books on that shelf like a grotesque man-child starved and crazed, afraid at the same time of what would happen once I had finished them, when I would be forced out of this enchanted zone into the fullness of real time and my present life.

When I was a child we played a game in which tiny footholds of land lay far apart within a torrential stream, and there was a ravenous, thrashing crocodile that could kill you with the faintest touch of its flailing arms. The river was narrowly bounded on all sides, there was always one less spot of land than there were desperate humans, and you had to move from one chalk-circle to another through the dangerous water every few seconds. My shelf of books was now my only island: I could think of nowhere else to leap after that, and yet inch-by-inch the land around me was unstoppably disappearing under.

And I haven't stopped running since, nor have I ceased to fall. The chapters of a novel you'll find among these papers are nothing but fiction, Ellery. But it was my obsession with the undisclosed principals of Sharon's phantom book from which arose its peculiar vision of all-encompassing alliances and indecipherable interests, and it was that same fixation that set me running. Perhaps, in my ill-chosen mode of hothouse seclusion I completely lost the plot, yielding to the most unjustifiable hysteric paranoia, but it became increasingly clear during that period that I couldn't imagine resuming normal life until the motives behind her murder had been resolved.

I furnished myself with several reasons – originating from long before Sharon entered my life – why I too could well be in their sights. After all, you only had to examine my career cursorily to agree that the same track record which qualified me to be her aide, might also make me an equally undesirable irritant to such a coalition. Unknown as their names were to me, wasn't it supremely likely that I had baited more than one of them in a column at one time or the other? If big shots were ganging up and issuing 'fatwas', was it so improbable my name would be mentioned during the awarding of contracts? And the threat I posed was far more specific – it would not have escaped their notice that Sharon visited me twice within four days. Perhaps they too were hunting for the notes of *The Leap*. What if Sharon had made me a partner and revealed to me where they were? That would explain their gesture of intimidation, the overcoated figure charging at me with such menace. What worse might unfold if I remained passive?

Once I allowed myself to proceed along those lines, the pieces fell into place thicker and faster. Day or night, various sentences and portions of text from different articles and books of mine drifted through my head. In my personal crusade to be involved with everything around me, while remaining rigorously independent-spirited, I had given so many influential parties reasons for wishing me dead. Just as one example, I remembered my syndicated series of articles on last year's gang wars in Rio, in which I prominently discussed before an international audience da Lima's (yes, my erstwhile pa-in-law's) interest in encouraging the escalation of the drug feuds of the past three decades, both to eliminate rivals as well as to influence outcomes in forthcoming local and national elections.

In the same vein, numerous sections floated before me from hundreds of columns about India, and there were other opinions, countless others: on dams and patents, treaties and their unreported clauses, Indo-Pak relations, Islamic machismo, landless movements, privatization, military rule and caste and education, tax havens in Monaco and refugee camps in Lebanon, the geopolitics of water in the Occupied Territories and of hydrocarbons in central Asia, Maoists and hospitals in Bengal – a different subject each fortnight for the past fifteen years. Understand me clearly: I wasn't exceptional for writing about these subjects, and certainly not alone in any of my views. What singled me out was that I had written about such thorny matters regularly in at least three different countries, with no ideological consistency or programmatic loyalty whatsoever. It was a career which at different times succeeded in pissing off *everyone*.

And what had probably been especially irksome was that I was friends with many of those I bitterly criticized, and friends with many of their enemies. I was disloyal, duplicitous, ungrateful, impossible to predict or control. Which is why that night and whenever I have thought about it since, whenever I have begun a mental list of those with reasons (and the required reach) to organize my disposal on such a scale, I came up with so many names that after a while I gave up, convinced of the preposterousness of such an exercise.

Because the implications were as absurd as they were terrifying, evidence either of a frightening degree of insanity, or worse, of truth! I was discovering that I couldn't bring myself to rule out almost any of the powerful people I knew. It could well have been someone acting alone, potent enough to undertake such steps out of sheer irritation, without any need of consultation or alliances; or perhaps a tacit syndicate had been formed by various parties with nothing else in common, who had agreed to co-operate covertly in this small, one-off and mutually beneficial matter. Even at sixteen, my son had spotted the danger when he repeatedly wondered how it didn't bother me that I was considered 'friends' with everyone, 'people who hated each other, as well as people hated by everyone else'. And Ana, who hadn't spoken to her own father in fifteen years, would reply to him that it had never been enough for me to be a writer, that I had always considered it a minor-league occupation to sit behind a desk and merely describe the world. No, his father had to go out and play-act with the big boys who 'ran' it.

Now suddenly, after years of surprisingly elastic tolerance, they weren't play-acting any more. They had decided – correctly – that my friendship had gained them nothing while it cost very little to finish me. Quite characteristically, the hunt had begun without any last chances or warnings. Their cunning was remarkable: they could have simply blown a vehicle or room of mine into orbit. But that would have betrayed the involvement of major players and initiated an equally high-profile investigation. Sharon's murder and the (probable) attempt to attack me in New York deliberately had the mark of the crazed amateur working alone. When the real blow came, the detectives would go off looking for a non-existent Mark David Chapman, rather than a much murkier front-man working for an inconceivable coalition of interests. Plus, in the meantime, they earned themselves the inexpensive pleasure of watching me scurry.

I had always wanted to dance with wolves: apart from all my hot air to Sharon about curiosity and involvement, I suppose I simply had a childish weakness for the glamour, the thrill of sheer proximity to those who jerked the strings of power. Well, here I was finally savouring a first-hand prey's experience of the very qualities I wished to understand, tasting the whip-end of the ruthlessness that had made my 'friends' the 'never encountered but ever present kings of the world.'

There was one other remarkable night during that first week, which might have been thoroughly incongruous or a gift only made possible by my particular state of mind. I was lying in the dark as usual, unable to sleep, when I began to dwell upon this or that instant from among my memories. It began predictably enough, with sex – I was idly trying to hold down different phases of my life by evoking the women from the period. But an hour later I found myself on my back, enchanted by what had passed, yet certain that I hadn't slept. I realized I had been going over entire first encounters, recounting first undressings frame by frame: kisses, expressions, my first glance at the curves of various shoulders and breasts, each so particular that the phantom women actually began to move, touch me back, alter expressions and speak. What returned overwhelmingly in the darkness during that bewitched hour, along with the varied settings, the rooms, the voices and life-stories, was the force of the obvious yet suddenly vivid truth that there had been *other people* – each of whom had drawn close to me, but had somehow long since vanished. And people led on to people, and places, and walks, and shops and habits once so regular and present, yet carelessly unvisited in decades.

When I finally fell asleep that night, I dreamt of flying over a much emptier earth. I was showing my mother around Edinburgh, where I wrote my first novel. It lay below us, recognizable enough at first, though different bits of the city had been reordered in the usual manner of dreams, discontinuous in space as much as in time, so that we wandered through New Town streets I knew well, only to turn and arrive among crowds in a misplaced market scene from five hundred years ago. Later on, I was flying with my father beside me, in a light pre-Great War aircraft in extremely watery yellow-green sunshine over what I recognized to be the rolling fields and the shallow loch surrounding the volcanic plug upon which Edinburgh castle would one day come to stand. And afterwards I was skimming exhilaratingly unsupported on a clear day over an empty, densely forested Gangetic plain, rich and wetly green, before heading gradually over the Himalayan foothills and its higher, barer areas towards the first traces of snow.

As this chewed-up, discontinuous account nears its close, I see it has not been without rhythm or the binding undercurrents of common themes. I find that I have meditated insistently on the recurrent fact of absence, my absence from almost all the lives that have mingled with mine – the important ones as much as the episodic; an absence of care, understanding and attention which seems to have added up lapse by lapse to an immense absence from my own life. Who were my parents? What became of my father after we quit that room? How did my mother really feel about my decision not to live in India? What were Ana's reasons for not returning to me? Who is Sebastião becoming, and where was I while all this happened? How was Vera killed by Bryan whilst I lived between them?

In trying to reach out to everyone, I find that I repeatedly failed to arrive inside of anything. Far from being the ringmaster of a varied, stupendous circus, it looks as though I might well have been one of its dumbest animals. So vainly absorbed with my gift for juggling multiple lives, countries, masks and disguises – joker, dabbler, genius, clown, born free and impossible to imprison – I ended up being taken in by everything and noticing nothing.

Perhaps it has been an error that will ultimately prove to be deadly, yet today I'm moved by the thought that so much of my unvisited, under-lived real life returned to me that night just as I was on the verge of losing everything, and I interpret those later dreams as an obvious longing for escape. But then I must have been swayed off-direction by the winds because I landed south of where I was headed, in the tiny narrow pathways of the medieval temple town of Bhubaneshwar. I wandered away from the market crowds around the temple walls, looking for a suitable point from where I could again launch myself and fly off unnoticed. I was afraid of being shot down as a wizard or a shaitan in case I was spotted.

(A sequence of dreams noted in my diary, from April 2006, just after I left the flat in New York)

I've dreamt of Ana often these past few weeks. The first time was many nights ago, and I was trudging a long distance over various parts of the city. Ana never actually appeared that night, but it was a dream about her, because I knew throughout my walk that she was my destination. I covered many bridges: we lived in a hilly, medieval town and once I even came across a cricket match being played on an extremely sloping crossroads, where the bowler sent the ball down to the batsman a few feet below him, and the fielders were positioned down the smaller streets that branched away. The surface beneath their feet was cobbled.

I remember wooded lanes along railway lines, and greeting a group of friends seated outside a café behind a white fence, separated from me by a fast-flowing river. Though it was a fine day, I shouted that I couldn't stop and even told them why. Most of it was in the daytime but it seems to have grown darker as I walked. At one stage, I raced down a wide grassy slope on a bicycle until I arrived at the gates of a huge estate. I followed a red earth road and by now it was pouring, so I took shelter in a folly designed to resemble a Roman temple. Later I was still walking, but found myself trapped in a snowstorm on broad eighteenth-century streets that resembled Kensington or Edinburgh but all opened in parallel onto vast white meadows at either end. I tried each of them but failed to find a way out of this open maze.

I remained awake for a while, trying to fix a print of every stage before it faded from memory. When I fell asleep again, I was miraculously returned to its sequel. After a brief climb through the streets of the medieval centre – where the buildings tower to one side and I can see the town spread out in the valley on the other, with a train arriving through the woods covering the opposite hill – I emerge through a narrow alley on my way to a restaurant in which I work, and who should I bump into but Ana and one of her men. She is aware of my purpose, and despite being with her present boyfriend glances at me sympathetically, draws me aside and gives me a promise and a time. That is when I wake up, exultant at first, but gradually I realize there might never be such a meeting.

But I am proved wrong a few nights later when I arrive at her house, which is just beyond a small bridge over a narrow river. She lives in a mock castle, with windows and turrets at its many corners. The thick wooden door is open, and I walk up the wide stone stairs to the first floor. I'm about to continue upwards when I notice Sergio, whom I haven't seen or thought about in twenty-five years, packing his things in a small room in one corner. He is working by the early morning light, and his suitcases are on his bed that occupies most of the tiny area. Sergio was in love with Ana when I met her, and even though he didn't get anywhere and I assumed his place, I decide his leaving must be a good sign. But I'm cordial enough to disguise it, and stand by the door making polite conversation to keep him company while he packs.

This is when I notice Ana walking down the stairs from the second floor. She is radiant even at such an early hour. As I approach her, she signals to me to keep quiet; we should slip out while her man is asleep.

But slip out we don't, and our date never begins because that is when I wake up. I spend the whole of that day inconsolably weeping, even though I'm supposed to be on the lookout for assassins, and am expecting another interview with detectives from London that evening. It is as though I'm being toyed with and denied even in my dreams, or that even in fantasy I'm unable to elude my fate.

For many nights afterwards there is just darkness, whether my eyes are open or shut. Then suddenly Ana and I are on the streets of Calcutta, near Golpark, a few minutes from my childhood neighbourhood. It is almost dawn, there is no one else, and I find her very close to me – we are walking with our arms around each other. And now we are kissing, and though it is a dream I vividly sense my lips melting: I feel myself turning weightless. The kiss continues forever and I know it is a good omen. This is the return my life has been leading up to. Everything else has come true, the false starts, the disappointments, the delays. I reason even as I kiss that after all these years I would not have been granted such a meeting if it is to culminate in nothing.

The Perfect Worker

Derangements

(New York, March 2006)

So I am reminded it is a very thin line I'm treading, with everything to lose. Not just in the present context: I mean my sanity itself. It is not improbable I am losing my mind, and my grip on events is imperceptibly slackening. (Perhaps the effects of this are already evident to others; even my walk gives it away, and that is why the target last night sensed something odd and ran before I could approach him.)

The next few days will be crucial: my last window of opportunity, the last chance I might have to weigh the situation and make an independent decision. I have an eerie feeling things will speed up not long after that (if they haven't already) and I will confront the consequences of my choice, one way or the other. In the night and a day since the attempt that never was, I have felt a definite shift in mental balance, a slow but certain erosion in my capacity to line up happenings and view them clearly. In fact, I have done little else in this time besides wandering around and trying to focus. I have sat down on benches and steps, and tried counting up pros and cons on my fingers to see if it would help. But every time I get to about three arguments on each hand, I lose the thread or something happens to wash them away, and I'm forced to begin walking quickly, because for some reason stillness suddenly seems the more dangerous alternative.

I began writing to help the process of assessment. I have tried my best to be clear, most of all because I haven't much time. I tried to follow my hunches about what episodes it would be vital to remember, and thankfully there haven't been any obstructions, until now, until this moment. The rest of the story hasn't happened yet, which is one obvious problem. But this wait has caused me to cast my eye over the writing from the beginning, and an uneasy sensation has appeared on the horizon. It might only be a matter of literary composition, one of the normal stages of writing, and my worry may simply be that of a novice. Or else it is another trick of the pressure I feel in the present situation. Whatever the cause, I have noticed that the words I set down don't always remain where I put them, and there are huge stretches of time about which I have said nothing at all.

Why did I choose the events of Chapter One so readily as a point of departure? What are the threads that run through each of the episodes that follow? Where are all the years that went missing? Have I been aware at each stage of the crux of what was unfolding, and the choices that were leading me deeper into *this* life rather than any other? If not, where was I while my life occurred, and how am I expected to arrive at the correct decision now, in this hour of greatest urgency, when I need most of all to see a clear way into the future?

(New York, Summer 2006)

One day, three months after my dismissal, I realized over a tinfoil tray of spaghetti that I no longer cared how I looked while I ate, even though I ate in full view of passers-by. I noticed this after I bit upon a piece of bone and immediately used my fingers to bring out the meat as a reflex. Once I had it, I set down my tray, and used my left hand to go over the meat until I had picked out the shard and thrown it away. Then I put the half-chewed piece back into my mouth, licked the oil off my fingers, and picked up my dinner again. It was at this moment that I grew aware of myself, and my gaze fell upon my beard, from which were hanging four noodles besides scraps of meat and blobs of red sauce. I put my tray down for the second time and held out my beard to search better, threw out the food I could see and tried to dig away with my fingernails older spots that had dried on the hairs.

As to my resolve to keep the target's front door under constant watch in case he should emerge at an advantageous moment, I had worked out a routine in which I circulated undisturbed between a particular unused doorway, a spot beside a cigar store opposite, and a bench a few metres away, where I could rest occasionally and still be close if ever an opportunity arose. Yet, despite every effort, I found myself spending large parts of the day half-asleep even while I was seated, or so I would realize when something happened to break my torpor.

On one such out-of-body journey I was seventeen, and running along with the envelope containing my university application, which my mother had sealed and assigned me merely to deliver. She assured me she had filled in everything exactly as required and I had no reason to worry, yet twice I put my hand in the letterbox and my fingers refused to drop it. Finally I decided there was no harm in opening it just to check; all I had to do was buy another large envelope and re-address it. Mummy never even needed to know.

I vividly remember the relief I felt on awakening because when the papers fell out, they were pages from the diary I had rigorously maintained while in Brazil: pages in my own hand, writing on unlined sheets in every direction, points and memoranda in code incomprehensible to anyone but me. Mummy had clearly made a mistake, and thank god I had checked before posting it.

But when I return to that other world, it has turned into a dazzling aquarium of glass and white – a spacious, high apartment with white walls, brilliant sunlight and sliding doors, and the ongoing life of Manhattan far below us. There is very little furniture, but the rooms are full of people sitting around on white sheets spread out on the floors, also in white as if at a Hindu wake. New mourners are being guided to different spots, and everyone has been warned in advance about the apartment's outstanding feature: the occupied areas make a crescent around the largest room, which is suddenly revealed to be full of water. The new faces press against its glass doors at three corners, expressing eagerness and terror in equal measure. I, though absent from the scene, am as bemused as the others, but suddenly there is a muffled crash as a white shark shoots out from the sides to hit against one of the doors with malicious force. Amid screams on the outside, it turns and charges for the door opposite, teeth bared, fin upright, and body quivering in a faint hum that runs through the entire mass of water. This is the heart of the funeral, around which they are trying to conduct things normally, this is the menace the silence surrounds.

On my final transport that day, I'm in a wood at the edge of the desert. Behind me in the distance are dry red rolling Central Brazilian highlands to one side and the desert on another, and ahead lies a path of red earth continuing into the heart of the forest. As I venture further I take a keen interest in the movements of two bright beetles visible even from standing height. I am aware that my eyes feel as sharp as the lens of a camera and I can view them in exactly as much detail as I please. One is chasing the other but together they move in patterns so effortless, it seems as though they are gliding.

The silence is disturbed only by a pounding that approaches nearer until I can see one rhinoceros running in my direction down the red path, followed closely by another. Both of them are shimmering in the heat and dust as they leave the cover of trees behind, and I step aside to watch them rush past. Not very far though, because suddenly they stop in their tracks almost exactly where the grassland ends and the chase is reversed, or perhaps this is merely their sport. I can smell them as they run past this time, feel their sweat slam into me in boiling blasts and their footfalls beat up my body and lodge behind my temples.

I decide to follow them and begin running, but soon it is evident that something unusual is happening. I am not making any effort, yet I'm racing faster than I normally can. When I look down, my feet aren't moving; in fact, they are a few inches from the ground. I'm flying along behind the animals and the ability does not disappear even after I have grown aware of it. Soon I begin to control it, but I'm still afraid to try and rise higher.

After we have gone a long way inwards, the animals disappear into the dry foliage but I have lost the wish to follow.

Besides, I'm not sure my newfound gift won't be withdrawn if I stray from this clear path and entangle myself amidst the trees. So I decide to return the same way.

This time as I near the end of the forest, the path is a little more crowded. Small groups of people wait by its edges, wrapped in thin white cloth as if they are pilgrims or mourners. I suddenly notice I too am dressed like them. The first gathering fails to spot anything unusual as I skim past, but someone in the second group notices my otherworldly smoothness. I have raised myself a few inches so that I am more conspicuous. As I show no signs of slowing down, he points me out to some others and gradually a cry is raised. They begin to run after me with appeals to stop. This, and the fact that I'm now proceeding a good few feet above the ground, attracts the attention of those in the next, larger gathering, who attempt to block my way. As I sail over their heads I can clearly hear their shouts turning into pleas. Now I can make out the edge of the forest, and below me the voices grow more frantic. The fastest few have managed to keep up with me, and suddenly I'm struck by terror about what might happen if I fall into their hands. Also, there is the desert ahead and I do not know how long I can keep this up without tiring. I'm thirsty at the very thought of such distances, but to the west behind the hills I am aware the sun is setting and I will lose my way if I return into the forest.

By now I've arrived high above open earth, and I cannot hear them any more since the desert is still too hot for their bare feet to touch, and they too would be afraid of getting lost in the dark. But I can sense their desperation pulling me downwards. I make a quick chart in my head, working from the position of the sun: I know I live not far to the northeast of here. Yet the red mountains call to me with their unblemished surfaces, the late evening gold and the shadows striping them in large wavy shafts, the clear air lighting up the way straight to the sun. And that is the direction I take, assuring myself it is a small diversion and that I will resume my proper course long before the sun disappears.

The Writer of Rare Fictions

'So Great a Sweetness...'

(Autumn, 2006)

So, the gift I've believed in my entire conscious life – for penetrating and synthesizing disparate realities – has proved to be no more than an empty-headed self-obsession, a bimbo's fascination with appearances; or perhaps the gift has been degraded because it was I who proved to be a bimbo. Ana could recall for you a time when I seriously discussed the possibility that I was some sort of anti-Faust who had made a pact with God in exchange for special gifts. I often claimed I owed Him a life, that He was the great designer behind the scenes and I was just a model on assignment, strutting and winning accolades, none of which were really mine. That seemed the only explanation for the numerous unmerited blessings, and all the turns of fortune I merely followed.

In return He must have a set of tasks for me, I argued, and it's what I believed until not many years ago, despite Ana's unrelenting scorn – that from the beginning the course of my life had never truly been mine to direct. I was a custodian entrusted with responsibilities far beyond myself. Beyond family, beyond country, beyond mere vocation and even love, I deciphered and defined my mission. I was to be curious about 'all of life', I was sent to be involved with 'the world'. I felt I'd been equipped with all the endowments – the learning, the travel, the suppleness of spirit, the capacity to create and recognize so many forms of beauty – that were necessary to reach out to every corner of it, to mingle freely in its variety, because my objective was unique. I was meant to know the world's laws but not to own it, to see as much of it as possible and yet to love it, to accept and describe its awesome fullness and also to change it.

And I failed, and lost it all. In what grand terms I had determined my own purpose and yet, drunk on those very myths, I fell prey to the oldest suspects of all – hubris, arrogance, ego – the most obvious and foreseeable nine-times-out-of-ten afflictions. I lost, not just blinded by my pretensions of divinity, but because I signally underestimated the ruthlessness of earthly interests and motivations, the very things I had spent my life diagnosing. To the exclusion of everything else, I concentrated on making 'friends' who would come together to kill me. 'The infinite variety of the world' – the principle to which I have paid lip service throughout these years: perhaps it has been decades since I was last in touch with any of its actual content. Instead, I churned out opinions by the thousand, forgetting that to merely name things was never my end. I thought my best chance to catalyze change would be to arrive directly to the heart of events, which I associated only with those whose actions moved lives by the million. Because, as I once proclaimed naked to Sharon, 'they might be good for the soil, but you only find worms happy among the grassroots.'

The young man always in a hurry, who cannot rest anywhere for long, the man of promiscuous curiosity who cannot fully embrace anyone because he must have time to reach everybody, who cannot ever let himself be ordinary because the world itself is his extraordinary duty, to view in its entirety and affect from its very top. How quickly, in just nine chapters, he aged and ran out of steam.

Which leads me to one last thing. I wish I could guide you to *The Leap* and play my part in publicizing its findings, or at the very least establish its existence. Without that evidence, I realize I resemble a certain raggedy knight-errant jousting with the arms of a windmill, or one of those actors in dinosaur movies, as they perform their scenes running away from thin air. Yet, I remain certain that book has already cost a life, so I hope this will encourage anyone who can help locate it to step forward.

Of course, *The Perfect Worker* is not much more than an indulgence and a pastime. Whatever his role in my life has been, Sr. da Lima's long proximity to two artists will permit him to see beyond a libel action, through to the humour in my depiction, and understand my request for such licence. Besides, any killers-to-be biding their time in the shadows would certainly be unequivocal professionals for whom I am a simple job. I spent the last few weeks chasing a whim that grew on me and grew into this story: the image of Charles, with the inexplicable blockage that exists to insulate him from the consequences of his actions, making him some form of ideal corporate employee. I suppose the conditions of personal stress have provided an extra impetus for this piece, but after all this time, it is a weightless fiction, nothing more, and its beauty is its only argument.

The Perfect Worker

Brooklyn Pyre

My train speeds smoothly out of the earth and climbs onto a high bridge in the middle of a wide street. On both sides are continuous grey-brown tenements; black people in kitchens and living rooms are visible through their windows. It has started snowing.

After a few stations have gone by, I get off and begin to wander. I'm looking for somewhere to settle at least for a while, one uncontested spot where I will not be intruding on someone's territory and from which I will not be beaten off. For the nights I'll find a shelter.

The blocks go by one after the other: straight, unbroken for long periods, and without storefronts. I pause at a certain point to watch someone from across the street before I decide whether I'll talk to him. He has made a little tent by covering himself with a blanket, but his head pops out every few minutes as if to check whether anyone is passing. After a while I notice that his hands are working away furiously beneath the blanket, so I move on, having decided not to disturb him.

Several blocks later I arrive at a huge store, as high as the building itself, with a large green awning in front. It is a showroom for beds and mattresses, and since it is open I enter to warm myself a little. It has turned more overcast and the snow continues to fall.

The ceiling inside is at least three floors high with hanging fluorescent lights, and everywhere there are columns of beds piled on top of each other. In another section there are towers of different-coloured mattresses, and the store has mirrors everywhere so that I'm often surprised to find a large bearded man with dishevelled hair and an ill-sized overcoat carrying a plastic bag and coming at me. What is not so curious is someone in a suit behind him who is also always in the frame. I would like to sit down on a bed for a few moments but I know he will show up to prevent me.

When I step outside I notice a mattress lying a few yards away from the store. There is no one around, and it is still quite dry, so I pull my blanket out of my bag and lie down. I watch the building in front of me and try and follow the descent of some of the snowflakes, until gradually I'm thinking of nothing. In just those few seconds before I fall asleep another person beds down beside me. I decide not to protest, since it might be his mattress. Anyway, he is lying with his back to me, under his own blanket, and no one is bothering anybody.

A while later I am awakened by a weight across my upper legs: someone else has laid himself horizontally across us. As my eyes open, I realize there is also someone lying across our feet. They both have their own blankets, they have their backs turned to our faces, and are looking for somewhere dry to rest. The snow is beginning to soak into us, so I reason these extra bodies will keep us warm and protected.

But when I next wake up there are two more men asleep vertically across the two above us: one pair of feet lies upon my chest though I still cannot see even one of their faces. While asleep I felt nothing, but now I am aware suddenly of the weight upon my middle. I can tell how long I have slept because of how much snow covers my blanket; I even feel it encrusting my face. I should get up and shake my limbs, but how to achieve this without waking everyone, all of whom seem so comfortable and quiet?

I lie there gazing at the view, only now everything has grown much whiter. The only other warmth besides the sleeping bodies all around is that of an old woman in a first-floor window who seems to be readying her dinner. But warm I am, and with another man's head in front of me. And slowly, even though I'm now awake, the bodies turn weightless again, my palms grip each other under the blanket, and I realize that for now, I could be nowhere better.

Day turns to evening in this way.

Editor's Note

And that is all I received. I'm allowed to divulge that the relevant essentials in this account do not differ from what Raj has consistently repeated to the detectives. Like them, I have combed these pages countless times, both as an amateur sleuth as well as an editor, and still nothing else about his claims seems actually verifiable, including the clever weaving-in of the yet-unknown commons murderer from five years ago. All the crucial events in Raj's story happen without any living witnesses, and with nothing concrete to go on, in which direction does one begin to search, especially when no one is sure if the supposed book at the heart of it still exists?

These have been the conclusions of New Scotland Yard, where I deposited my package a day and a night after it arrived. The investigating inspector turned out to be a book-lover and a long-time fan of Raj's work, and it was his considered suggestion that the best plan might be to publish everything: the publicity could force things into the open. Someone might make a move out of panic, or indeed be dissuaded from acting in case Raj was actually in danger. Alternatively, it might jog a few memories – witnesses, interviewees, bank managers in charge of safe-deposit boxes. Nobody knows who else Sharon confided in, apart from Raj. But such a titanic, eighteen-month, globe-spanning effort must have left a few more footprints.

The inspector also confirmed for me that Raj had phoned the police in New York and reported a 'near-assault', or at least his perception of one. But despite round-the-clock plain-clothes surveillance for a fortnight, no one unusual was noticed again. He then asked to leave town, and requested that his whereabouts remain a secret.

That is where things stand. So far, Ana da Lima is the only person to have read these pages, apart from the police and myself. A few weeks later, she insisted on the right to respond to certain chapters, since they were labelled as non-fiction and referred explicitly to her and Sebastião. She asked if I could include her reply as part of this same volume. An unusual request, and I contacted Raj at all of his known email addresses asking for his consent. After a month of silence, I made what you might call an editorial decision. I hope it balances the account, and puts right some of the reservations she expresses about me.

Ana and I have been friends for twenty-five years, and if there is one thing that rings true in Raj's 'autobiography', it is that there is no quantifying her significance in his life. The pages below speak for themselves and require no preamble: only Ana and Raj know their actual relationship to the truth, and even she cannot be certain where the truth has got to these last few months. All we have therefore are angles, and none more precious than Ana's. My only suggestion is to judge their testimonies not just in relation to each other, but also to everything else that is not here, everything else that grows to exist between two people, the formative stuff of all our lives, including anger, hurt, love, hope, regret, blindness and dream.

I know Ana would not mind me attaching such a caveat, because whatever truth there is in either account, these things cannot but be a part of it. Whatever the as yet unknowable truth about Raj's disappearance, these things are always true for every one of us.

I will end my contribution to this volume by reminding Raj of one of our shared favourite moments in literature. We are beside the deathbed of Don Quixote, and the much-harried Sancho – despite grumbling his way through nine hundred pages of delusion and chimera, not to mention innumerable, all-too-real beatings and ignominies – cries out (on behalf of all of us who have accompanied them to this point) to the knight whose eyes are disenchanted at last:

> Oh, don't die, dear master... Take my advice and live many years. For the maddest thing a man can do in this life is to let himself die just like that, without anybody killing him, but just finished off by his own melancholy. Don't be lazy, look you, but get out of bed, and let's go out into the fields dressed as shepherds, as we decided to. Perhaps we shall find the lady Dulcinea behind some hedge, disenchanted and as pretty as a picture. If it's from grief at being beaten you're dying, put the blame on me and say you were tumbled off because I girthed Rocinante badly. For your worship must have seen in your books of chivalries that it's a common thing for

> one knight to overthrow another, and the one that's conquered today may be the conqueror tomorrow.

Come back soon, man, let's go tilt at some more windmills together.

Ellery King
London, 2006

An Epilogue

I AM NOT ROSEBUD

by Ana da Lima

Memory says, I did this. Then pride intervenes: I can't have done that. A struggle ensues, but pride is adamant. Finally memory relents.

– Friedrich Nietzsche

Do not forsake me, oh my darling,
You made that promise when we wed…

– from the title song of 'High Noon',
starring Gary Cooper and Grace Kelly

Poor chap, he always loved larking.

– Stevie Smith, 'Not Waving but Drowning'

An Ordinary Story

He always wanted fans, not friends; he secretly preferred the distance between an audience and a platform to real closeness. Yet, no matter how large the crowd and distant the platform, the price of entry was never less than absolute adoration. Each faceless soul in the dark had to love him as if they'd known him all their lives, as if he had been a turning point in every life. He treated that love as his due, forgot about it the second after it was offered, but could never have enough of it. No amount of reiteration truly satiated him, no evidence remained fresh long enough to convince his memory. It had to pour forth again and again, from new faces as much as from the known ones.

I'll stop speaking of him in the past tense. Everyone knows Raj is prone to proclamations, and he launches into them even more frequently in private than on a stage. These torrents are usually the consequence of minor disagreements, such as when I asked him two summers ago how he had managed to be absent for each and every one of Sebastião's eighteen birthdays, and he orated Castro-style for an hour on the iniquitous conspiracy of the bourgeois family. He could turn anything into an idea, spin any idea into a position, and pour molten feeling into any position until it had bubbled into a role of high drama, involving planetary-scale issues. He's been generous enough to provide examples throughout this book, but let me add with all affection that when I came across Bellow's *The Actual*, I felt an instinctive sympathy for the woman Amy, who had to train herself to write off at least sixty per cent of what the narrator spouted during any of his rambles of indefinite duration. But what is revealing today is that I still recall most of those rants verbatim, even though I mocked or ignored him at the time.

It also seems ironic that someone with such a clear sense of purpose could fall prey to temptations he had so thoroughly diagnosed. Ellery is right: I too perceived him as a Don Quixote figure, and for several years I went along with it, deciding to be entertained, and played an amused but willing Sancho. Yet he was never just a cartoon, no matter how well he played one – his Cassius Clay persona with its chest-thumping rants was one of his favourite routines, except it hid much more than it showed.

Even now, I think it wonderfully schizophrenic how he habitually reveals different dimensions in his stories, playing scared characters, small characters, cowards, losers, weaklings. I have always loved the care with which he creates such lives, and the detail he infuses them with: Raj could create them because he was all those people, he carried them within him. He was the little boy bewildered in the backseat of his father's car, and the young man who never forgave himself for leaving his mother when he was seventeen, just as he never forgot what happened to Vera and Bryan.

The reason he was photographed so often in slums and ghettoes during the early years was simply that he wandered through them all the time – angry and powerless. And at least at the beginning, the reason he sought audiences with ministers and tycoons was his impatience. Immature though it was, it was most of all that quixotic impatience that first turned him into a courtier of power. Because he's right about one thing – he never had the time to toil honourably, hidden somewhere amid the grassroots. He was going to muster his gifts to be the great galvanizer, the one who would affect millions by animating those who ruled their lives. 'Hearts and minds will come round later,' he used to say, 'they have all the time in the world to read my novels.' Systems had to be transformed first. For this, their workings had to be understood and then exposed, as also the ways of their masters. He only had contempt for those who ran in the opposite direction from worldliness and power, fearing to be tainted by their touch. Incorruptibly, inexhaustibly, he would inspire change from the very top, send it rolling downwards, gathering force, until it was an unstoppable avalanche.

Today the question has become, is he merely stuck amid all that manure or is he well and truly buried? Of course, he discovered very soon that writers don't affect anything visible, and certainly never on the scale that he envisioned. His achievements outside the literary have remained as lacking in shape and focus as his proclamations: he would have made probably the same footprint if he had stayed at his desk and merely written all these years, invisible behind the words.

It also strikes me that perhaps he was especially ill-suited to any such transformative efforts, simply because of his laughable attention span. Or, as he says, it was his self-defined mission to touch and discuss 'everything', so how could he have spared the time to follow through on any one process he had initiated? He was the universal man: his voice was required everywhere. It was all he could do to imagine, diagnose (and decry), join the dots and reveal the big picture; other people had to dedicate themselves and seize the cue to action. He treated entire societies and their issues as mere stops on one of his gigantic rock-star tours. Many, many times he sparked off controversy and debate with one or another of his essays and interviews, in Europe, Brazil, and most frequently in India. Often there was tremendous support, but on each occasion it dissipated because Raj was never there to ask the next set of questions, or duller still, to repeat himself patiently until there was a measurable response. He couldn't afford to be: by the time the fortnight had come around, he was on another continent, raising hell over an unrelated subject and managing to be spotted at two premières and an awards-night party within the same period.

This approach became a habit. Despite periodic bouts of frustration, he never experimented with the other way – settling into a rooted involvement with any one matter that had moved him. It's all very well to be obsessively independent, but to truly dislodge any single thing, you have to allow yourself to belong somewhere. Some corner of the world has to be granted the right to claim you, however temporarily. Even during the recent years of criticism and ridicule, which I have admittedly watched from a distance, it was as if he refused to recognize his lack of impact. Each time, his frustration fizzled out in grumbling that 'the world' hadn't met him halfway, had never rewarded his energy with action. And of course, with Raj, such complaints were always a complaint about not being 'loved' enough as well.

Perhaps he is right, and it boils down to something as simple as getting soft on the lifestyle. The stream of essays and interviews that habitually caused a few hours of discomfort had become his comfort zone long ago, and then there was the effect power had on him – his lifelong attraction to the secrets and mannerisms of those who wielded it. It was already obvious twenty-seven years ago, on his first visit to my father's fazenda, a few months after we met; he was fascinated by the way Pai dealt with a servant he suspected of stealing. It had been going on for some weeks while Pai was away in São Paulo, but that first day after we arrived, he watched the man as he cleared the breakfast things and soon after took him aside and confronted him. The man confessed within fifteen minutes. Pai closed the door while he questioned him and emerged an hour later. Even I don't know what his punishment was, all Pai said was that he'd realized the truth from the way the man's eyes met the gardener's during one particular exchange of glances.

Raj was hypnotized, and it was the beginning of a friendship that has long outlasted our marriage, and my own relationship to my father. He hated my amateur psychoanalysis, such as when I (frequently) theorized to him that the reason he was so attracted to my father was his memory of his own. Raj remembered his Baba as a weakling, a man who managed to mess up the simplest tasks (who couldn't even steal a file with panache), who toiled away pointlessly at a job he hated, who didn't have the courage to leave the family roof even though it cost him his own family.

It was amusing in those early years how he unconsciously imbibed certain gestures of dismissal that Pai used. At the time I thought it male and childish, but perhaps it was the weakening resolve of a Bhishma, that Raj was having doubts about his own vow to keep clear of wielding power the more he glimpsed of its possibilities. He was also bothered by that old dichotomy, of being ultimately a describer and not a doer. And though he insisted he wanted to learn the qualities required by a 'warrior' without ever wishing to wage war, it is not just a matter of style how much he loved striking the poses.

Striking the poses: it seems odd that Ellery who knows him so well should not have considered the possibility. Raj has always been openly fascinated by the quality of mass charisma. Playing the part, before as large a public as possible – maybe to shift a few books – but more to know and feel for himself – for Raj – what it is to be hunted, and stripped down (metaphorically) to a bum. Yes, another shade to add to his spectrum, because Raj has always been multiple, expects himself to be multiple, just as in the past he sought after the roles of celebrity, lover, artist, father, amateur diplomat, television activist and general bearded 'saviour', each performance so operatic, so public. Besides, everyone does what they can to grab themselves a headline: some have sex in the pool on *Big Brother*, and Raj Chakraborti is supposedly on the run from murderers.

So what are we expected to do, I wonder. I could put out a multi-media appeal saying 'come back home, we love you, all is forgotten', but perhaps I would just be luring him out for some grateful sharpshooter to take aim? I know my response sounds a lot like the village that ignored the fantasist's cries of wolf, but is Raj really helping his own cause? Is it really believable that Sharon chose him to reveal so much about her book, and did not drop even a single name?

Please Raj, either admit you're genuinely afraid, and let us empathize with you. There's no shame in abandoning your integrity in the face of such a threat. Or else, Ellery, there's been enough hoopla already. If the two of you are trying to stage a comeback by making a splash, the end of this volume is just the time for a confession. It is beyond vulgar to build all this on the back of a young person's killing. This absurd game of hide-and-seek can stop, and I'm sure Raj will stand up and admit it was his idea. Why would so many world-important people (including, it appears, my father) risk being implicated in his murder, when no matter how much he annoys them, they have him exactly as they want him, flitting about from place to place with steadily increasing irrelevance? As a social force, he couldn't be less influential now than if they'd specifically designed him.

I went up to London myself and spoke to the detectives concerned: there are many aspects to his testimony that strike them as genuine and troubling. But there were other options open to Raj besides involving the whole world in his conspiracy theory. Just a quiet disappearance under protection would have been honest, but he would never be content with the simple humanity of a leave-of-absence. For many years now he has been humble only in his novels. Only in those does he concede his smallness, his bewilderment, his great fear of drowning in the all-ness of the world. That is why his true gift emerges there.

The rest I always thought pathetic and slightly scrawny: all of the personas he considered so influential and glamorous were to me the weakest of his fictions.

The Ghost with Lovely Eyes...

(India, June 1988)

> Calypso, ah Calypso! I often think about her. She loved Odysseus. They lived together for seven years. We do not know how long Odysseus shared Penelope's bed, but certainly not so long as that. And yet we extol Penelope's pain and sneer at Calypso's tears.
>
> – *Milan Kundera,* Ignorance

We spent a week in Bombay before moving on to meet Raj's mother in Calcutta, on the visit when I first heard of Sunayani. We arrived at his friend Ajit's house in Bandra, and on Sunday afternoon we were moving to another friend's in Cuffe Parade at the very bottom of the city. Raj decided it would be a great idea to make the trip on a horse-drawn carriage, driving along the shoreline. He would brook no discussion and at eleven-thirty had even arranged for the carriage to draw up and wait outside our building.

But he was right; it had rained hard the night before, and we wound our way down Mahim and Worli, fanned by a churning sea on one side and enjoying the overcast washed-ness of the city to our left. Everything was perfect, trotting down Chowpatty and even through the smells of the reclamation, but just when we were taking our suitcases off the tonga opposite the World Trade Centre, the tongawallah decided to stick us up with a knife.

Perhaps it was our obviously foreign-returned look and the sheer hippie dopiness of hiring a Victoria for such a long journey that convinced him we were easy game, but it was a deserted afternoon and we couldn't take any risks screaming. Raj had just about opened negotiations with him when two men scrambled through a hedge behind us and made off with a large suitcase.

The tongawallah was the first to notice and he couldn't help shouting out 'Saab, woh dekho, Chini log suitcase lekar bhag gaya' ('Look Saab, the Chinese ran off with your suitcase'). A quite baffling remark from your average mugger, especially if you haven't noticed what on earth he is referring to, but Raj, thinking equally quickly, responded with 'Come, follow them with me and I'll give you a huge reward,' and set off through the hedge.

The tongawallah, who had a sweet smile, had given us no previous impression of being either a toughie or a rogue, and the sudden acceleration of the situation brought out the boy in him once more. He too had very little time in which to decide, and ordered me 'Memsaab, wait here,' forgot all about the stick-up and set off right behind Raj. 'Keep the knife in your hand,' Raj shouted.

Two men trying to get away with a suitcase were no match for two men chasing them without one, especially when one of them had a large switchblade. I could hear Raj blustering away loudly at the thieves, and when I made my way through the hedge, holding Seb, I realized they were indeed Chinese. They too were passers-by who had just been trying their luck because they didn't even have a getaway car nearby or a weapon. Anyway, Raj let them off with a big shouting (in which Hari the tongawallah joined in as well), and we sent him on his way with a hundred-rupee tip. He was so pleased, he smiled and waved all the way until he turned the corner.

That was our life the week before we arrived in Calcutta. Exactly a week later, the two of us were standing at the gate of an asylum for women, outside Ranchi. We'd left Seb with his grandmother. Someone called Sunayani had been admitted here about three months before, someone whom Raj said he'd briefly dated in his teens. It must have been brief but important, because we were on a train here the day after he heard the news from his mother. I was requested by her to go since Sunayani had apparently especially asked to see me.

We were standing at the large, locked gate, waiting to sight a watchman. Far away in the distance, at the end of a six-hundred-yard drive, we could make out a long, low single-floor cluster of buildings. All the rest of the area was an immense playing field fringed by familiar-seeming trees, some of whose Indian names I already knew – flaming orange gulmohur, the magenta of bougainvillea, deodar, neem and mango. In one lonely corner we watched a large group of women in white saris playing together. They were throwing upwards what looked as light as a beach-ball and following the direction of its float.

As we watched, one of them caught it and ran away from the others, throwing it ahead of her and arriving below to catch it again just in time. She was approaching the gate and a few yards behind her – giving hard chase but looking as weightless an apparition as the multi-coloured ball floating in the breeze before them – was a much larger group of women. I can still recall the image just before we heard their shouts: it was as noiseless and rapid as a dream, especially with the waves of heat that shimmered and warped our vision.

That is why I didn't immediately realize Raj had run away. He had fled along the wall and was now hiding where he couldn't be seen from the other side of the gate. That was where he collapsed and threw up, and even after he refused any discussion of going inside and we returned to the hotel, I stupidly continued to believe he was reacting to the heat.

For a couple of days he insisted she had been a lifelong friend who was going through a difficult period. We remained in Ranchi, though he kept postponing a return to the institution. It was his mother – once we were back in Calcutta – who felt she owed me the truth, that Raj and Sunayani had been in love for years before he left for England, they were planning to be married, and that his remaining there without her, followed later by our relationship and marriage, had been successive shocks from which she'd never recovered. He was supposed to return for her, that had been the understanding, and this was the latest stage of a long decline.

'But he never told me anything,' I said. 'He never gave any sign that something was wrong. Did he know what effect it was having on her?'

'Yes, he knew. He even decided to move back once, and make a go of it here. He found a job in a boarding-school and promised her they'd soon be married. But he hated the atmosphere there, and had to give it up after a month. This time he went back for good to England.

'She wrote to him a few times but afterwards, when she was too ill, I begged him to visit at least once, just to face her while he said his goodbyes. He asked me to explain that things had changed, and you had entered his life. Don't misunderstand me, Ana, I had no idea who you were, but I had known her for years. They had been friends in school since he was fourteen, and I was watching her fall to pieces.'

There isn't much more to say, at least not for me who never even met her. I saw a picture once and it justified her name – she had exquisite, drawn out, bright eyes, like close-ups of stars. And I certainly wouldn't have mentioned it here, if Raj hadn't managed not to mention it *at all!* This epilogue arose in response to two specific, supposedly 'non-fictional' sentences that I couldn't allow to go unchallenged: when Raj recalls pleading with me, 'you're the only person I ever craved,' and when he tells Seb in Rio that he broke up our family because he suffered from the disease of big ideas.

What an extraordinary portrait he has drawn of our relationship, without providing any background or history, selecting only the occasions when he caught me out with other men as if that was the reason we combusted – two sad, wrinkling swingers out of Updike. Yet, he found enough room to include lengthy excerpts of his favourite speeches – about waste and error and loss – as well as the characteristic lament for me from which I emerge appearing either deaf, incredibly heartless or plain stupid.

But not a word about Sunayani and the effect she had on our marriage. It is the most astonishing of omissions, because from that visit onwards I literally watched us emptying: first the content drained out slowly and then rapidly the forms fell to dust. Initially there was a lot of resistance from me in the way of shouting and tears, but soon there remained only exhaustion. The strange thing is, he refused completely to discuss her but sometimes, during those nights when we didn't even bother talking, I swear I could see her lying behind him, on her side, gazing over him straight at me, expressionless.

She seemed to show signs of recovering during the winter, and we heard she was being brought back home. But she never arrived, because on her way to the bathroom, while her mother waited in the compartment, she fell out of a moving train. Or, as Raj immediately interpreted, she jumped to her death. And that also turned out to be our final period as a couple, because he disappeared a fortnight later without even a goodbye note, much as he has done now. At first we were sure he had left for Calcutta, but there was no sign of him there. Then, after six months, a friend of his took pity on us and told me he was in Hamburg. Raj had wired him for some money.

We found him in a large single room in a converted warehouse that stood on a narrow canal, facing the endless brick walls and windows of the warehouses opposite. Very little light made it into the corridor, and two-year-old Seb didn't even recognize the thickly-bearded man who opened the door. His room was filthy and so was he. Our conversation was insignificant. I don't know how much time passed, but both of us had barely spoken before I noticed that the door was open and Seb was missing. He was nowhere in the hallway where all the other doors were shut, he wasn't on the staircase or on any of the other floors, and when I arrived downstairs the door leading straight onto the water was open.

It seems amazing that Raj, otherwise so rigorous with himself, so profoundly and publicly confessional, could narrate a testament without a *single* mention of either Sunayani or those twelve months of living in her shadow. I hadn't come to Hamburg with any decisions, I was far too worried and relieved for that, but I remember exactly that it was the second when I re-entered the room with Seb to find him lying in bed just as I had left him, that I understood I would be leaving with a divorce. It was as if I suddenly saw he didn't care at all about us, because there was no way he could have missed hearing my frantic cries down the hallway and up the stairs. He made it easier by admitting he had no intention of returning home. He said whatever measures I was going to take, he agreed to in advance: now that I knew where he was, I should just send him anything that required his signature.

And that is why I am not his Rosebud. I do believe there is a lot of truth to the feelings he has described about me, but I know even now that it remains a tremendous denial, a willed attempt at illusion, for him to substitute Sunayani and pretend that I am what he needs to be complete. I'm not sure if he wished to exclude her memory from the gaze of others (in which case I'm guilty of disrespecting his wishes), or for his own sake. Perhaps it is what he sincerely wants to believe, but it is not the truth, even though I too have wanted to believe it for most of these intervening years, though part of me still wishes to believe it.

But Sunayani can never die, not since she fell off that train. She remains alive in every story. She turns into a kitten and falls down a stairwell, and returns more alive than ever.

...And a Story about Myself

I have one last memory with which to close this epilogue. I suppose I felt guilty when I recalled it, and perhaps I am including it out of a spirit of expiation.

It's from the time I shot my film *Shakuntala* in India, about seven years ago. I was on a train leaving Calcutta, on my way to a location near the Nepal border in North Bihar, to assess its suitability for shooting. One of the assistant cameramen who had grown up there had described the setting so evocatively, it sounded ideal for our purpose – decaying palace, marble rocks, fast-flowing river and unspoilt forest. He had left already to make arrangements for my stay and would receive me early next morning.

I had laid out my sheets, answered as many questions from my co-passengers as briefly, politely and untruthfully as possible, and the compartment light had been switched off. I was soon in the state where I kept realizing I had nodded off only when I abruptly awoke again. I'm sure it was already the third or fourth time when I noticed I was waking up on the same note each time, with the sense that someone was repeatedly asking me to get off the train. I would start up, wonder what had happened, try and hold on to the fading wisps of the voice and form an impression of what I had heard. But a clear tone eluded me, though its words were always the same: 'Leave this train at the next station, the *next* station, leave this train at the next station.'

My way of ignoring it was to try and sleep by turning over and closing my eyes, but when it had happened more than five times, I sat up feeling overwhelmingly ill. The metal shutters on the windows had been brought down. I had no choice: I felt that whatever happened, I needed fresh air. Trying to lie down was useless because it only weighed harder upon my chest. But once I sat up I needed to stand, when I stood I had to walk around, and when I'd walked the length of the carriage and even visited the toilet to no avail, I knew voice or no voice I was getting off the train. It didn't matter that it was one in the morning, I had no idea where we were arriving and there was no one still awake I could ask.

I spent the night in the first-class waiting room at Sitarampur, where a very kind but extremely puzzled railway policeman laid out as much bedding as he could muster on a bench for a crazy memsahib, whose story was that she realized in the middle of the night she was on the wrong train. 'But why did the TT not warn you, madam, when he saw your ticket? Then you could have got off at Burdwan or even Asansol and gone to a hotel. Here there is just a circuit-house, ten minutes from the station, but I can knock loudly and wake them up if you like.'

I assured him that all I needed was to rest until daybreak when I would take the very first train back to Calcutta. After he left me with repeated guarantees that he would be only a shout away no matter what the time was, I lay back to find I was feeling absolutely fine. The memory of being unwell now seemed nothing more than a stupid fit of hysteria. I had never experienced anything of the sort before, and wouldn't have imagined myself succumbing to such a feeling. Watching the still shadows in the dim moonlight stealing through the window, I considered the possibility of continuing onwards in the morning. But I couldn't face the thought of telling my benefactor this, not after the midnight harassment I'd caused him. So I decided I would return within the next two days, rather than embarrass myself before him once more.

I woke up at very early dawn, and spent a few minutes watching the play of dust particles in the first pale beams of sunlight. I was thinking of my final dream, in which I was a girl strolling down an icy path somewhere in the English countryside. All around me was the sparkling sunlessness of snow-covered fields and a few houses on both sides, far away. Underneath the ice were clearly visible hundreds of brightly coloured snakes, red and green and blue, all unmoving. I continued down this bejewelled path, trying not to tread too hard, when an equally young and unfamiliar Raj approached me. He stopped with some elaborate explanation about how the cold forced the snakes out of their holes and they emerged only to be trapped in the ice. I said to this beautiful boy that it reminded me of Coleridge's *Kubla Khan*.

I wanted to phone my cameraman as soon as it was morning, but within a few minutes a policeman knocked loudly and entered with two other excited railwaymen, one of whom was the stationmaster. 'This is the memsahib,' he announced by way of introduction, and then turning to me, he continued, 'Madam, a very strange thing happened. You were very lucky to get off last night. Thank god it was the wrong train. Do you know, it derailed at three a.m. two hours north of here?'

'What?'

'Yes, madam,' said the stationmaster, 'we are not getting the exact casualty position yet since it happened in the middle of the night. But policemen are already at the scene, four or five bogeys went off the rails, and they have telephoned up and down the track. The entire route is closed for the time being.'

Perhaps their opinion of the memsahib's nerves fell even further, because I found myself overcome by helpless sobbing. But they brought me tea, which I gratefully accepted, and a big railway breakfast I couldn't face. They sat opposite me until I'd calmed down, and the stationmaster kept repeating, 'Madam, this is destiny, no one can overturn it. You were not meant to be on that train. You mustn't feel bad. It has nothing to do with you.' I felt very grateful for their attention during what must have been a frantic time for them. Even when they went to receive calls they left a deputy to attend to me, right until I was safely on another train that came in from further west and was going on to Calcutta.

The story has a small sequel. We found our palace afterwards, near Murshidabad. But two days later I went to see Raj's mother, and she was the first person to whom I described every detail of that night. I hadn't told her about the trip before because she would have worried about me in North Bihar. We were sitting in the safari park by the Dhakuria Lakes and what surprised me, as much as her words themselves, was the absolutely unruffled, even tone of her voice.

'Sitarampur,' she said. 'But that must be along the same route on which Sunayani's accident happened.'

This time I didn't react. I merely asked her if she was certain. She said the track bifurcated soon afterwards and Sunayani's train would have been approaching from the west.

Neither of us said anything more. I was watching the birds on the tips of one of the bare trees up ahead. Then my eye fell upon a little slum girl who was walking absent-mindedly towards a lone couple seated at the far end of the lawn. Her hands were outstretched above her head, and her feet were following the swoop and rise of one of the many crows flying low above her: now she would run a few steps, and then slow down again. Almost disinterestedly, as if it were an annoyance and a chore, she went up to the couple and asked them for money. But she didn't stay a moment after their first refusal; she had done her bit and no one could accuse her of not trying. She re-crossed the lawn in the same way, making for another couple who were about to take the bench a few yards down from us. She pestered them a little more conscientiously, but with highly original methods. She plucked a flower off the bush beside them and tried to stick it in the lady's hair.

By now I had looked in my bag and found a five-rupee note to give her, but for some reason she didn't even glance in our direction and again made for the far end of the lawn, part skipping, lightly running, but never in a straight line, never with a sense of purpose. A little child was about to kick a plastic ball in the direction of her older sister, and this was the game that had caught her eye. She ran to retrieve the ball, rolled it back to the baby, and entered into the circle easily and enthusiastically, as if they were well-known to her and she had been expected to come along. But the parents were lying on the grass a few yards away, and they shooed her off. She stayed a moment and then continued in the opposite direction, unburdened as ever, tracing the flight of another crow along the grass, gaze upwards, arms outstretched.

(Those of you who know my film *Shakuntala* will have recognized its opening moments. I found an excellent seven-year-old to play the part, and we gave her a big beach ball to throw in the air and catch, with me standing at different spots towards which she was asked to run, but whenever I watch that sequence, I find I have failed to convey the sheer blitheness of my real-life model.)

As dusk gathered and we walked out of the park and along the bank of the largest lake, Raj's mother smiled and pointed out thc dozens of couples on all the benches and under the trees. She wondered if some of them were students of hers, looking away as she went by. It suddenly occurred to me that Raj and Sunayani would have been regular visitors here as well, during their courting years, since they had lived just up the road.

Acknowledgments

First of all, I'd like to thank my editor, V.K. Karthika, for believing in this novel when she saw it at draft stage, and her invaluable help in bringing it to its final form. Thank you also to Shivmeet Deol at HarperCollins, for her assistance in this regard.

I owe a large debt to the editorial team at my agency, Osian's, Renuka, Kavita and Amrita, for their encouragement and detailed feedback.

A big thank you to Claudio, Clare and Chloë, without whose hospitality I would simply not have been able to imagine a Brazil to write about.

And to my friend Ibrar, for the constant warmth of his welcome in London.

I'm especially grateful to my friends and colleagues in the Department of English Literature at the University of Edinburgh – too many to name here – for their support over the last few years, which has taken so many different forms. Thanks also to Jennie and to *Textualities* for publishing extracts from *Derangements* while it was a work-in-progress.

Thank you to Christophe and Karen at *La Bagatelle* restaurant, Edinburgh, for very useful details that fed into the restaurant episodes in this novel. I'd also like to mention two books from which I've adapted a couple of anecdotes for use in that same section: *Surely You're Joking, Mr. Feynman!: Adventures of a Curious Character* by Richard P. Feynman et al., and *Life Is a Menu – Reminiscences and Recipes from a Master Chef* by Michel Roux.

There are a few works from which I've quoted excerpts in the novel: *High Windows* by Philip Larkin, *Don Quixote* by Cervantes (translated by J. M. Cohen), *Fury* by Salman Rushdie, and *William's Treasure Trove*, by Richmal Crompton.

A big hug each to Rob and Ankur, and to the Sens for their love and support; and finally, for every other uncountable, unspecific thing, my acknowledgments to Sasha, and to Ma and Baba.